From *Death at The Dog*

It was a bright, chill evening. The hunters' moon, a sharp-edged sickle, was rising into a galaxy of stars. Over the woods, the long-fingered searchlights moved and hovered; there was a grimmer sport afoot than fox-hunting this year. Better not think of that; it only made you curse the day when you'd become a policeman, so that now, when other men were hunting U-boats, drawing the sky for enemy aircraft, all you'd got to hunt was some poor devil who had been misguided enough, or exasperated enough, to take the law into his own hands and deliver this hedge-bound hamlet from its local Hitler.

Guy came out on the green. A rough road crossed it. The macadam, turning left, led him past cottages powdered with starlight, to a long, low house, which a sign, depicting a small white terrier of uncertain parentage, proclaimed as The Dog. There was a white fence with a gate in it, which led to a garden. *No Dogs Allowed* and *Please Shut the Gate,* said notices. In the shadow of the house he struck a match, discovered a door that said *Public Bar,* opened it and found himself in a square, blue-lighted room, smelling comfortably of beer, old oak and tobacco. There were several men in the bar, and a small, dark, depressed-looking woman in a flimsy, pinkish overall was serving them. He hesitated for a moment and then noticed *Lounge Bar* painted on the door opposite him. He went through to an unlighted lobby and the sound of voices brought him round left-handed. He opened a door and his first impression was of a particularly charming room, softly lit, chintz-hung, cozily warmed by a bright fire, made, so his nose told him, of apple logs. Murder? he thought, and then it flashed across his mind that not one of the murder cases he had had to do with had been suitably set in sordid or horrific surroundings; it was an undercurrent, this desire to kill, a crawling thing, deep down under the placid waters. . . .

Mysteries by Joanna Cannan

Featuring Inspector Ronald Price
Murder Included (1950)
In the U.S.: *Poisonous Relations*
and *The Taste of Murder*
Body in the Beck (1952)
Long Shadows (1955)
And Be a Villain (1958)
All Is Discovered (1962)

Featuring Inspector Guy Northeast
They Rang Up the Police (1939)
Death at The Dog (1941)

Death at The Dog

An Inspector Guy Northeast mystery by
Joanna Cannan 1898

with an introduction by
Tom & Enid Schantz

The Rue Morgue Press
Boulder, Colorado
1999

Death at The Dog
Copyright © 1941, 1969
Reprinted with the
permission of the author's estate.

New material © 1999 by
The Rue Morgue Press

0-915230-23-2

The Rue Morgue Press
P.O. Box 4119
Boulder, Colorado 80306

PRINTED IN THE UNITED STATES OF AMERICA

Meet Joanna Cannan

SET IN LATE 1939 during the first anxious months of World War II, Joanna Cannan's *Death at The Dog* is a wonderful example of the classic English detective novel that first flourished between the two World Wars when writers like Agatha Christie, Dorothy L. Sayers and Ngaio Marsh began practicing their trade. Like so many books of its period, *Death at The Dog* is set in a picturesque village filled with thatched-roof cottages, eccentric villagers and genial pubs. As well-plotted as a Christie, with clues abundantly and fairly planted, it's also as deftly written as the best of the books by either Sayers or Marsh, filled with quotable lines and perceptive observations on the human condition. Cannan had a gift for characterization that's second to none in Golden Age detective fiction, and she created two memorable lead characters in *Death at The Dog*.

One of them is Inspector Guy Northeast, a lonely young Scotland Yard inspector who makes his second and final appearance here and finds himself hopelessly smitten with the chief suspect in the murder of the village tyrant. The other unforgettable character is the "lady novelist" Cresy Hardwick, an unconventional and ultimately unobtainable woman a number of years Guy's senior, who is able to pierce his armor and see the unhappiness that haunts the detective's private moments. Well aware that all the evidence seems to point to her, she is also able—unlike her less imaginative fellow villagers—to see how very good Northeast is at his job.

Most of the other villagers in *Death at The Dog* aren't at all impressed with Northeast. "Practically no education," snorts one, snobbishly proclaiming that the detective probably went no further than grammar school. Northeast wouldn't really disagree. "Detectives aren't any more brilliant than anyone else," he explains. "They've experience in putting jigsaw puzzles together, that's all."

Observing Northeast in action, Crescy realizes why her own attempts at writing a mystery novel had failed. "I tried to make my detective a brilliant kind of person—like Dr. Priestley [the plodding sleuth in John Rhode's innumerable detective novels], only young and attractive. But Northeast isn't brilliant."

Yet Crescy recognizes that Northeast is blessed with other talents far more important in a detective, and she dismisses his lack of a proper education in a line worthy of Oscar Wilde: "Education's all very well for dining-out on, but it can't make fools wise. A wise lad, Northeast, and wisdom is common sense lit by imagination."

With his unassuming manner and uncommon ability to dislodge information from suspects by means of seemingly casual conversation, Northeast gradually worms his way into the confidence of the villagers, sharing a pint or two over a game of darts as he tries to discern who had the most to gain from the death of the terrible old miser who ruled over the village and his family with a fierce iron will.

The present case marks Northeast's second visit to Loamshire. The first was recounted in the 1939 novel *They Rang Up the Police*, which appeared only in England. He's not pleased to make a return visit, given "the prospect of working with two men he disliked, in a county he despised, during a war in which he wasn't allowed to fight."

After *Death at The Dog*, Cannan deserted detective fiction for nine years. When she finally did take up the genre again it was with a new character, Inspector Ronald Price, who was introduced to the reading public in 1950 in her most famous novel, the frequently reprinted and retitled *Murder Included*, first published in the United States as *Poisonous Relations* and twice later reprinted as *The Taste of Murder*.

Cannan's daughter Josephine Pullein-Thompson, herself the author of three crime novels, said her mother dropped Northeast as her sleuth "because he was too nice. She much preferred her hate relationship with the awful Price," possibly because "it was too difficult to write about good or nice people." That may be, but Northeast is too complex a character ever to become boring, and the final scene in *Death at The Dog* will tear at the hearts of all but the most hardened readers. Perhaps Cannan felt that Northeast deserved a little peace.

"Awful" is a good description for Price, who foreshadows the equally loathsome sleuths Jack Rosher and Inspector Dover, respectively created many years later by Jack S. Scott and Joyce Porter. Critics Jacques Barzun and Wendell Hertig Taylor, in their highly opinionated *A Catalogue of Crime*, praise Cannan's work but admit that "Price is a caricature" whose "genteel-vulgar traits, speech, and habits" are "deliberately overdone in order to permit a hostile kind of humor at his expense." In spite of the success of the first Price book, the other four in the series have never been commercially reprinted in the United States (an edition of *The Body in the Beck* designed for libraries was published in 1983.)

"Loamshire" in *Death at The Dog* is a thinly disguised version of rural Oxfordshire, where Joanna Cannan settled with her husband and four children in 1932. "The Dog" is based on a real pub, The New Inn at Kidmore End, which is still in operation and lies near Reading. During the war, especially, the pub was the center of village social life, and in *Death at The Dog* the close-knit relationships of the villagers, particularly those who gather around the moody but convivial Crescy, are primarily played out there.

Before she tried her hand at detective fiction, Cannan's books dealt primarily with the aftermath of World War I and life in England during the Great Depression, although several of her novels did have elements of crime fiction in them. All show her keen interest in the social mores of the day and how people behave in difficult times.

During the war, Cannan devoted her energies with great success to writing fiction for young readers. According to daughter Josephine, her mother's "pony" books changed the horse book genre. "Pre-Cannan the central character had always been the horse or pony," Josephine said. "She introduced the first human heroine, a pony fanatic called Jean." Altogether Cannan published nine books for children between 1936 and 1957. She died in 1961 after a long bout with tuberculosis.

Born in Oxford in 1898, Cannan came to the literary life quite naturally. Gilbert Cannan, the novelist who ran off with Mrs. Barrie, was Joanna's cousin, and her father Charles was an Oxford don and Dean of Trinity who became Secretary to the Delegates of the Oxford University Press. Many of Charles Cannan's friends were poets and publishers who made frequent visits to his home.

Joanna's sisters also embraced the literary life. Dorothea married John Johnson, printer to the Oxford University Press, but didn't write herself, while another sister, May Wederburn Cannan, was a noted World War I poet who was engaged to Bevil Quiller Couch, son of Q., who, having barely survived the fighting, died of the black flu shortly after the armistice. With her sisters (to whom she gave most of the credit) Joanna helped edit at the age of ten *The Tripled Crown: A Book of English, Scotch and Irish Verse for the Age of Six to Sixteen*.

All four of her own children became writers. In addition to her crime fiction, Josephine Pullein-Thompson has written numerous books for older children while Christine, the most prolific, has written for a younger age group. In addition to books for children, Diana also wrote a biography of Gilbert Cannan and two other books for adults. Like their mother and aunts, Josephine and her twin sisters collaborated as teenagers during the war on a book for children. Publication was held up until 1946 due to paper shortages. Joanna's only son, Denis, is a playwright whose first play was performed at the Citizens Theatre in Glasgow after he returned from the war. His second play was directed by Laurence Olivier and was a West End success and went on to New York. Joanna Cannan would no doubt be pleased that her children continue to carry on the family's long-time love affair with words.

Why Joanna Cannan's mysteries haven't been more successful in the United States is something of a mystery itself. Perhaps it's because Northeast was too realistic a character for a time when readers were looking for distractions from the war, while the unlikable Price might have been a hard sell for an American audience used to sophisticated and well-mannered British sleuths. That was unfortunate. Cannan's books deserve a place on the bookshelves alongside the works of Tey, Allingham, Sayers, Marsh, Brand and Heyer. She's that good. We hope the present volume will help to introduce modern readers to this very talented and much under-appreciated practitioner of the literate English village mystery.

Tom & Enid Schantz
February 1999
Boulder, Colorado

Death at The Dog

CHAPTER I
THURSDAY

AS FAR AS business in the lounge bar was concerned, the blackout, thought Eve, spilling a few drops of beer on a soft duster and beginning to polish the shove ha'penny board, was proving disastrous. It was a quarter to nine and, though the public bar was filling up, here the only customer was old Mathew Scaife, glowering over his second double whiskey in the corner seat by the door. Eve was not often sorry for herself; at forty-three she had abandoned extravagant hopes; but tonight she was tired. It was only six weeks since the beginning of the war, but already the blackout shutters of laths and black paper, which Peter had made for the twenty-eight differently shaped windows of the sixteenth-century building, had begun to warp, tear and split where the knots in the wood were. Peter, on leave from his duties as a War Reserve policeman, had only arrived at tea time, and Eve had spent the entire afternoon in the backbreaking, thumb-crushing and exasperating job of repairing the shutters. Her back ached; her ankles ached and her thumbs ached. Scaife had already been pretty offensive; and it did seem hard that, after all the trouble she and her brother had taken to build up a really solid connection, to create in the lounge bar of The Dog a club-like atmosphere, attractive to local people like the Days and the Franklands, which should make them independent of the possibly ephemeral attentions of bright young things from Melchester, this wretched blackout, coupled with petrol rationing, should reduce the usual cheerful evening crowd to one customer and he unwelcome.

Scaife was the local squire and the largest landowner on this side of the county. His family was one of the oldest in Loamshire, the Chancery Rolls recording in 1103 the receipt of sixteen shillings and eightpence, the scutage of Willielmus Scaife of the manor of Witheridge, while, according to the Pipe Roll, in 1150 Rogero Scaife was fined ten marks for

11

breaches of forest law. In the dim little chancel of the village church reclined the stone effigy of a Scaife crusader, and on neglected head-stones in the graveyard you could trace the direct line down to Mathew's father, John, who died 'honored and beloved by every station' in 1874. John Scaife may have been honored and beloved by every station, but his son, emphatically, was not. During the half-century of his steward-ship the beautiful Queen Anne mansion, built on the site of the Tudor house destroyed by Cromwell, had decayed into a ruin in which only a few rooms were now habitable; under the noble oaks of the park, pigs routed, rabbits burrowed and thistles and nettles advanced like armies; throughout the estate, tumble-down farms, condemned cottages, der-elict barns, tangled hedgerows, rotting fences and pasture humped with molehills and overgrown with thorn bushes bore witness to the decay of agriculture. Scaife wasn't without knowledge of farming, but he had got his knowledge at a time when a farm laborer's wage was ten shillings a week; obstinate as a mule, he had refused to move with the times and slowly, inexorably, brutally, the years had beaten him. Now his hand was against every man's. He was constantly in the Courts to answer for such misdemeanors as allowing horses to stray, permitting the growth of rag-wort, supplying milk deficient in fat, omitting to stamp insurance cards and disobeying the regulations of the Pig Marketing Board, while he, in his turn, freely summoned his tenants for nonpayment of rent, pros-ecuted trespassers, mushroom-gatherers and persons in search of co-nies. In spite of all that and more, there were men now in the public bar who would, Eve knew, speak up for him. Squire's orl right if you knows 'ow to take 'im. . . . Sooner 'ave Squire than some of them there jumped-up folks. . . . So does the feudal instinct linger in the hamlets of hedgebound, elm-muffled Loamshire.

But whatever brief was held for Scaife in the public bar, Eve didn't want him in the lounge, leering at her women customers, annoying the men, sprawling and snoring over her Tudor Rose cretonnes. His ap-pearance was unappetizing. He wore shapeless suits which smelled of the cowshed; his linen was dirty; he left straggling gray hairs on the cushions in the 'cozy corner'; his deeply lined face, with its small, blood-shot eyes and out-thrust lower lip like a Hapsburg, gave an impression of morose ferocity. But she had no excuse for refusing to serve him. He was offensive when sober, but after two or three double whiskeys, he would fall asleep and at closing time someone would shake him up and he would go off muttering, walking over a couple of fields to his ruined house and presumably to the ministrations of the wretched old woman— a poor relation, some said, and others, a former mistress—who waited on him. During the last six months he had been less of a problem. His son—Edward, not the impossible Mark—had come home, having, through no fault of his own, lost his job of land agent to Lord Deddington, and Edward seemed a decent young man and the wife he had brought with him a sensible, quiet kind of young woman. Sometimes they came to The Dog and then Eve comfortably felt that she could rely on them to handle any awkward situation. She wished they would come in tonight, for already, with an unpleasant leer at her shining gold-brown hair, the old man had muttered something about fancying fair women. She could cope with him, of course; she could cope, she thought a little wearily, with anybody, but it left a bit of a taste in one's mouth, and Peter was apt to go off the deep end if he heard of it. And now the old beast was stirring. His slow, bloodshot eyes, that had been fixed on the table, rolled round to her. He pushed forward his glass and muttered, "The same again," and, "You're quiet here tonight," he said as she took his glass and went round behind the bar to fill it.

Eve answered brightly, "Oh, it's early yet," and, bringing his glass back, she went on, "The other bar's pretty full, considering the black-out."

Scaife pulled some change out of his pocket. "It 'ud take more than a dark night to keep 'em away from their beer," he grumbled. "They've got money to burn—everything's given 'em—education, doctors, dentists, now the dole when they're out of work, the loafers—and the money that ought to be going back into the land, goes into the brewers' pockets." His voice was thick and indistinct, and Eve, without straining to catch the words, made assenting noises. If she neither annoyed nor encouraged him, he might grumble himself into somnolence.

". . . This blasted government," muttered Scaife, and ". . . this miserable country . . ." and then the door was thrown open and somebody did come in. Eve, who was polishing a glass, looked up and saw with joy that it was Cressy Hardwick, and it was Cressy in her red Breton trousers and short-sleeved navy-blue jumper, which meant that it was Cressy in one of her good moods. Eve liked Cressy. Most people liked Cressy sometimes, but Eve liked her always, even at those times when it seemed that someone had placed an extinguisher neatly and quietly over the shining spirit and Cressy sat in silence as morose as Mathew Scaife's or chatted cozily about hens or hairdressing to casual customers, uninteresting matrons or twittering girls, whom young men had driven out from Melchester and quickly tired of. Cressy's appearance, like her behavior, was unpredictable. Sometimes she would come in dashingly dressed, her face made up, her nails varnished, but she was just as likely to appear in threadbare tweeds, with straws in her hair, grime in her nails and holes in her stockings. These inconsistencies precluded friendship. Dashing people didn't like the shabby Crescy; quiet people didn't like the dashing one. The Highbrow resented her descents from Olympus; the Lowbrow were perplexed by her flights of fancy and the academic wisecracks she exchanged with Adam Day. Only Eve, who had troubles of her own, analyzed a nature passionately in love with life, once and forever disillusioned and still bitterly resenting it. As for the banal conversations, to explain them you had only to read Crescy's novels. In that queer contrary soul humility persisted. She had kept the common touch.

It was three years almost to a day since Crescy had first appeared at Witheridge Green. The harvest had been a poor one. Mathew Scaife had dismissed several of his farm hands. Little Bottom Cottage was vacant and Crescy took it, spent a hundred pounds on repairs and a hot water system, and settled down there. It was a white cottage, isolated, standing in a fold of the hills, approachable only by a wagon track leading to the woods beyond, but except for two dogs, three cats and a one-eyed pony, Crescy lived there alone. She was by way of doing her own housework and sometimes it was done and sometimes it wasn't, she told Eve, but she disliked cooking, and she soon began to drift into The Dog for her lunch of a pork pie or a sausage roll and half a pint of beer. At first she had been utterly uncommunicative, but presently she had told Eve that, for first time in her life, she was living as she would have chosen to live, and another day, talking about knowing oneself, she had remarked that the whole miserable business with Hugo could have been avoided if only she had known earlier what constituted happiness for her. As Crescy wore a wedding ring, Eve assumed that Hugo was her husband, but what the miserable business was and whether Crescy were divorced or not she had never discovered. She was increasingly anxious to know because of Peter. He was six years younger than she was, and, since they had been left motherless when he was quite a child, her affection for him, without being possessive, was protective. Lately, particularly in Crescy's presence, he had seemed absentminded; he had given people the wrong change, poured out drinks they hadn't asked for, handed them Players for Goldflake and *vice versa;* worse still, he had a different face for Crescy and took a grip on his voice before he spoke her name.

" 'Evening, Eve," said Crescy gaily and, shutting the door behind her, she positively skipped in. "Nobody here? Defeatists!" She swung herself up on one of the high stools at the bar.

Eve made a hushing face and pointed to Scaife in the corner. "Oh," said Crescy, and she swivelled round. She had snatched a sausage roll and her mouth was full, but nevertheless she contrived a grimace of disgust at the sight of the squire.

Scaife, who was sitting with his arms on the table and his head bowed, looked up. "Ah," he said, "Mrs. What's-her-name from Little Bottom Cottage. I wanted a word with you. You haven't answered my letter."

Crescy wrinkled her nose at Eve. She had a small, oval face, which she could contort like india-rubber. With her mop of honey-colored curls and her green eyes, she didn't look English. People guessed Viennese.

Taking another sausage roll, she announced to Eve, "That's elevenpence." Then she swung round and faced the squire, her green eyes blazing. "I didn't reply because I couldn't believe you were sober when you wrote that letter. You can't turn me out of the cottage. Look what I've spent on it!"

Heavily Scaife shifted his limbs and sat at his ease, leaning against the partition. "I was as sober as a judge when I wrote to you. It was ten o'clock in the morning. I've given you a month's notice to quit and that's all you're legally entitled to. You've got a copy of the lease. You go back home and look at it, Mrs. What's-your-name."

"I daresay you can do it legally," said Crescy, speaking as though legally didn't matter much to her. "But it's a dirty thing to do after what I've spent and what I've done to the garden and everything. Besides, what's your reason? I've always paid my rent, haven't I?"

"Oh yes," said Scaife, "you've always paid your rent, but what have you paid? Fifteen bob a week. Now, when I've got you out, I can shift some furniture down there from the Hall and let the place furnished for eight guineas a week to people who've run away from London on account of the air raids."

Crescy said, "You bloody profiteer."

Eve said, "I don't think that's very patriotic of you, Mr. Scaife. I don't think it's very wise of you either. People will get to know about it. . . ."

"Let 'em," said Scaife. "Clack, clack, clack. They talk about me enough already. What do I care?"

"I never . . ." began Crescy, but Eve interrupted her. "If I were you, Crescy, I wouldn't say any more. I should go into Melchester tomorrow and see a solicitor."

Scaife gave a derisive snort.

Crescy, all her brightness gone, turned round, put her elbows on the bar and her head in her hands. "Solicitors aren't any good," she muttered. "I'd like to murder him. Oh, Eve, it's my home."

"Rotten luck," whispered Eve. "Finish up your beer, Crescy, and have a whiskey and soda to pull you together. After all, there are other places."

"They wouldn't," said Crescy, "be the same. There's the orchard for One-Eye—it's almost impossible to get a small place with enough land. Besides, you can't get a cottage now. They're all let to London people.

I've been planning murder ever since I got his letter. I'd like to kill him, the bloody old profiteer."

Eve was silent. She sympathized deeply with Crescy, but all the same, this wasn't, she considered, the way to take a blow. *Not with an outcry to Allah or any complaining* was the way one should bear the bludgeonings of fate; besides, Cresy, over forty, was old enough to know that *tout lasse, tout casse* and, mercifully, *tout passe.* Dignity certainly wasn't Cresy's strong point. She was taking her whiskey like a lamb, but she was still muttering. "Filthy old beast," and, "Dirty devil," and, "I'd like to stick a knife in his insides." Perhaps Peter would be able to do something with her. Eve opened the door that led into the public room behind both bars.

Peter and Mrs. Chandler were serving beer. The room was full of smoke and rather dark because, although there was a door into the same lobby through which one entered the lounge, there was also a door which opened directly on the road, and this was the entrance which the patrons of the public bar were accustomed to use. By the simple process of removing the bulb from the electric fitting in the lobby, Eve and Peter had been able to make a light trap for those who entered the lounge, but they had thought it better not to bring the public bar people up the dark garden path to the lobby door. The entrance from the road was, therefore, still in use, and, instead of erecting a light trap and losing much-needed space, Eve and Peter had fitted up the public bar with blue electric bulbs. The effect was rather eerie, the blue light giving a sinister look to the homely faces round the bar. Eve, peering in, was struck by the thought that the room looked less like the bar at The Dog than like an *apache* den. And something had gone wrong with the conversation. They weren't talking about the size of their marrows. Bert Saunders was cursing. "Damn and blast 'im," said Bert Saunders, "to 'ell."

Eve quickly shut the door behind her. Peter, noticing her, raised his eyebrows. Eve said, "Cresy's come."

"I'll be through in a minute," said Peter. "Scaife there?"

"Yes, that's the trouble," whispered Eve. "He's given her notice to quit. She's—taking on."

"Well, listen to this," said Peter.

Eve listened. Saunders was speaking. "My grand-dad lived there. My dad lived there. Born there, I was. What right's 'e got to turn me out now?"

" 'E's got legal right," said Stanley Janes, the carrier.

"I'll show 'im legal right," said Saunders. "Turnin' me out after a matter of nigh on an 'undred year. 'Tain't jannock. And what's 'e doing it for? Just so as 'e can get more money out of them excavated London folks, that's all."

Someone spoke up for Scaife.

"When all's said and done, it's Squire's cottage. 'E needs the money. Things 'as turned out like that. You can't blame 'im."

"Blame 'im? I'd like to wring 'is bloody neck. Only that's 'ow we kills chicken—that's too good for 'im. 'E may need the money, but what about me? Where am I going with seven kids to look out for?"

Someone suggested a council house. "I ain't going to no council house," said Saunders. "There ain't room to swing a cat in them kitchens and the wind blows under the doors and lifts the oilcloth off the floor. Besides, look at the rent. 'Ow can I afford to pay eight and six-pence a week, and extra for a lot of mucky electric light what no one can't afford to use? I'm lucky if I see two pounds at the end of the week, and with seven kids opening their mouths it don't make sense. Squires nor councils, there didn't ought to be no bloody landlords."

An old voice said, "There's always been landlords and there always will be. I'd sooner 'ave Squire than the council. Squire don't do no re-pairs, but 'e don't make a lot of rules and regulations. Mustn't do this and mustn't do that. Gar . . ."

"Orl very well for you to talk," said Saunders. "You ain't 'ad notice to quit. Notice to quit! Ar, well, perhaps 'e won't find it so easy, Squire or no Squire. . . ."

Saunders's face disappeared into his tankard and Eve took the op-portunity to slip back into the lounge. Crescy was still drooping at the bar and Scaife still lolled in his corner. As Eve came in, he pushed his glass across the table and said, "The same again." Even when she was very busy and the room was full and he had to roar before she heard him, he never got up and brought his glass to the bar.

Eve went to take his glass, but before she reached the table the door opened and Edward Scaife came in. "Good evening, Mrs. Hennisty," he said. "Good evening, Mrs. Hardwick." Edward Scaife was a tallish man of round about thirty. He had a long head, mouse-colored hair and gray-ish-blue eyes. The only feature in his face which expressed the least individuality was his mouth, which was small, immobile and crowded with sharp white teeth. He was dressed in a suit of gray herringbone tweed, which was clean and well pressed, though worn.

" 'Evening," muttered Cresy.

"Good evening," said Eve brightly. "Nice to see you. Haven't you brought your wife along?"

"No. She's gone into Melchester to the flicks," said Edward. *The Four Feathers*. Very good, I believe." He looked down at his father and said, "Hullo, Father, nothing to drink? Have one on me?"

Scaife made a sucking noise through his teeth and lifted his old red eyes to his son.

"Thought you were hard up for money, Edward? Thought what I'm paying you wasn't a living wage. Yet your wife can go gadding off to Melchester to watch a lot of trash and you can stand drinks. . . ."

Edward had flushed scarlet. He stood for a moment silent, the veins in his high forehead swelling, his fists clenched. Then he gave a short laugh.

"Well, of course no one's got a bean, these days, but it's no use sitting at home and moping. Everyone—a woman especially—needs a change from the house sometimes. Isn't that so, Mrs. Hennisty?" He walked away from his father and sat down on a stool.

Eve said, "Definitely. Nothing's worse for you than never going anywhere or seeing a fresh face. And it's no economy really, because you only end up with a nervous breakdown." She filled Scaife's glass and took it to him. He paid her and in a thick voice grumbled, "It's bloody cold. Where's the draft coming from?" With an unsteady forefinger he pointed to the electric fan. "That damned newfangled thing."

"Well, we can easily put that right for you, Mr. Scaife," Eve said soothingly. She reached out to the switch of the fan, turned it off and went back to Edward. "What will you have?"

Edward asked for half a pint of bitter. Eve was drawing it when she heard footsteps and laughter and the Days and the Franklands came in.

The Days lived in a small white Regency house on the Green. Adam was an architect. Normally he was a cheerful, chatty, highly intelligent person, but since the beginning of the war he had become quite impossible, sitting all evening at the bar with his head in his hands, only occasionally looking up to say, "I *wish* someone would tell me how to get into the Army." He was thirty-three. He had been too young to fight in the Great War and was, it appeared, too old to fight in Hitler's War. Since the declaration, his job had been nonexistent, but was a reserved occupation. He was tired of other people dying for him and he didn't know where next week's housekeeping money was coming from. His young wife, Valentine, was a gentle, decorative, dense little creature. She couldn't understand why Adam wanted to leave her and their charming home.

Bridget Frankland was of sterner stuff than Valentine. The Franklands lived in a drafty farmhouse on a windswept hill on the opposite side of the Bottom. David was on the staff of a weekly paper, which struggled to provide the Thinking Man with reliable foreign news. Bridget farmed. She farmed very seriously, working from dawn till dark, driving everyone in her household to equal efforts, and at the end of her finan-

cial year she generally found herself in pocket to the extent of six or
seven pounds, which she greatly prized. She was tall and dark, and when
the long day's work was over, she changed out of corduroys into picturesque garments of tawny colors, and decorated herself with long, swinging earrings, of which she possessed a great variety. Her husband was a
well-informed little man of feeble physique, which defied the harden-
ing processes his wife forced on him. For Freudian reasons, he had grown
on his girlish face a small blond beard. He usually drank mild ale, but he
was subject to colds in the head, for which Eve recommended whiskey.
Considering the state of trade, she could not help feeling pleased to see
that he had a cold in his head now.

The Days and the Franklands greeted Eve and Edward Scaife and
Crescy, who scarcely looked up, but they ignored old Mathew, now half-
asleep. Bridget, who always did the ordering for the Franklands, asked
what everyone would have, and the Days and Edward had bitter beer
and Crescy had another whiskey and Bridget herself had mild ale, and
David, after consulting with Eve, had whiskey because of his cold. Bridget
began to tell Valentine how to feed evacuees on nettles rubbed through
a sieve, and David gave forth information on the history of Poland. Edward Scaife listened to him. Adam Day, after asking Eve where Peter
was, because he wanted to ask Peter if he had heard anything in London about how one could get into the Army, sat with his head in his
hands, and Crescy made a starfish on the bar with her forefinger in
some spilt beer.

Eve was wondering if it was any use trying to cheer up Crescy and
Adam by pulling herself together and engaging them in conversation,
when Mark Scaife came in. This was an extraordinary occurrence, because Mark usually drank with his father's laborers in the public bar. No
one knew why, but then no one knew much about him. According to
Mrs. Chandler, he had not been seen or heard of in the village until he
had arrived there at the age of fourteen. Some people said that he was
illegitimate, some that he wasn't Mathew's son at all, but the son of his
sister, who had run away with a gypsy, others that he was Mathew's son
all right and born in wedlock, but after Mathew's wife had left him and
returned to her own home. This story went on to relate that poor Emily
Scaife had never revealed to her husband the birth of his second child
and that, after her death, the boy's arrival at the Hall had surprised his
father as much as anyone. It was in order to pay back his wife, these
people said, that Mathew had at once set the boy to labor on the farm;
Edward had been educated at the local grammar school and had subse-
quently got himself a scholarship to an agricultural college, but Mark
had had no schooling after he was fourteen. Bridget Frankland had

something to say about him. She had come across him when she had
taken a cow to Scaife's bull to be served. "And never again," she had told
everyone. Scaife's yard had been indescribable; the dung of ages had
seeped over the tops of her rubber boots and she had been terrified
that her lovely Cowslip would catch some dire disease. She hadn't been
afraid to tackle Mark Scaife about it. He replied with oaths in broad
Loamshire, prefixing 'bloody' to every noun.

When Mark Scaife came in, everyone stopped talking. He swaggered
in and stood for a moment looking round him with hot brown eyes.
Physically, he was a far finer specimen than Edward; about the same
height but broader across the shoulders and handsome in a dark, wild,
gypsy way.

Bridget Frankland, as usual, took the lead. She said, "Good evening,
Mr. Scaife." Mark had nodded at Edward. He now turned to Bridget and
spoke without a trace of Loamshire accent. He said, "Good evening,
Mrs. Frankland. I never heard what luck you had with that cow."

"She dropped a bull calf," said Bridget.

"You haven't been back again," said Mark, and asked for a pint of
bitter.

Edward had been staring at Mark, and it was Eve who was now listening to the history of Poland. She moved to the other end of the bar
to draw the beer. David Frankland spoke on for a few moments and
then realized that no one was listening and ceased. Edward, addressing
Mark, said with a tight mouth, "I don't wonder, considering the state of
the place."

"The place is all right," said Mark.

Edward said, "Tch," throwing back his head in scorn. Mark, with a
glance back at the corner where the old man was snoring, said, "I'd
sooner have the old man's methods than yours."

Eve felt that tact was called for. Preferring to address Edward rather
than Mark, she said something about women on the land. Edward described how girls were being trained at the agricultural colleges. Adam
said to Mark, "I suppose you don't know any way for a man of my age to
get into the Army?"

Mark said he didn't. He said he was twenty-eight and had gone into
Melchester on the first day of the war to enlist and had been sent home
again. Then he turned back to Bridget. They began to talk about pigs.
David Frankland moved up and stood beside them. There was a queer
look in his pale hazel eyes.

What was happening to The Dog? Eve asked herself. The old cheery
evenings had come to this: Adam with his head in his hands, unable to
utter except for his tiresome question about getting into the Army,

Bridget talking coarse stuff about farrowing sows to Mark Scaife, who had never before ventured beyond the public bar, David looking queer about it, Edward Scaife tightly controlling himself, but liable to blow up at any minute, silly little Valentine gazing, puzzled, at Adam, Cresy in the depths of despair. What could she do about it? She helped herself to a drink and tackled Cresy. "Well, Cresy, how's the book getting on?"

"Bloody."

"It's about an architect, isn't it? Why don't you collaborate with Adam?"

"Adam?" said Cresy. "I couldn't collaborate with anyone, Adam least of all."

"Why not me?" said Adam. "Or do I mean, why me? What I mean is, why me, least of all?"

"*I am a reed and the wind blows through me,*" said Cresy. "I might collaborate with David, who knows obscure things like the history of Poland, but there'd be no point in collaborating with another reed."

"I see your point," said Adam. "I thought it might be because I had B.O. When I get into the Army I shall know obscure things—about forming threes and the mechanism of the Bren gun and how Colonels' wives go on. We might collaborate then."

"How can we, if you're in Egypt or Bessarabia or somewhere?"

"Oh," said Valentine, "I hope Adam won't be sent abroad."

Adam groaned.

"And anyhow," said Cresy, "it seems to be doubtful whether I shall be here much longer. That misbegotten old reptile"—she nodded towards Scaife—"has given me notice to quit the cottage."

"Good God!" said Adam, "but he can't do that, Cresy. You can't go away from here. I—we can't do without you."

Cresy gazed gloomily into her golden liquor. "Looks as if you'll have to, unless he dies in the night or something. I wish he would. He's no use—mucking up his land and annoying everybody."

Adam shot a furious glance in Scaife's direction.

"Foul old beast. Why's he doing it?"

"Money. He thinks he can get a bigger rent by letting it furnished to people who've run away from London."

"Good God! What people won't do for money!"

"The root of all evil," said Cresy. "No, perhaps that's not fair. The evil's in human nature. God, how I hate people."

"If you go . . ." said Adam and fell silent, and Cresy was silent too. Further along the bar, Mark Scaife was lighting a cigarette for Bridget and David was looking queerer than ever. Eve said, "Nine o'clock—shall I turn on the news?"

Everyone said no.

Then Peter put his head through the door. He said, "Eve, Waller's here. He says we're showing a light from a window upstairs."

Eve said, "Where?"

"On the garden side," said Peter.

Eve pushed up the flap of the bar and walked through the room into the lobby. She heard Mathew Scaife's heavy breathing as she went through the door. She groped her way along the passage. The door into the garden was open and the solid form of Waller, the village constable, stood there.

Waller was a popular man in the village. He had been in the Irish Guards, had seen the world, and couldn't bring himself to consider seriously the petty offenses of the inhabitants of Witheridge Green. "You really mustn't drive on the wrong side of the road, madam," he had said once to Valentine Day, and, "Bed's the place for you, my lad," he told the drunk and disorderly, and to owners of senile spaniels he remarked, "Don't you forget to take out a licence for that dog when he gets to be six months old." He now said, "Sorry to trouble you, madam, but there's a light showing in one of the upper windows and the Air Warden may be round this way tonight."

Eve said, "Which room is it?"

"Well, madam," said Waller, "if you'd just amble out . . ."

Flashing his lamp, he guided Eve on to the lawn.

It was a very dark night. The stars were obscured. A southwest wind went shivering through the elms in the hedgerow that bordered the lane. From Eve's bedroom window, through rosebud chintz curtains, a light was shining. It looked very pretty . . . a kindly light, but that was wrong. . . .

"Oh dear," said Eve, "that's my bedroom. Peter *will* be annoyed."

"Oh, well, madam," said Waller, "we all make mistakes sometimes. If you'd just amble in and turn it off. . . ."

"Of course," said Eve. "Actually, there's a shutter. I can't imagine why I forgot to put it up tonight."

"Well, who's the culprit?" said Peter coming out on the lawn.

"Good heavens," said Cresey from somewhere. "I believe I left my bedroom light on."

"No, you didn't, madam," said Waller. "At least, there was nothing to be seen when I cycled along the Cold Harbor road just now."

"I must say," said Peter, "I think the village deserves full marks. Compared to us, Melchester's a blaze of light. Noticed it, Waller?"

"It's not good. It's the small shops, mostly. They have to keep their lights on and they can't afford proper materials, like the big firms. What's

London like, sir?"

"Pretty good. Of course people have aberrations, like my sister to-night."

"That's human nature," said Waller.

"Feminine nature," said Peter.

"How you do harp on the he and she business," said Crescy irritably.

"Well, I'll be off," said Waller.

"Won't you have something?"

"No, thank you, sir."

He went away down the path, his footsteps scrunching the wet gravel. Eve's light was out. "The he and she business," said Peter, "is rather important to me."

Crescy said, "If you want to tell me your difficulties, you must do it where it's warm. Not out here. Especially with this smell of chrysanthemums. It's melancholy. My God, I think it's the most melancholy smell in the world!"

"I wasn't going to tell you my difficulties," said Peter. "I haven't any. Except you."

"You can't call me a difficulty," said Cresy. "I'm the cat that walked by itself. I don't ask anything from anybody. Let's go in. You go first, Peter. I'm paying a call on the way."

The door was open. David Frankland was standing just inside. He said, "One thing about Waller is that he's not out to make trouble. Not like some of these officious air wardens. Jack's in office!" He followed Peter back into the lounge.

Eve had just served another round of drinks, for which Adam, defying fate, had paid.

"Waller gone?" she asked Peter.

"Yes," said Peter. "Bad show, that, for a policeman's house."

"I'm awfully sorry," said Eve. "Oh, I've drawn some beer for—the other Mr. Scaife and he's gone."

"Yes," said Bridget, stubbing out her cigarette. "He went before Waller came."

"We ought to go home," said David.

"Good lord," said Bridget, "why? It's not nearly bedtime and one can't sit about doing nothing these days."

"I can," said Cresy as she came back into the room. "In a crisis I always do nothing. . . ."

"My first instinct," Bridget said, "is to act." She began a story about a motor accident in which she had shown up well. Nobody paid any attention. With the possible exception of Edward Scaife, they had all heard the story before.

Peter went back to the public bar. It was less crowded now. Bert Saunders was there. Usually a sober man, he had had plenty. He was finishing a game of darts with Sidney Smallbone, the village butcher's young roundsman, and he swayed unsteadily, but alcohol did not, apparently, affect his eye. With his first dart he got the double six he wanted and lurched back to the bar and his tankard of beer.

"Well done, Bert!" "That's a Brahma!" and "Told you 'e'd get it!" said Janes, the carrier, Bligh, the postman, and Cox, a jobbing gardener.

Sidney Smallbone wanted another game. No one else seemed keen, so Peter suggested that perhaps someone in the lounge would like to play. There wasn't room in the lounge for a darts board, but enthusiasts like Adam and Bridget Frankland often went into the public bar for a game. He put his head through the door and said, "Anyone like a game of darts?"

Adam said at once, "Yes. Me."

He went with Peter. Valentine said, "Oh dear! He'll be in there for ages and we ought to go home."

Eve said rather tartly, "It's good for him. It will take his mind off things."

"We're all in the same boat," said Edward Scaife. "The Army won't have me."

"I'm glad they won't have Adam," said Valentine.

Crescy gave her a malevolent look. "Don't you understand," she said, "how Adam feels?"

"About this? No, I don't," said Valentine.

Crescy sighed.

Then David proposed a game of shove ha'penny, and he and Valentine played Edward Scaife and Eve.

Presently Adam came back. He came in by the lobby door. He had beaten Sidney Smallbone and his mood had changed. He stood watching the game of shove ha'penny, applauding hilariously. Suddenly Crescy cheered up. She slipped off her stool and stood beside Adam, laughing and making derisive comments on the play.

It was odd, thought Eve, how the temper of the room had changed.

Eve and Edward won. At Crescy's invitation, everybody had one for the road. Edward said that he must be off or his wife would be home before he was. Bridget said, did that matter? Edward said, well, he had promised to meet Janet at the bus stop and he thought that first he'd better see the old man home.

He went across the room to his father. He said, "Time to go," and then he laid a hand on his father's arm. Round the bar, the others were talking. Suddenly they heard Edward say calmly, but in a voice that was an octave higher than usual, "I'm afraid something's happened. I'm afraid he's gone."

It was Eve's job to cope. While the others merely stared, she came through the bar and joined Edward. He had hold of the old man's hand. He lifted it and let it fall. "I'm afraid," he repeated, "he's gone."

Eve, conquering a certain amount of distaste, put her fingers round the bony wrist and felt for the pulse.

"There's nothing," she said. "Will somebody call Peter, please."

At that, everyone was crowding round her. Valentine, said, "Oh, how awful!" Bridget said, "Heart I should think." David said, "He mayn't be dead. Perhaps it's a stroke." Adam said, "Don't you do something with a mirror?"

Crescy called Peter, but before he came Bridget, remembering that in a crisis her first instinct was to act, pushed past the others, walked up to the old man and unbuttoned his coat and waistcoat. She felt for the heart. "He's dead all right," she said. "Dead as mutton."

"What's the matter?" asked Peter.

"My father's passed away," and, "The old man's dead," said Edward and Bridget simultaneously.

"Adam!" said Crescy.

Valentine had fainted, crumpling at Crescy's feet, and Crescy, down on her knees, was supporting Valentine's head and shoulders. "Shove her head between her knees," said Bridget. "Eve, can we have some brandy?" Adam, Crescy, Bridget and Eve attended to Valentine, while Edward Scaife, David and Peter bent over the dead man. Peter was feeling his heart. Bridget said, "I've done that," and pulled out a cigarette.

"Let's move him into the light," said Edward.

"Better not," said Peter. "First thing is to ring up the doctor. David, you might do it. Phone's in the sitting-room."

David said rather helplessly, "What's the number?'"

"Witheridge 2100," said Peter.

David went through to the private sitting-room, which opened out of the lounge. Edward still bent over his father. Valentine had come round. Bridget and Adam had carried her to the sofa and Adam was sitting beside her and she was saying, "Oh, Adam, does everyone think I was silly?"

"Of course they don't," said Crescy. "I feel sick myself."

Bridget said it depended. Death didn't upset her at all. On a farm you got used to it. She wasn't squeamish either. Last week she'd helped to castrate a colt. . . .

"Oh, shut up," said Crescy.

Then David came out of the sitting-room. In a dispirited voice he explained that Doctor Judd was away and his assistant, Harvey, was at a confinement at a farm where there was no telephone.

Peter said, "Damn that fellow, Judd. He's always away. We'll have to ring someone in Melchester. Try Baker, David. He's this side of the town."

"What's his number?"

"Can't you look it up?" said Peter.

David went back to the sitting-room. Valentine called out suddenly, "Oh, why don't you move him? I can't bear to see him sitting up there. As if he was alive. Why don't you move him to the sofa?"

"Oh, don't be so silly," said Bridget. "He's dead. It doesn't matter if his body sits up or lies down. If you're so squeamish, you needn't look that way."

Peter said, "It's better not to move him till the doctor's been here. I suppose there'll have to be an inquest. Unless he was under a doctor?" he said to Edward Scaife.

Edward said, "No, he wasn't. He loathed doctors. Wouldn't have one in the house. Not even when Janet had influenza. If he'd been dying we couldn't have done anything."

Peter said, "But why don't you people go out of here? Go into the other bar. You'd better all have a drink on the house to pull yourselves together."

Eve said, "Yes, come along," and she shepherded the Franklands, the Days and Crescy into the public bar and asked what they'd like. Her manner was hospitable, but she couldn't help feeling that Peter's generosity was an unnecessary extravagance. Business was bad enough already and Scaife's death wasn't going to make it any better. Nobody would fancy that corner seat again; Valentine probably wouldn't fancy the room at all and it was no use pretending that Scaife was a loss to anybody. If, as one assumed, Edward inherited the Hall, the whole village would benefit. Though he wasn't exactly a kindred spirit, didn't add much to the gaiety of nations, he seemed a decent fellow, with up-to-date ideas on farming. He might make something of all those derelict acres, and since he'd had hard things to say about profiteers, it was to be supposed that he'd allow Saunders to stay in his cottage. And Cresy. Eve, handing Cresy another whiskey, looked at her and wondered what she was thinking. She wasn't a person whose thoughts would be cluttered up with sentiment about death. She must be feeling pleased, but she didn't look it. Her small, expressive face was white. She turned her glass in her hands and stared and stared at it. What was she thinking?

Cresy was thinking: Little Bottom Cottage. Little Bottom Cottage. One-Eye under the apple blossom. Pablo and Vincent and Marie Laurencin lying on the window ledge in the sun. And the smell of the wood fires of ages and the smell of stocks. And the firelight dancing and Vicky and Olivia with their heads on their paws. After all, am I any better off? He's a decent man, but decent men with small mouths have their price. Hugo's girl had a small mouth. It didn't stop her screaming. Little Bottom Cottage. Little Bottom Cottage *where peace comes dropping slow. . . .*

Peter stuck his head in and said, "You people all right?" and, since Saunders and Sidney Smallbone, now the only remaining patrons of the public bar, were staring, he told them, "The Squire's been taken ill. I might as well tell you he's gone."

Smallbone said, "Cor!" Saunders said, "Gorblimey, that's the best bit of news I've 'eard for years. 'Ere, Else," he said to Mrs. Chandler, "fill up me glass. Christ lumme! 'Ere's a bit of luck at larst."

"Shut up, Saunders," ordered Peter. "If that's how you feel, you should keep it to yourself."

Mrs. Chandler, a depressed dark widow with a beaten look, put in a word for Saunders. " 'E's 'ad a lot to put up with, Bert 'as. So 'ave we all."

Eve remembered some gossip about the Chandlers. Before she had come to Witheridge Green, while Scaife's old housekeeper was in bed with a bad leg, the Chandlers' younger daughter had gone to the Hall to help with the housework. One day she had returned home unable to speak, dumb as a beast. Some kind of shock, said the doctor, and sent her from one hospital to another, but no medical skill could undo the wrong that had been done to Edna Chandler at the Hall. But you had to keep up the decencies. It would never do if it got about that the Squire's death had been celebrated at The Dog. She said, "Well, the man's dead. Let's leave him alone."

Crescy laughed.

Peter gave her a reproachful look, which was interrupted by a squeal of brakes outside. He went to the door, and Dr. Baker, complete with bowler hat, dark overcoat and black bag, came skipping in.

Baker was a lively little man. He began to talk at once. "Scaife, is it? Tch, tch. I've heard of him. Hates doctors. Well, he's got to have a doctor now." Peter said, "This way, sir," and, "That way," and got him through the passage into the lounge. "You're dark here," chirped Baker. "I can't quite imagine the Boche wasting bombs on Witheridge Green. Still, we're all under orders. So this is the casualty. Oh, yes. Oh, yes. Tch, tch."

"We found him like that," said Peter. "He usually sits in that corner and he often goes to sleep, so we didn't notice anything till Mr. Edward Scaife, here, thought of going home. He came over to wake his father and found him dead. We felt his heart and so on, but we haven't moved him."

"I see. I see," said Baker. "Heart, I expect. He's not a young man. . ."

"Seventy-five," said Edward. "At least, so I believe. I say, Conway, I was going to meet my wife at the bus stop. I'd better shoot down there while this is going on. I'll bring her back with me."

"Right," said Peter. "We can manage."

Edward went out through the public bar. "I'm going to meet Janet. I'll bring her back here," he told Eve. He opened the door and collided with Waller. Waller let him pass and then came in.

"Excuse me, madam," he said, addressing Eve. "I expect your clock's out of order, but it's past closing time."

Eve said, "Help! Waller, haven't you heard? The Squire's dead. We found him dead in the lounge."

"I'm sorry to hear that, madam. A nasty upset for you. I quite understand, of course, but, if these ladies and gentlemen will kindly drink up, I really think you'd better close the bar."

"Yes, of course," said Eve. "Come along, everybody. Closing time."

Obediently everyone emptied his glass. Saunders and Smallbone called, "Good evening," and went out. The Franklands followed them. Adam jerked a thumb towards the lounge and said, "Do you think they'll want a hand in there?"

"I don't think so," said Eve. "There's Peter, and Edward will be back soon. You'd better take Valentine home."

"I'll stop a bit," said Crescy. "Janet Scaife may take on."

"There! I knew you all thought I was silly," said Valentine.

"Nobody thought you were silly," said Adam. "You can't expect to be as tough as Crescy and Eve." With his arm round his wife's shoulders, he went out, saying, "Good night."

Mrs. Chandler was collecting glasses. Waller said, "I wonder if I could be of any help to the gentlemen in there?" Eve answered, "Yes, I expect you could," and then Sidney Smallbone came in.

"Oh, Mr. Waller," he said from the doorstep, not daring to set foot in licensed premises after hours, "me bike's been took."

"Your bike?" said Waller. "Where did you leave it? I expect you've missed it in the dark."

"No, I ain't," said Sidney. "I left it right under the winder. And now it's gawn. Some bloke's took it. This won't 'arf cause it. It's me sister's bike. She cycles to work of a morning and I borrowed it without arsking 'er."

"Well, you shouldn't do such things," said Waller. "You get along, young Sidney—it won't hurt you to walk home. I daresay you'll find your bike where you left it, in the morning. We've got a corpse here I can't bother about your bike now."

Sidney's rabbit face fell. He made himself scarce, and Waller walked through to the lounge. Eve said to Crescy, "Let's go to my sitting-room. You're nearly finished, aren't you?" she said to Mrs. Chandler.

"I'm just off," said Mrs. Chandler, reaching for her coat and beret. "This 'as, as you might say, been an evening! I wonder where Squire is now?"

"I wonder how long it takes?" said Crescy. "I mean, to hell."

Eve said, "Crescy!"

"Not long," said Mrs. Chandler, fixing her beret. "At least, I 'opes not. Unless 'e 'as to wait for the day of Judgement, in which case I 'opes I'm there."

"I 'opes I am, too," said Crescy, ignoring Eve's faces. "And he's not the only one I'd like to see sent down. God!" she said fervently, "I hope there's hell."

"Crescy, how can you? . . . Good night, Mrs. Chandler," Eve said pointedly.

Mrs. Chandler tucked in her muffler, picked up the paper carrier, which, optimistically, she took with her everywhere, said, "Well, I'll love you and leave you. Good night, ladies," and went out. She didn't usually speak like that. Usually she said, "Good night," and nothing more. Either the squire's death had sent her spirits soaring, or else Crescy's *camaraderie* had affected her.

Eve said, "You're so unwise, Crescy. You know, everything you said will be all round the village tomorrow."

Crescy was lighting a cigarette. She said, "I'm glad I'm unwise. I'd hate to be careful. Aren't we shut off enough from one another anyway? Listen—that sounds like Edward and his consort. I'll let them in."

She went to the door, which Eve had locked behind Mrs. Chandler, and Edward and his wife came in. Janet Scaife was small, sturdy, dark. She wore a brown and green checked jacket over a green dress. Her head was bare. Her long black hair, smooth and shining, was parted in the middle, drawn back from her pale, intelligent face and twisted into a Grecian knot. She was perhaps a year or two younger than her husband and rumor had it that they had met as fellow students at an agricultural college, and that she knew as much about farming as he did. They were childless, but had not been married, it was gathered, for more than a couple of years.

"I wasn't long, was I?" said Edward.

"No," said Eve, glancing at the time. "The bus must actually have been on time. I'm so sorry about this, Mrs. Scaife. It must have been a shock to you."

"Yes," said Janet. "Of course, he didn't look well. But he had a complex about doctors. I daresay his heart was in a bad way."

Edward said, "You'd better have a whiskey or something, Janet. Do you good."

"My knees do feel a bit wobbly," said Janet with a faint deprecatory smile.

"You'd better come through to the sitting-room," said Eve. "I can't serve you here. The Eye of the Law is on us. I forgot all about the time, and Waller came in, and he's in the lounge now. But you can have one on the house in the sitting-room, Mrs. Scaife. Supposing we go out into the garden and in at the sitting-room window, Cresy. Then we shan't disturb them in the lounge."

"I'll go and see what the verdict is," said Edward. "Thank you, Mrs. Hennisty. You're being most kind."

In the lounge he found that the doctor's examination was finished. The old man's body had been laid on the sofa and covered with a counterpane. Peter said, "Oh, here you are, Scaife. We've rung for an ambulance."

Edward said, "Oh, is that necessary? I mean, I could have got some of the men and it's not a quarter of a mile to the Hall."

"I'm afraid I must have him taken to the mortuary," said Baker. "He hasn't had a regular medical attendant and I can't give a certificate."

"You don't mean you want a postmortem?" said Edward, looking horrified.

"I'm afraid so."

"But really," protested Edward, "it seems unnecessary. He was an old man. It was probably heart."

"My dear sir," said Baker tartly, "it generally is."

"In any case," said Edward, "it can't be anything very complicated. I'm not a rich man, Doctor. I don't want to run into a lot of expense." He turned to Peter. "What about getting a second opinion?"

"I really think," said Peter, "that if I were you, Scaife, I'd leave it in Dr. Baker's hands." He dropped his voice so that it wouldn't reach Baker, who was fussing angrily with his bag. "I know he's not impressive, but he's got the reputation of being the cleverest doctor in Melchester. He's the police surgeon, too, so he knows the routine. I mean, if you've got to have an inquest . . ."

"I think that's the ambulance, sir," said Waller, interrupting him. "Shall I amble out and see? And it would be best, wouldn't it, to take him out through the garden? A bit cramped behind the bar."

"I'd take him out through the lobby and the other room," said Peter. "Wait a minute, and I'll move a bulb into the lobby light." He went into the sitting-room for a bulb and Eve took one out of a reading lamp.

"I want," he explained, "to put it in the lobby for the ambulance men."

"Why an ambulance?" asked Janet. "Edward said he'd rouse some men and have him carried home across the fields. He would have preferred that."

"They're taking him to the mortuary," said Peter. "Baker won't give a certificate."

He took the bulb from Eve and went out.

Janet said, "Oh dear. He would have been annoyed. He told me once that he wanted to die in his fields."

"I don't blame him," said Crescy. "I hope I die out of doors."

Eve said, "It gives much less trouble to other people if you die in bed."

"You can't always be thinking of other people," said Crescy. "Unselfishness is a most dangerous virtue. The martyr. I've worked my hands to the bone for you. While you've been enjoying yourself, I've been slaving on my hands and knees. If one does anything unselfish one ought instantly and automatically to forget it." Cres5y always expected other people's minds to skip, like hers.

Eve said, "The world would be a funny place if you were in charge, Crescy. Wouldn't it, Mrs. Scaife?"

"Sorry," said Janet. "I'm afraid I wasn't listening. I was thinking of my father-in-law."

"What were you thinking?" asked Cresc5y. "Of course, when it's someone you care for, that's obvious. But was there anything about the squire to make even you regret him? Had he *any* virtues?"

"Yes," said Janet. "He was a strong man. He had the courage of his mistaken convictions. He had the guts to be wicked. Very few people have. They're good, but only out of fright. Just inoffensive. But he had outlived his time; he was against any kind of progress and people like that are definitely public enemies."

"That," said Cresc5y, "is just why I *should* regret him. All this beastly buzzing progress. . . . The virtue I find in him is that he loved his land. He wanted to die in his fields with the smell of wet grass and dusk spreading in from the hedges. . . ."

"He may have loved his land," replied Janet, "but it was a rotten diseased kind of love. He loved it, but he ill-treated it. I don't suppose you know much about farming, Mrs. Hardwick, though I daresay you like the smell of cows and the look of a hayfield. To me, a farm that doesn't pay is like a car that won't go, or an unhealthy body. . . ." She broke off as Peter opened the door.

"They've taken him away. It's all clear now."

"Well," said Janet, setting down her glass, which was not quite empty, "my husband and I had better be off home." She got up and the three women went through into the lounge.

Edward was standing by the fire, gazing into the still glowing ashes. He looked up and said, "We might as well be off now, Janet," and again he thanked Eve for her kindness. Then Crescy said good night. In a vague search for comfort, which she was unlikely to give him, Peter went with her through the lobby. The door into the public bar was open. Waller, at his ease on an oak settle, was enjoying a glass of beer.

Peter, stooping to look for something Crescy had kicked, so that it had tinkled across the lobby in front of her, said, "You've been awfully good, Crescy—staying on. Was Mrs. Scaife upset?"

"I don't think so," said Crescy. "She seemed to take it very calmly, but then she's not one for laughing or crying, is she? What is it I've been playing football with, Peter? Did you drop anything?"

"No. Did you?"

"Not as I knows of." Crescy stooped. "Look, it's a dart."

"Damn people. They're careless. No wonder we're always having to buy new darts, if that's how they treat them. I bet it was young Adam. God, I'm tired," said Peter.

But Crescy didn't say, poor Peter. She said, "Well, I suppose the sun will rise again tomorrow," and then she said, "I'll restore this to its shelf. A place for everything and everything in its place . . ." and she slipped into the public bar and was quickly back again.

Peter held the door open to light her down the path. They called good night and he went back indoors and into the public bar. Waller set down his glass and rose. "I'll be ambling off now, sir."

"I'm for bed, too," said Peter. "Very trying this sort of thing. I wish people would die in their beds and not on my premises."

"You must look on the bright side, sir," said Waller. "However trying it may be for them as is left to clear up the mess, the old gentleman's out of his misery. Well, sir, thanks for the drink, which was very acceptable, and good night to you."

Peter, yawning, saw him out, locked up behind him and went back into the lounge. Eve, limp with fatigue, had a damp cloth in her hand and was wiping the bar. Peter said, "For pity's sake, stop pottering."

"I'm not going to potter tonight," Eve told him. "Only it's fatal to leave wet rings on the bar." She put away the cloth and said, "What a dreadful evening! I keep on looking at the corner seat. I've a feeling he's still there."

"You go to bed," said Peter. "It's no use having feelings about Scaife. We'll all be much better off without him—Crescy, Saunders, Edward and I suppose that mysterious fellow, Mark. I wonder why tonight, of all nights, he came in here."

"It was odd, wasn't it? He didn't talk to anyone but Bridget. He seemed friendly enough with her."

"If you ask me, she'd get off with anyone. A predatory female."

Eve yawned.

"We're getting gossipy. Good night, Peter dear."

"Good night," said Peter, turning out the lobby light and locking the lounge door. "You were splendid, Eve," he called after her as she toiled limply upstairs.

CHAPTER II
SUNDAY

ON SUNDAY MORNINGS between twelve and one the Days, the Franklands and Crescy Hardwick usually forgathered at The Dog. Eve and Peter took a variety of Sunday newspapers and the party amused itself by answering the questions in General Knowledge Competitions and reading out strip advertisements and the future, foretold by the stars. On the Sunday following Scaife's death, it was some time before the papers were opened. The Franklands hadn't come and Adam and Cresc talked about Scaife's death and advanced wild theories on why the inquest had been adjourned after only formal evidence, until Valentine began to look green. Eve made faces at them and presently they saw what she was driving at. Adam said, "Well, what about the future?" and opened a paper. "Cresc, I believe you're a fish. Pisces . . . pisces. . . . Here it is. My God, you're in for it. Listen to this . . ." He was interrupted by the opening of the door. Expecting to see the Franklands he turned round, but it wasn't Bridget and David. It was a man in the uniform of a police superintendent, who came in.

Adam turned back to the paper. "Pisces people . . ." he began, but the Superintendent, a broad-shouldered man with steel-gray eyes, clean-cut features and an impressive chin, walked straight to the bar and said to Peter, "You're Mr. Conway, the licensee here, I believe?"

"No," said Peter. "My sister, Mrs. Hennisty, is the licensee. I'm her manager. What can I do for you, sir?"

"I'd like a word with you and Mrs. Hennisty. In connection with the death of Mr. Mathew Scaife, which took place here last Thursday. I'm Superintendent Dawes from Melchester."

"What's wrong?" asked Eve, and added, "I'm Mrs. Hennisty."

"I don't know that anything's wrong, Madam," said the Superintendent snubbingly. "I have a few routine enquiries to make, that's all. Have you another room?"

"There's our private sitting-room," said Peter. "I'll take you in there. But you'll have a drink first, won't you?"

"No, I thank you," said Dawes.

Peter came round from behind the bar and the Superintendent followed him into the sitting-room. No sooner was the door closed behind them than Crescy said, "Foul creature! By Henty out of Ethel M. Dell."

"What's it all about?" wondered Adam. "That remark about routine enquiries sounded familiar to me. I believe you were right, Crescy—the inquest being adjourned means there was something phony. . . But it doesn't make sense. Though we didn't know it at the time, we all saw him die."

"Ugh!" said Valentine, green again.

Eve said calmly, "There can't be anything wrong. Perhaps they can't find out what he died of and they want to know exactly what he drank and so on."

"But why the police?" asked Crescy. "And why a Superintendent? They're very elevated."

Trust Crescy, thought Eve, to ask tiresome questions. She said, "Well, we shall know soon enough. Let's get on with Crescy's birthday."

"No, don't let's," said Crescy. "I wonder what he's asking Peter? Do you think he'll want to question you, Eve? What will you tell him?"

"What he wants to know, of course," said Eve.

"Of course," said Crescy, "you're so public spirited. So's Peter. My own reaction to the police is obstructive. What's yours, Adam?"

"Oh, definitely obstructive."

"I do think that's silly," said Valentine. "I mean, we pay the police to protect us, don't we, Eve?"

"It's motoring," said Adam, "which has made them our enemies."

"Nonsense," said Crescy. "It's something fundamental. I'm against all authority. Down with everything!"

Eve said, "That's sheer affectation."

"It's not," said Crescy. "You don't understand me, Eve. Neither you nor Peter has the least idea of my nature. Have they, Adam?"

Eve said, "Has Adam?"

"Yes," said Adam. "Crescy and I are both born hooligans." He didn't look at Crescy, or Crescy at him, and it was absurd . . . he was ten years younger than Crescy . . . he had his lovely little Valentine; but there was a queer note in his voice and Eve, thinking of Peter, was suddenly afraid.

She began, "Nobody understands anybody . . ." but, as she spoke, Peter came out of the sitting-room. He looked grave. He said, "Eve, the

Superintendent wants to speak to you."

Eve went through the bar at once and into the sitting-room. Peter, taking her place, said, "I'm afraid you people will be in for it next. From the questions that were put to me, it looks as if Scaife didn't die a natural death. I believe there's a suspicion that he was poisoned."

Valentine made an incoherent shocked sound. Adam repeated, "Poisoned?"

"But how? When? Do you mean someone put something in his drink?" asked Cresy.

"I haven't the least idea. I only got that impression. Of course I oughtn't to pass it on, but I want you to realize that this is a thing which must be taken seriously."

"Good lord, yes," said Adam. "Eve served his drinks and there was a glass in front of him the whole evening. Any of us could have slipped something into it."

"It would have meant taking an awful risk," said Cresy. "Murderers in books do it—they change cocktail glasses about in front of a whole dinner party. But there were lots of us at the bar. Anyone might have turned round at any minute."

"But would they have seen anything?" said Adam. "The fatal tablet could have been held between the fingers and the thumb, as in Up Jenkins. Then as the murderer, excusing himself on the grounds of answering Nature's call, passed Scaife's table, he would only need to stretch his hand out a few inches. And it's dark over there in the corner."

"Much better not discuss it," advised Peter. "We shall only get preconceived ideas, and then . . ."

"Oh, Peter, don't be so proper," said Cresy.

Eve came back. She said, "You now, Cresy."

"Oh God!" said Cresy. "Is he what he looks like?"

"I don't think he'll approve of you," Eve whispered.

"Not in these trousers, anyway," said Cresy.

Making a face at Adam, she walked sulkily across the room. "It feels," she observed, opening the door and addressing both Eve in the lounge and Dawes, seated at Eve's writing table, "like being summoned to the Headmistress's study."

Not a muscle moved in the firmly set face of the Superintendent. He said, "Would you mind closing the door, Mrs. Hardwick?" Cresy shut the door ungracefully by leaning against it. The Superintendent said, "You're Mrs. Cresy Hardwick, of Little Bottom Cottage?"

"That's right," said Cresy.

"Will you sit down?"

Cresy perched on the arm of a chair and her rust-colored nails picked nervously at the sea-green cover.

"I understand that you were here on Thursday night when Mr. Mathew Scaife was present?"

"Yes. And when he wasn't present. I mean, when he had passed out. But I didn't see anything. . . ."

"I understand that, with the exception of the deceased himself, you were the first to arrive in the lounge bar. What exactly was the time then?"

"God knows," said Crescy.

"Well, Mrs. Hardwick, perhaps we can get at it like this: what time did you leave home to come here?"

"I don't know," said Crescy. "I haven't got a watch. It's no use my having a watch. I'm one of the people whom watches won't go for."

"But you must have *some* idea of the time," said Dawes incredulously. "Had you had supper?"

"No," said Crescy. "I forgot to have supper. I ate some sausage rolls when I got here. Does the time matter?"

Dawes didn't answer that. He said, "When you came in, Mr. Scaife was in his usual seat in the corner?"

"Yes," said Crescy.

"And you spoke to him, I think?"

"He spoke first," said Crescy.

"Can you give me an account of the conversation?"

"Well, not word for word."

"The gist of it then."

"Well, I expect Eve—Mrs. Hennisty—told you. He asked me why I hadn't answered his letter."

"His letter? What was the subject of it?"

"It gave me notice to quit my cottage. Scaife is—was my landlord."

"And you hadn't replied to the letter?"

"No. I was thinking it over."

"And when he asked you why not, what was your answer?"

"Well, I said he couldn't do that to me. You see, I'd spent a lot on the cottage and planted things in the garden and so on."

"In fact," said Dawes, with a piercing look, "you were angry and upset about this letter?"

"Well, nobody likes being turned out like that, do they? But I didn't consider that all was lost. I mean, it's three years since I signed the lease and I'd forgotten what was in it. I told Scaife—at least Eve told him— that I should consult a solicitor."

"You're very forgetful, aren't you, Mrs. Hardwick? People don't usually forget on what terms they are occupying premises, any more than they forget to have supper."

"Well," said Crescy, "I'm not like other people. I am," she said with pride, "an artist."

"Mrs. Hennisty," said Dawes, "informed me that you were a lady novelist."

Crescy said, *"Painter and poet are proud in the artist list enrolled."*

Dawes said, "Pardon?"

"Browning. It means it's all the same thing," said Crescy.

"But which *are* you?"

"A novelist," said Crescy. "A woman novelist, if you like, though what that has to do with it I can't imagine. But not a lady."

"I see," said Dawes. "You write fiction and you're naturally forgetful. I suppose it's no use asking you in what order the other customers came in?"

" 'Strewth, no. A lot of them came in together. The Days and the Franklands did. Edward and Mark Scaife drifted in at odd times. Mrs. Edward didn't arrive till it was all over."

"Vague statements like that don't help me at all," said the Superintendent. "When did you first notice that the deceased had passed away?"

"When everybody else did. When Edward Scaife told us."

"And when did you last notice that he was alive?"

"Well," said Crescy, "he spoke to Edward. Edward offered him a drink and he refused it. That was after we had had our row about the cottage."

"And when the constable came to complain about the lights, were you one of those who went out into the garden?"

"Yes, I was."

"Why did you go out?"

"Oh, just to see what was happening. And because Waller's always good value."

"As you went out you must have passed quite near the table where the deceased was sitting. Didn't you notice then whether he was breathing?"

"No, I didn't," said Crescy.

"That seems rather curious," said Dawes. "Mrs. Hennisty told me that he was breathing heavily."

"Eve's a noticing sort," said Crescy. "I'm not. And I wasn't thinking of him. I was thinking how depressing these everlasting blackouts are. Besides, nobody does notice Scaife. After he's had a couple he always goes to sleep till closing time. He used to, I mean."

"And when you went back into the lounge?"

"Well, let me see," said Crescy, staring at the carpet, with her hands dangling between her knees and her curls over her eyes. "Peter—Mr.

Conway—and I stayed out in the garden chatting of this and that, and then he went in and I paid a visit."

"A visit?" said Dawes.

"Yes," said Crescy, "for what I believe the police call a certain purpose. When I got back into the bar, Waller had gone, but everyone else was there."

"Everyone else?"

"As far as I remember."

"And after that—did anyone leave the room?"

"I don't think so. Why?"

With an edge on his voice Dawes explained. "It's important because anyone who went out by the passage door must have passed quite near to the deceased. It's curious that you can't help me, because Mrs. Hennisty informed me quite definitely that during the period that followed the business about the lights, more than one person had occasion to leave the room."

"Oh. Who?"

"Mrs. Hardwick, I'm here to get information, not to give it. Do you remember that a game of shove ha'penny was played?"

"Oh, yes."

"The shove ha'penny board was quite near to the cozy corner, I believe?"

"Well, fairly near. But it would have been impossible—I mean, if Scaife was done in, nobody could have done it in that crowd."

"Who was playing?"

"Oh, I don't know," said Crescy. "Just some of us. I didn't play. I stood by the table looking on."

"Who won the game?"

"Hasn't Mrs. Hennisty told you?"

"Yes," said Dawes, "but we like to get every statement corroborated. We also like to see who is withholding information. That helps us a lot."

"I see," said Crescy. "Well, I'm afraid I'm so terribly unobservant that I can't help you in catching people out."

Dawes shut his notebook. "It's a pity," he said, "but I daresay a lot will come back to you when you're in the witness-box. Thank you, Mrs. Hardwick. I won't trouble you any further at the moment. Would you ask the gentleman to come in—or the young lady—Mr. and Mrs. Day?"

Crescy said, "All right, but I hope you won't bother Mrs. Day much. She's quite young and rather a timid sort of girl."

Dawes said, "That's quite unnecessary, Mrs. Hardwick. I know how to deal with all types. I can sum up people the moment they enter the room." The tone of his voice said, And I've summed up you.

Crescy went out. She shut the door carefully behind her and said, "My God, my God!" Adam asked, "What's the matter?" "He didn't like me at all," said Crescy. "I think I'm Suspect Number One."

"Oh, Crescy," said Eve, "you *are* an idiot. I suppose you simply set out to rub him up the wrong way."

"He rubbed me up the wrong way," said Crescy, perching herself on one of the stools. "He didn't believe me when I said I didn't know what the time was and things like that, that I *never* know. And then he asked me who went in and out and who played shove ha'penny and where everybody was and when, and then I did pretend I couldn't remember. Damn it all, I wasn't put on earth to inform against my friends."

Eve said, "You're a fool, Crescy. If murder's been done, the only thing is to tell the truth, isn't it, Peter? You only get the wrong person into trouble otherwise."

"I didn't get anyone into trouble," said Crescy. "I didn't tell him a damn thing. Eve, duck, give me a drink. A small whiskey, please."

The Superintendent appeared at the door of the sitting-room.

"I asked," he said icily, "for Mr. and Mrs. Day to come in."

"Oh, sorry, I forgot," said Crescy.

Adam said, "I'll go first. Make Valentine drink something, Eve." Dawes had gone back into the room. He was sitting at the table, his notebook open before him, when Adam went in.

"I've no time to waste," he said ominously.

"No," said Adam, who prided himself on handling clients. "I expect you're a busy man."

Dawes almost smiled. He said, "I am. Now, Mr. Day, about Thursday night. At what time did you arrive here?"

Adam said, "My wife and I arrived at approximately twenty minutes to nine. We came into the bar with the Franklands, whom we met outside."

"And whom did you find in the bar?"

"Old Scaife; Edward Scaife; Mrs. Hardwick; Mrs. Hennisty. Conway wasn't there. He was serving drinks in the public bar."

"You passed near the deceased. He was alive then?"

"He didn't speak and his eyes were closed, but I didn't get the impression that there was anything wrong. In fact, I made some comment about him to Frankland. I said, 'Damn it, the blot's here.'"

"And then," said Dawes, "I presume you all settled down at the bar. And in the course of the evening, did anyone else come in?"

"Mark Scaife. He came in and threw back two pints and then he went off again. A bit later Conway put his head in to say that Waller had come about the lights."

"And who went out?"

"Mrs. Hennisty. Then Mrs. Hardwick. And Conway came in afterwards, so I expect he went out by the other door and round. And Frankland went out. He came back with Conway and after a minute or two Mrs. Hardwick followed them. Mrs. Hennisty came back first though. She had been upstairs to put out the light."

"Thank you, Mr. Day." The Superintendent was silent while he wrote. Then, "And did any of them pause, even for a second, near the deceased?"

"I'm quite sure none of them did," said Adam firmly.

"How can you be so sure?"

Adam had resolved to tell the truth—as Eve had said, you only got the wrong person into trouble otherwise—but he couldn't say, because they're all my friends, so he said, "Well, I'm sure I should have noticed it. I was looking towards the door."

"And why were you looking towards the door?"

Adam said, this time truthfully, "I was wondering if Mrs. Hardwick was coming back, or if she had gone home."

"I see," said Dawes, and Adam hoped he didn't. "And then?"

"Well, let me think," said Adam. "Conway went back into the public room. He used the communicating door behind the bar. After a bit he came back and asked if anyone would like a game of darts. I said I would, so I went with him—through the communicating door. I played with Smallbone, the butcher's roundsman, and then I came back. Oh, by the way, as you want to know about everyone's movements, before the game of darts and I *think* before the fuss about the lights, Mark Scaife had gone. When I came back, I came by the passage door. People were playing shove ha'penny. Mrs. Hennisty and Edward Scaife were playing Mr. Frankland and my wife. I stood and watched. I was quite near old Scaife, but I didn't notice that anything was wrong."

"And where was the lady novelist—Mrs. Hardwick—then?"

"She was sitting at the bar to begin with, but when the game got exciting, she came and stood by me."

"Near the deceased?"

"Well, no nearer than I was."

"You were standing side by side?"

"Yes."

"Then one of you was nearer to the deceased than the other."

"I suppose so," said Adam.

"Which was the nearer?"

"Well, actually she was. But she didn't go up to him. We were talking and laughing and actually we were standing arm-in-arm."

Dawes said disapprovingly, "Oh. All the time?"

"Yes," said Adam, "We're old friends. And then the group broke up and Edward Scaife said he must be getting along. He went across the room to wake his father and found him dead."

Dawes wrote. Then he said, "Thank you, Mr. Day. All that seems quite clear. Now can I see your wife?"

"Yes," said Adam, "but don't frighten her, will you? She's a bit highly strung and the corpse and everything rather upset her."

He opened the door and held it open saying, "Your turn, Valentine." Valentine didn't hesitate. She swung off her stool and, with a smile for her husband, went in to Dawes.

The Superintendent liked little women, feminine little women, with sweet voices, soft faces and small smooth hands. He liked Valentine. He smiled.

"Now, Mrs. Day, you mustn't think I'm an ogre."

"Oh, but I don't," said Valentine, widely opening her big, blue eyes. "I know the police are here to protect us. I'll help you all I can."

"That's very nice," said the Superintendent, almost beaming. "That's the right way to look at things. But in any case, I wasn't going to trouble you with a lot of questions. I only want to know this: did you at any time during the evening notice anyone standing near Mr. Scaife, or stopping beside him as they went by?"

"I don't think so," said Valentine. "You see, I was sitting at the other end of the bar. Of course, when we went to play shove ha'penny we were all fairly near him—that was Mrs. Hennisty, Edward Scaife, David Frankland and I."

"And the ones who looked on."

"Yes, my husband and Mrs. Hardwick. We were all fairly near."

"Anyone nearer than the others?"

"Well, Mrs. Hardwick was nearest. She and my husband stood at the top of the board. But she just stood there. I mean, she didn't go really near."

"Still," said Dawes, "you weren't watching her."

"No," said Valentine, "but I expect I should have noticed. I mean, it would have been funny if anyone had gone up to Mr. Scaife. He was a horrid old man. We just left him alone. I mean, he was quite dirty and rough-looking. I always said he ought to have sat in the public bar."

"I see," said the Superintendent. "Well, that's all, I think. Thank you very much for your cooperation, Mrs. Day."

Valentine smiled at him and went out. He picked up his notebook, pocketed his fountain pen and followed her. Peter, behind the bar, said, "Now for a drink, sir."

"No, I thank you," said the Superintendent. "I must be getting along now. Can you direct me to Mr. Frankland's place? I know the Hall."

Peter said, "I'll come out and put you on your way, sir." The door closed behind them. Cresy said, "Did you see the dirty look he gave me, Eve? How did you get on with him, Valentine?"

"Beautifully. It was quite easy. He just asked me questions and I answered them."

"I don't know how you people do it. You must all be very noticing," said Cresy with faint but unmistakable scorn. "Or perhaps I'm the odd one. I suppose you could all tell him exactly what I did—I hope you didn't tell him what I said about Scaife, Eve?"

"What did you say?" asked Valentine.

"I said I'd like to kill him."

"Oh!" cried Valentine.

Eve said, "No, I didn't tell him that. I thought it was unnecessary. Actually, I didn't even tell him that Scaife had given you notice. I said there had been some conversation but he didn't ask what about."

"Oh, I told him that," said Cresy. "He asked if I had been upset and I said no, because I felt doubtful whether Scaife could turn me out. If he questions us again, you might forget what I said, Eve, there's a darling. I know he suspects me."

Eve said, "You're dramatizing yourself, Cresy."

"Well, whom do you suspect?" asked Cresy. "I know whom I do."

"It's funny," said Eve. "I hadn't thought of it in that way. Of course someone must have done it. Someone who was here. Someone we know. It's rather ghastly. Or, perhaps, it was done before he I came here. I do hope so. Anyhow, it's no use starting to suspect anybody till we know how it was done."

Adam said, "Whom do you suspect, Cresy?"

"Don't . . ." began Eve, but at the same time Cresy said, "Mark Scaife."

Adam said, "Why?"

"Because he came in here. For the first time in history."

"Well, I don't suspect him," said Adam. "He looks much too much like a murderer. And besides . . ."

Eve interrupted him. "Look here, you two: if you're going to start 'naming names,' I shall close the bar."

"You can't," said Cresy. "It would be illegal. You're bound to supply alcoholic refreshment when called upon. However, Adam and I were nicely brought up and we can take a hint, can't we, Adam? Let's have the one o'clock news. . . ."

Eve had said, it's no use starting to suspect anybody . . . but after her customers had gone and she was cooking lunch for Peter and herself, she couldn't keep her mind off the ghastly possibility that murder had been done not by some low-browed, queer-headed, monstrous-minded stranger, but by one of these charming people, whom she knew. She read murder cases. She was aware that many murders are committed in smug villas by mild little people exasperated beyond endurance by this and that; but she had never got it out of her head that the murderer's a monster, an abnormal creature, whose mind works differently from yours or mine. The Franklands . . . she thought. Well, according to Peter, Bridget's a predatory female, and perhaps David knows that, and is unhappy, but there's no connection with Mathew Scaife there. Valentine couldn't swat a fly, and Adam has nothing against Scaife; only Saunders and Crescy have, and Saunders seems a violent creature, but he wasn't in the lounge bar. And Crescy . . . Crescy's unpredictable. She's bitter. She's reckless. She doesn't know how to take a blow. I'd like to kill him, she said, and, I'd like to stick a knife in his insides. And she doesn't eat enough and after all those whiskeys. . . oh, rot, thought Eve, pulling herself up: Crescy's my friend. If it was anyone here, it must have been Mark Scaife, she thought, putting everything into the simmering oven; not Edward—he's a decent sort of bloke; if anything *too* righteous—but Mark's a mystery and, as Crescy said, it was odd that last night, of all nights, he should have come into the lounge. Mark Scaife . . . she thought, getting the ice out of the refrigerator, and then there were sounds through the house and Peter came in.

"Sorry I'm late," said Peter. "I've been making friends with Mammon. I piloted the Superintendent up to the Franklands and footed it home."

"Oh, Peter," said Eve, "who do you think did it?"

Peter said, "We don't even know that it was done, but if it was, considering motive and psychology, Mark Scaife's my guess."

CHAPTER III
MONDAY

DETECTIVE-INSPECTOR NORTHEAST, C.I.D., had not been pleased when he received orders to investigate a murder case in Loamshire. A couple of years ago he had had enough of Loamshire. The Marley murder case had been a puzzling business with an end that had left a nasty taste in his mouth, and he hadn't forgotten the cavalier treatment he had received from the obstinate Melchester Superintendent and Loamshire's roaring red-faced Chief Constable. According to Superintendent Hannay, Witheridge Green was south of Melchester and a good fifteen miles from Marley; but Northeast, Wiltshire born, despised all Loamshire as a stuffy, tree-bound, rabbit-eaten county of small pastures, overgrown hedges and uninspired bankrupt farming. The country round Marley was about the best in Loamshire; there was the open stretch of ground rising to Marley Clump; but he never thought of Marley Clump without thinking of Marley Grange and its household of unhappy women. The prospect of working with two men he disliked, in a county he despised, during a war in which he wasn't allowed to fight, had disgruntled Guy Northeast and it was in no pleasant mood that he arrived in Melchester. Remembering the dishcloth soup and cabinet pudding at the Red Lion Hotel, he resolved to blow the expense and install himself at the Randolph, the only really good hotel in the town, but, on arriving there, he discovered that the premises had been obscurely taken over by the Government. Cursing his taxi-driver, he proceeded to the Red Lion, where he was informed that, owing to the closing of the Randolph, there was only one room vacant, and this turned out to be the same depressing room in which he had racked his brains over the contents of Delia Cathcart's suitcase.

It was late afternoon. Early that morning the Chief Constable, Major Carruthers, had rung up Scotland Yard to ask for assistance in a

murder case, for which the Melchester police, harried by air-raid pre-
cautions, lighting offenses and cases of profiteering, could spare neither the time nor the men, but Northeast, himself afflicted by the general disorganization, had missed the morning train and would now, he
thought, dumping his suitcase on the bed, have to endure the re-
proaches—the Yard takes its time, was their old phrase—of the Superintendent and the Chief Constable. He had better give tea a miss, he
thought; anyhow, tea at the Red Lion was an inadequate affair of soft
biscuits and tepid water poured over yesterday's tea leaves; and, since it
had begun to rain, he struggled into his mackintosh, picked up his hat
and hurried through Melchester's now soaking streets to the Police Station.

He was welcomed, this time respectfully, by the station sergeant.
The Superintendent was busy with the Chief Air Raid Warden, but, on
receiving the information that Detective-Inspector Northeast was in the
outer office, Dawes evidently decided to terminate the interview and an
elderly man of the retired naval officer type walked out, looking offended,
and Guy was shown in. The Superintendent rose with an outstretched
hand. "Glad to see you, Northeast. A real bit of luck for us, getting you
back again."

Guy hoped that his face wasn't expressing the surprise he felt. Well,
nothing succeeds like success, he thought, grasping the Superintendent's
hand and trying not to wince as his bones seemed to crack in that grip
of iron. "I'm glad to be back, sir," he said mendaciously. "Melchester's
becoming quite a home from home."

"Staying at the Red Lion again?"

"Yes, sir."

"Good pub, that," said Dawes judicially. "Good plain English fare.
Can't stand the continental muck they serve at the Randolph. Well, I
suppose we'd better get down to this business at Witheridge Green."

Guy said, "I understand they've poisoned their squire. I suppose it's
murder. You've ruled out the possibility of suicide or accident?"

"Bar wasp stings, you don't get a dose of poison in the back of the
neck by accident."

"In the back of the neck? That's a new one on me."

"And on me too," said Dawes. "Dr. Baker—you remember that little
cock sparrow who was in the Marley Case?—well, he's all over himself.
He brought the postmortem report round on purpose to explain what a
clever, observant fellow he is. Here's the report—seven pages of foolscap."

"I suppose it will have to be read," said Guy dolefully. "But couldn't
you give me the gist of it?"

"Boiled down," said the Superintendent, "it comes to this: before opening up the organs, Baker, who's a very precise little fellow, went over the corpse with a magnifying glass and, in addition to a discharge from the ear and a boil on the buttock, he discovered a small puncture in the back of the neck."

"Inflamed?"

"No. I'll come to that later. With the idea, I suppose, of earning his money, or else because he's naturally a Nosey Parker, he probed the puncture and pulled a minute piece of sponge out with his forceps. As you might expect, he sniffed his find and it smelt of tobacco."

Guy sat up.

"That sounds like nicotine . . ."

"Well, that's what we're waiting to hear. Sparkes, the county analyst, is on the job at this minute."

"So that's why the inquest was adjourned?"

"Yes, and why you're paying another visit to Melchester. Baker's theory is that Scaife died of heart failure all right, but it was induced by poisoning. He says that but for his smartness, skill and general superiority over other police surgeons, it would have been the perfect crime. You see, death took place instantaneously so the puncture hadn't time to inflame—only, of course, Baker puts it more scientifically."

Guy thought for a moment. Then, "We're up against someone with brains," he said reflectively.

"That's what the Chief said to me after our conference with Baker. Scaife was a heavy smoker and his heart was rotten. All our murderer did was to hasten the end."

"I see. Someone with brains but without patience. Any family complications?"

"Not that I've heard of. There are two sons, but, by all accounts, the old man's left nothing but debts behind him. On the other hand, he wasn't a nice piece of work and there are many that owe him a grudge in his own village. You talk to them up there and you'll hear something. No, it's not why that's the mystery, but *how*—in a bar full of people."

"You've got all their names and addresses?"

"Yes, and I know all they've condescended to tell me. But they're all friends—a little click, as you might say."

"No one saw anything peculiar?"

"Not if you're to believe their stories. In my opinion everyone who was in that bar should be requestioned and damn well put through it. With the exception of the Scaife brothers, they're as thick as thieves, and it's my belief that they've got together and decided what not to say. Look at it like this, Northeast—Scaife was sitting by himself in a corner away from the others: it's obvious that at some time in the evening our man went over to him and sat down beside him, or bent over him and pretended to give him a pat on the back—that's how I see it."

"Who found him dead?"

"His elder son, Edward Scaife. He made up his mind that it was time to go home and went, as he thought, to wake him."

"Could he have done it then?"

"I thought of that," said Dawes, "but according to Mrs. Hennisty—she's the licensee—he hadn't time. It's all in my notes here." Dawes turned over a page of the typescript and read out, *"Edward Scaife then went across the room to his father and said, 'Time to go,' and then we heard him say, 'Something's happened. I'm afraid he's gone.' I should estimate that approximately three seconds elapsed between the two remarks. I went through the bar and felt Scaife's pulse. It had stopped. I served as a V.A.D. in the last war.* Well, the poison worked instantaneously, but still, the murderer must have had it tucked away somewhere and three seconds isn't long. . . "

"And Edward Scaife's an outsider? I mean, he isn't one of this matey gang?"

"I gather not. He seems a decent chap, but actually he's new to the district. Lived there as a boy, of course, but hadn't been back for years till he lost his job as a land agent to one of the notes over in Oxfordshire, and came home. But you can get that bit of Mrs. Hennisty's corroborated by Adam Day. He's not a bad witness, though he's definitely in the click. Or his wife. She's a nice little woman, but women aren't so reliable when it comes to estimating time. The Franklands—" He shuffled through his notes. "Well, they were rather vague. Mr. Frankland—he describes himself as a journalist—said he was talking and didn't notice, and Mrs. Frankland, who calls herself a farmer and seems a practical sort of woman, didn't hear the first remark, but noticed Edward going across to his father, and says that the second remark was made as he bent over him."

"Well, sir," said Guy, "I'll get on to these notes of yours and I'll go out to this pub tonight—with any luck the gang will be there, talking things over. I'll have a look at them without letting them know who I am."

"O.K.," said the Superintendent. "I know you're keen on the psychological point of view. Personally, I prefer hard facts, but you go about it in your own way. The Chief hoped to see you when he was in this morning—thought that whoever was coming would be down by the morning train. But he'll be here tomorrow at nine-thirty, if you'll make a point of calling in then."

Guy took his leave and, still marvelling at the Superintendent's change of heart—'Go about it in your own way' was something new indeed—he went back to the Red Lion and settled down in a plush armchair under a dusty palm, with a drink beside him, to study the Superintendent's notes. Eve Hennisty's statement was clear and practical; it surprised him, coming from the licensee of a village pub. Peter Conway, as a War Reserve policeman, ought, he felt, to be reliable, but the information he had supplied was scrappy, as he had spent so much time in the public bar, away from the scene of action. Dawes had evidently taken a dislike to the lady novelist. At the end of her record of forgetfulness he had noted: *An apparently reluctant and probably quite unreliable witness. A fast type.* Adam Day's contribution seemed definite but rather glib. Mrs. Day, for some unknown reason, had been let off very lightly by Dawes. For a journalist, David Frankland seemed curiously unobservant, while Bridget Frankland, farmer, had supplied a great deal of irrelevant information about the farming methods of the deceased. Edward Scaife supplied nothing new, beyond his firsthand description of discovering that his father was dead. *It was a shock naturally,* Edward stated, *but it was not altogether unexpected. My father was an old man and violently prejudiced against the medical profession. He took no care of himself. He was out in all weathers. He didn't look well and, as a family, we are not long-lived.* Mark Scaife was indeed an unsatisfactory witness. He had left the inn halfway through the evening and where he had gone was his own business. Like the lady novelist, he had inspired a footnote: *M. Scaife definitely hostile. A surly, foulmouthed type.*

Guy pocketed the notes. He was interested in people and his spirits rose; he was looking forward to an intriguing evening with the fast lady novelist, the nice little woman, the decent chap and his foulmouthed brother, that was to say if his luck was in and he found them at the pub. If not, he couldn't, he decided, do better than reveal himself to Mrs. Hennisty and have a good look round the place. He ordered another gin and French and picked up Dr. Baker's report.

The deceased, he learned, was seventy-six years of age and in poor health. His heart was diseased; there were signs of cirrhosis of the liver due to prolonged overindulgence in alcohol; he had a neglected carbuncle on the left buttock and a discharge from a long-standing abscess in the right ear. A dirty old soaker, all the better out of the way thought Guy, and read on. A fragment of sponge, possibly steeped in poison, had been introduced subcutaneously into the back of the neck by means of some sharp instrument. Considering the deceased's state of health, death would have taken place instantaneously, and, roughly, within an hour of the doctor's examination at ten-forty-five. The remainder of the seven pages minutely followed Dr. Baker's processes of thought and paid handsome tribute to his sagacity. Well, it was all very interesting, Guy thought, but he'd be glad to have it confirmed that the poison was one which, when purchased, had to be signed for: this looked like being a difficult case and there were too many poisons which could be bought without record over any chemist's counter, to be left about in kitchen cupboards or on shelves in bathrooms, waiting for some poor devil's Ithuriel's Hour.

He folded up Baker's report and put it away, along with the Superintendent's notes, in his breast pocket; then he went into the long, cold, grained-and-varnished coffee room for dinner. Soup was crushed potatoes in boiled and watered milk; fish, unidentifiable under a white sauce, was followed by tough foreign mutton, boiled-to-death cabbage, scraps of mint afloat in vinegar, and potatoes, mashed without energy. Then came a slab of canary pudding, smeared with jam made from pulped marrows and colored red, and biscuits and your choice between Gorgonzola and a soapy triangle wrapped in silver paper. As Guy left the room, the first pangs of a formidable attack of indigestion were gnawing at his vitals.

He took the Melchester-Lesser Pocklington bus, which, he was informed, stopped at a crossroads, from which it was less than a five minute's walk to Witheridge Green, and for twenty minutes, now doubled up with indigestion, he bumped and swayed along the highroad at an apparently furious speed. As the bus drew near to Witheridge Green, people sitting behind him began to gossip about the murder: Squire Scaife was a rum 'un; there'd been a time when he was for everlasting writing to the *Melchester Mercury* to say how farm laborers had been better off when they were paid ten bob a week; by all accounts, someone had done a good job, putting him out of the way. The bus stopped. The conductor called out, "Witheridge." Guy got out and took the ascending road, which the conductor had indicated by a jerk of his thumb.

It was a bright, chill evening. The hunters' moon, a sharp-edged sickle, was rising into a galaxy of stars. Over the woods, the long-fingered searchlights moved and hovered; there was a grimmer sport afoot than fox-hunting this year. Better not think of that; it only made you curse the day when you'd become a policeman, so that now, when other men were hunting U-boats, drawing the sky for enemy aircraft, all you'd got to hunt was some poor devil who had been misguided enough, or exasperated enough, to take the law into his own hands and deliver this hedgebound hamlet from its local Hitler.

Guy came out on the green. A rough road crossed it. The macadam, turning left, led him past cottages powdered with starlight, to a long, low house, which a sign, depicting a small white terrier of uncertain parentage, proclaimed as The Dog. There was a white fence with a gate in it, which led to a garden. *No Dogs Allowed* and *Please Shut the Gate*, said notices. In the shadow of the house he struck a match, discovered a door that said *Public Bar*, opened it and found himself in a square, blue-lighted room, smelling comfortably of beer, old oak and tobacco. There were several men in the bar, and a small, dark, depressed-looking woman in a flimsy, pinkish overall was serving them. He hesitated for a moment and then noticed *Lounge Bar* painted on the door opposite him. He went through to an unlighted lobby and the sound of voices brought him round left-handed. He opened a door and his first impression was of a particularly charming room, softly lit, chintz-hung, cozily warmed by a bright fire, made, so his nose told him, of apple logs. Murder? he thought, and then it flashed across his mind that not one of the murder cases he had had to do with had been suitably set in sordid or horrific surroundings; it was an undercurrent, this desire to kill, a crawling thing, deep down under the placid waters. . . .

The fair, dignified woman behind the bar looked up and said, "Good evening." Guy walked to the bar. A woman, with green eyes and a mop of honey-colored curls, and an arty fellow, with a lock of hair over his forehead, drew in their elbows, and Guy, feeling pansy, asked for a *creme de menthe* which he hoped would settle his digestion. While Eve served it, he looked along the bar at the row of profiles. Besides the two who had tucked in their elbows, there was a dark, heavy-featured woman with swinging earrings, a little man with a blond beard, and a delightful 'rogue in porcelain.'

The 'rogue in porcelain' said, "Well, I only saw him once. I was walking across the right of way and he was forking manure or something out of a cart and he yelled at me to shut the gate, which of course I was going to. He was awfully rude—I mean, he could easily have said: Would you mind shutting the gate? or something like that, but he roared out, 'Shut the bloody gate, can't you—I don't want my cattle something-or-anothering out on the bloody highroad.' When I got into the next field, I met Mrs. Chandler and I asked her who the man was, because I thought Adam ought to complain to Scaife, but she said it was Mark Scaife. I thought that was all the more reason for Adam to complain, but he wouldn't."

The arty-looking fellow said, "I wasn't put on earth to complain," and for that he got a distinctly matey look from Green Eyes, beside him. But the 'rogue in porcelain' said, "Oh, well, if you don't mind your wife being sworn at . . ." Guy decided: Mr. and Mrs. Adam Day, threw back his *creme de menthe* and asked for a pint of bitter.

Earrings said, "Doesn't hurt you to be sworn at, Valentine. Enlarges your vocabulary. I'm fearfully foulmouthed myself, these days—you get so, farming. I must say my sympathies are with Mark on that occasion. Bloody fools leave gates open and not only are you up all night chasing stock, but you get fined for permitting straying."

Bridget Frankland, farmer, thought Guy, taking his tankard to the armchair by the fire, where he hoped he'd be forgotten.

Valentine said, "Well, I don't see any point in swearing. It's ugly. It's all very well for men . . ."

"Oh, God!" said Green Eyes. "How you do like to label everything. Women. Men. British. Foreign. Black. White. Good. Wicked. Oh, my God."

Obviously, thought Guy, the fast lady novelist. Fast? Well, she drinks and smokes and calls rather freely on her Maker, and that would be enough for Dawes. But personally, he thought, his first admiration for his 'rogue in porcelain' fading, I'd feel safer going over to post with her than with the nonswearing, nonsmoking Valentine. As for Bridget Frankland, farmer, practical she may be, but one has to consider those earrings and that husband. Wish he'd utter. . .

But it was Adam who uttered. He said, "Shut up, Cresry. Pity the young. They have to generalize."

That didn't please his wife. She said, "I'm not as young as all that, Adam. I know there are lots of quite womanly women who swear. Cresry herself, for instance."

"*Would* you call me womanly?" asked Cresry, blowing smoke through her nose.

"Oh, yes," said Valentine. "Very. I know you do lots of mannish things, but you can't disguise it. You're one of those people . . . well, I mean, even your trousers only make you look more feminine. And of course you've got a very feminine attitude toward men. . . ."

Miaou, thought Guy, and then he thought: Touche, for Cresry, with Adam, was sitting at right angles to the others, and he could see her face and it had turned scarlet. Her mouth opened, but whatever she was going to say was exasperatingly prevented by Eve Hennisty, who interposed, "Going back to Mark Scaife, I was surprised to find him so civilized. I had always heard that he was a complete boor." Afterwards, when she came to think things over, Eve blamed herself for giving this fillip to the gossip that all evening she herself had attempted to subdue, but she had had to say something quickly, or heaven alone knew what might develop from this incredible exchange between Cresry and Valentine. Her red herring proved only too successful. David Frankland said, "I know. I always understood he was completely uneducated. When I've been playing darts in the other bar, I've heard him talking broad Loamshire. It knocked me flat when he walked in here and started speaking like an educated man."

"Educated. Uneducated. Clean. Dirty," the fast lady novelist chanted angrily to herself.

Guy wished she'd shut up. This was interesting. His luck was in, however. No one took any notice of Crescy except Adam, who took her by the scruff of her neck, and Bridget said, "Well, I don't see why he shouldn't come in here, David. His father does—did, I mean, and his brother. Just because he works hard and gets a bit of honest muck on his clothes, I don't see why, while they're here, he should sit in the public bar with the laborers."

"There's no reason why he should," said David. "Only he always has. Isn't it a fact, Eve, that he never came into this room till Thursday evening?"

Eve said, "Well, it's true, but it's not very important, is it? I mean, it's almost like a club in here. He may not have liked to butt in."

"Till Thursday," said David. "Then he did like to butt in."

"What are you driving at?" said Bridget, looking him in the eyes.

"I'm not driving at anything. Only, it was curious and rather interesting."

"I don't think it was curious at all," said Bridget and between her swinging earrings, her full mouth, painted a dark, impossible red, slowly smiled. What that smile meant, Guy wished he knew. Was it a smile of self-satisfaction, revealing that Mark Scaife had penetrated into the lounge because Bridget Frankland was there, or did it mean that Bridget believed Mark Scaife to be his father's murderer? Anyhow, Guy was learning something. Dawes, for all his questioning, hadn't discovered that on the night of Scaife's murder, for the first time in history, Mark Scaife had entered the lounge bar.

"He's a very good-looking man, isn't he?" said Valentine, and, "Who's talking about good-looking men?" asked a large and not good-looking, but obviously good-natured, competent and cheerful person appearing from a door, which Guy presumed led to private rooms.

"Evening, Peter," said everyone, and Crescy said, "'Down, down, little flutterer.' Valentine wasn't talking about you, my dear."

"Shame," said Peter.

"She was talking about Mark Scaife," said Bridget Frankland.

Peter said, "He'd be better looking if he washed more."

"You would say that," retorted Bridget, reflectively tapping a cigarette on the bar. "Personally, I think he looks like a man, and that's quite a rare thing nowadays."

David said, "He looks like a brute, you mean."

"Perhaps," said Bridget, with another slow smile, "I do."

So you're like that, are you? thought Guy.

Eve changed the subject. She said to Crescy, "How's One-Eye?"

Crescy brightened up. "Getting his winter coat and looking very wuffy. I say, Peter, do you suppose that Edward Scaife knows that his father gave me notice to quit before he passed out?"

"It depends on whether the old man kept a copy of his letters."

"I should say he didn't," said Eve.

"Anyhow," said Peter, "I don't know the law. Perhaps Scaife's death makes everything null and void. But Edward's a decent fellow. He won't turn you out. The best thing you can do is to talk it over with him."

Crescy said, "I'm not so sure that he is 'a decent fellow.' I believe he's mean."

"So do I," said Adam. "If I were you, Crescy, I'd let sleeping dogs lie. If there was nothing in writing you're probably safe. It was obvious that Scaife didn't think much of Edward. Very likely he never discussed things like that with him at all."

"You don't know that he didn't," said Peter. "If you leave it like that, you'll find yourself in a mess, Crescy. I mean, you ought to start looking for another place, if you've got to leave."

"I don't want another place," said Crescy, like a child.

"I think it would be very stupid to stir up Edward," said Adam. "Decent fellers," he said in Peter's voice, "are a bloody lot—decent and that's all."

Peter said, "What more do you want people to be?"

"Either more or less," said Adam. "But decent—my God, no."

Peter shrugged his shoulders. "You're too bloody clever, young Day."

Adam appeared to take this as an insult. He said, "Thanks a lot—old Conway. I'm not clever. But I'm not a 'decent feller,' thank God."

"It might be an improvement," said Peter, "if you were. The straightforward thing would be for Crescy to get hold of Edward . . ."

"There you are, Crescy," interrupted Adam, tilting his stool. "Be straightforward. Play the game. The advice I gave you may be clever, but it's not cricket, chaps . . ."

Eve said desperately, "Would you turn on the fan, Adam? It's awfully smoky in here."

Adam stretched out an arm to the electric switch. Peter said, "All very well to sneer, but the simple, straightforward line of action usually pays."

"Ha!" said Adam in triumph. "Now we have it. The 'decent feller's' philosophy. *Whatever, Lord, I lend to thee, Repayed ten thousand times shall be, So gladly, Lord, I lend to thee . . .*"

"That isn't it at all," said Peter angrily. "Your type of mind simply

twists things. You can be as clever as you like about your own affairs—
that's your funeral—but when it comes to giving advice to Cresy—"

"I don't want anyone's advice," said Cresy firmly. "Do shut up, Adam.
I—" But neither of the men took any notice of her. It seemed to Guy
that something, which had been heating up for a long time, was going
to boil over. Adam said, "Why the hell shouldn't I give advice to Cresy?"

"Because it's bloody bad advice," said Peter. "And because you've
mucked up your own affairs enough without your starting on Cresy's.
And because if Cresy wants anything, she can come to me. You," he
said, glancing at Valentine, "have got your own responsibilities."

Adam's glass tankard was half full of beer. He picked it up and threw
it at Peter. It caught him on the shoulder. The beer ran down his neck
and over his navy blue sweater.

There was a horrid silence. Then one or two people said, "Adam!"
Adam said, "My God, Peter, I'm sorry."

Peter began to dry his neck with a glass-cloth, which Eve had handed
to him. He said nothing. Eve said, "This Scaife business has made us all
nervy." She stooped and picked up bits of the shattered tankard.

Guy found that he was standing up, in anticipation of a roughhouse,
he supposed. It might still come when Conway spoke; it would have
come if those two hadn't had the bar between them.

Peter gave his neck a final wipe. He threw down the glass-cloth and
said, "All right, Adam." Adam repeated, "I'm sorry." "Forget it," said
Peter and pulled out a packet of cigarettes and lit one. But that wasn't
the end of it, Guy thought as he sat down, for Peter's face was hard and
unsmiling. Adam might forget it; Cresy might forget it; but Peter
wouldn't . . .

"What will everyone have?" asked a small, embarrassed voice, which
was Cresy's.

Everyone had the same again, and they all began to talk about the
war, except Adam, who remained silent. Presently the Franklands left;
the Days faded out behind them; Cresy asked for a pork pie; Peter went
to get it and Guy moved over to the bar and asked for another pint of
bitter. Eve said, "Oh—I'm afraid I forgot you in your corner. I hope
you've had everything you wanted. I'm afraid it's been rather a stormy
evening. We don't usually behave like this, but an unpleasant thing happened here last week and it's made us all rather nervy."

"You mean Mr. Scaife's death," Guy said. "As a matter of fact I'm
here to investigate it. I'm from Scotland Yard."

"My God," said Cresy, before Eve could speak. "You might have
told us. You don't mean to say that you've been sitting there, listening?"

Guy faced her. There was a frown-line between her eyebrows; the skin at the corners of her eyes was what advertisements of skin foods call crepy, but her eyes were like green pools with the sunshine over them. He said quietly, "Listening's my job, I'm afraid."

"I can't think," said Crescy, "how anyone can be a policeman. It's worse than being a tax collector." The tone of her voice said, "Or a rat in the arras. Or a worm."

"Well, I didn't come here to talk about that," said Guy. "I came to get some information."

"We aren't informers," said Crescy.

"I know that," said Guy, "but I expect you're sufficiently public-spirited not to withhold information in a murder case."

"I'm not," said Crescy.

Though she was almost old enough to be his mother, Guy wanted to slap her. He said, "I'll come to you later. I'm talking to Mrs. Hennisty now. And to Mr. Conway," he added, as Peter reappeared with Crescy's pie.

"Peter," said Eve, "this gentleman's from Scotland Yard."

"Detective-Inspector Northeast," supplemented Guy.

Peter did not make the usual joke about preferring Southwest. He said, "Oh, I see. What can I do for you, sir?"

Guy said, "I've seen the notes the Superintendent made when he questioned you all; in fact, I've got them here with me. They're all right as far as they go, but, frankly, it seems to me incredible that a man could be murdered, as Scaife apparently was murdered, in this room without a single one among six or seven people noticing that anything was wrong. It's sillier than that, even. If I'm to believe what I'm told, no one noticed that anybody went near the man."

"Don't you believe it?" asked Crescy.

"No," said Guy. "Do you?"

"Yes," said Crescy. "But then I'm of a credulous nature. My God, yes," she added, as if remembering bitterly some previous occasion when she had been taken in.

"I must say, it does sound unlikely," admitted Peter. "I'm a War Reserve policeman, sir, so I've thought a bit about these things. My trouble is that I didn't come into this room until Scaife was dead and they called me not for keeps, that's to say. I came through after we'd been out about the light that was showing—and I looked in once to ask if anyone wanted to play darts, but I didn't look in Scaife's direction either time."

"And you, Mrs. Hennisty? You're quite sure he was alive when you went out?"

"I'm positive. I heard him snore as I passed and I'm afraid I thought what a blot he was."

"But when you came back he wasn't snoring?"

"Not that I noticed. As a matter of fact, I came in rather quickly, because I thought I might be wanted at the bar. What I mean to say is that I might have passed him between snores."

Guy turned to look at the corner seat. "The table," he said, "was between him and anyone who passed him. He was sitting upright. To touch him, it would have been necessary to lean across the table. Someone most have seen."

"I can only explain it in this way," said Eve. "People sitting at the bar had their backs to him and, at the same time, they were blocking my view."

"I can quite see that," said Guy, "but the times I'm thinking of are pretty definite; they are the times when someone was passing in or out. You went out behind the constable, Mrs. Hennisty, and Scaife was alive then. Mrs. Hardwick followed you." He swung round to face Crescy. "Mrs. Hardwick, why did you go out then?"

"For the reasons I gave the Superintendent—vulgar curiosity and because I dote on the constable," said Cresy, and her eyes met his, but they had changed. They were no longer green pools with the sunshine over them, but cats' eyes, wary and hard.

"And Mr. Frankland? Did he follow immediately behind you?"

"I haven't an idea," said Cresy. "You'd better ask him."

"And the Days could corroborate what he tells you," said Peter. "They stayed in the bar. So did Edward Scaife and Bridget Frankland. I expect they noticed Cresy's exit too."

"I shall be seeing them tomorrow. Now you, Mrs. Hennisty. Did you notice when Mark Scaife went out?"

"No. I only noticed that he'd gone. I remarked on it because I'd drawn him some beer. But Bridget told me that he went before Waller came."

"And now about Mr. Day. He went out for a game of darts and he went through the door behind the bar. Did anyone see him come in?"

"Yes," said Cresy. "He passed Scaife and stood by the shove ha'penny board."

Guy, who had his notebook out, ticked off a scrawl, which stood for 'Day comes back,' and wrote 'Hardwick' beside the tick, but, taking into account the scene he'd witnessed that evening, he'd need, he thought, some corroboration of whatever Cresy Hardwick might tell him about Adam Day. According to the Superintendent's notes, the two of them had stood arm-in-arm watching the game of shove ha'penny, but, trusting Cresy as little as he did, it was no use taking her over that again. He said, "Well, the Superintendent has got everything else, I think. Do you mind now if I ask you a few personal questions?" and Eve and Peter said, "Not a bit," and, "Not at all," and readily told him how Eve, a war-widow, had, after various experiments in other occupations, entered the hotel business, and how, three years ago, being tired of working for other people, she had taken The Dog and brought Peter down from London, where he had been working only moderately successfully in the motor trade.

Crescy, on the other hand, seemed reluctant to reveal her life's history. She asked, what did it matter? Pushing her hand through her curls, she wasted time quoting poetry to the effect that she was a reed and the wind blew through her, and then she delivered a lecture on the iniquity of common people poking and prying into artists' private lives. Guy said, "Quite," and asked if she were married? "Divorced woman," said Crescy, turning her glass in her hand. Guy dragged out of her that she had been divorced eight years ago; that her former husband's name was Hugo le Mesurier Hardwick; that he was remarried now and was living a Denis Mackail and A. A. Milne life in a smug smug smug west-end square, the name of which she had forgotten; that men were a joke, which, once seen, kept you laughing for the rest of your life; that she had taken Little Bottom Cottage three years ago, before which she had been knocking round Provence and Bloomsbury. "What were your reactions," Guy asked, "when Scaife gave you notice to quit?" "Well, I didn't want to go," said Crescy, fixing cats' eyes on Eve, "but there are other places. My reactions were philosophical." Guy doubted it. Mrs. Hardwick didn't strike him as a philosophical character and the look she'd fixed on Eve had said, for God's sake . . .

"Well," he said, shutting his notebook, "I think that's all for the present," and Crescy said she must go home and she hoped she wouldn't be followed by men in bowler hats, snooping and informing on their fellows. "When you think of the mess we're in," she said, munching a second pork pie as she drifted towards the door, "all whirling, no one knows why, on an ambiguous planet in incalculable spaces . . ." The door shut. Guy said, "A temperamental lady."

Eve said, "She writes beautifully. It's their work that is themselves. What you meet is the bits that are left over."

"Quite," said Guy, "but this business about the cottage—did she really take it philosophically?"

There was an instant's hesitation. Then, "Yes," said Eve. "After all, as she says, there are other places."

Guy climbed off his stool. "I wonder if I could look round a bit? This is where Scaife sat—upright, I gather. . . . The shove ha'penny board was where it is now. . . . People went through this door when they went to the garden or to the lavatory . . ."

"Quite right," said Peter, opening the door and switching the light on. "Only the lobby was dark then—I'd taken the bulb out and I put one back for the ambulance men—Eve, remind me to take it out again. This is the door into the public bar. When Adam Day had finished his game of darts, he came through here."

"And this is where Mark Scaife usually spent his evening," said Guy, turning the handle of the door. "Do you mind if I adjourn there?"

"Not at all, I'll be through myself in a minute. There's still a good hour till closing time."

"Remember I shall be anonymous," said Guy, and Peter nodded and went back into the lounge and Guy into the public bar, There were only four men there; a tall, dark, hefty fellow with a weather-beaten skin, whom he placed as a farm laborer; a rabbit-faced sixteen-year-old; an apple-cheeked man with bright brown eyes, and a genteel little person with a pale face and gold-rimmed spectacles. Apple-cheeks and Rabbit-face were playing darts and Rabbit-face was winning. The genteel little person said, "'Tis to be 'oped that 'is first action will be to 'ave them 'orrible dogs destroyed."

The laborer chuckled. With a broader Loamshire accent he replied, "What beats me is 'ow a chap like you, what's afraid of dogs, ever come to be a postman."

"I didn't reckon," said the genteel little person, "with folks like Squire Scaife. There's other folks got dogs, but they sees reason. At Little Bottom Cottage now—well, *she's* a lady. She fixed up a letter box on the gate after ter bloody great Awlsation went for me."

The laborer said, "I reckon it 'ud be a shame for Mr. Edward to 'ave them dogs destroyed. I reckon 'e will, though. Not because they bites the postman, but because they eats and don't pay for what they 'aves. 'E's the newfangled kind. Puts paid to anything what doesn't show a profit—man or beast. Reckon we shall all 'ave to jump to it in future, up at the 'all."

"There you goes," said the postman. "And only a few nights ago you was carrying on awful about the old squire."

The laborer expressed an unprintable opinion of Scaife. " 'Owsoever," he added gloomily, "I've lived for fifty years, I 'ave, and I've never seen no good come of any change."

His glass was empty. Guy asked what everyone would have. Everyone had beer. The game of darts was finished. Rabbit-face and Apple-cheeks came and stood beside him at the bar. Son of a long line of yeoman farmers, Guy knew how to talk to countrymen and he soon had the four men freely discussing the murder of the squire. Two-thirds of

the population of Witheridge Green had, it appeared, motive for murder, and he could only congratulate himself that two-thirds of the population of Witheridge Green had not taken it into their heads to patron-
ize the lounge bar on Saturday night. "What beats me," he said, "is how
a man can be done in in a roomful of people and yet none of them
notice a single bloody thing."

"Ah," said the laborer, whom he now knew as Bert Saunders, "don't
you believe it, mate. The gentry sticks together thicker nor thieves."

Then Smallbone, insatiable, challenged Guy to a game of darts.

Smallbone, who took the game very seriously, possessed his own set
of darts, but Guy picked up four at random from the selection on the
shelf. They tossed, and Smallbone opened with a double six. Guy made
a mess of his first two throws and then scored a double nine. When he
went to pull his darts out of the board, one of them stuck till he wrenched
at it. He gave it a casual glance. The shaft seemed flattish, improvised.
"Queer sort of darts you keep here," he said. "Looks as if this one had
been fitted with a homemade shaft. It's got an eye like a bodkin." "There's
plenty more on the shelf," said Smallbone in a hurry to throw, and Guy
tossed his dud back on the heap and picked out another dart.

The game was a quick one, Smallbone being an easy winner, and
Guy, resolving to concentrate in the hope of clearing his brain of the
seesaw—it was done and it couldn't have been done—suggested another.
Smallbone shook his head. "I've got to foot it 'ome. That night Squire
was done in, me bike was took. Me sister's bike it was, and cor lumme,
didn't she create? 'Asn't got over it yet. You'd think it was a bleeding
Rolls Royce instead of a rickety push-bike she paid the Rector's wife ten
bob for."

He finished his drink and went out. "He looks like making a good
darts player," said Guy.

"That's all 'e thinks of," said Saunders.

"That's why we get the Franklands' beef and they get our mutton,"
said Peter, who had been watching the game from behind the bar, and
the conversation was diverted to the iniquities of the younger genera-
tion; no wonder they got uppish, Saunders opined, when they were paid
out of all reason; at Smallbone's age he'd been earning ten bob a week
at what, compared to carting round joints on a bicycle, was skilled labor.
"Were you working for Scaife then?" Guy asked, and Saunders said that
he wasn't like some, always chopping and changing; he had worked for
Scaife all his life. Guy suggested that he must have had something to put
up with, to which Saunders replied with reminiscences of the Hall in
the days before Scaife had broken his wife's heart and she had left him.
Together Saunders and Apple-cheeks, now identified by Guy as Stanley

Janes, the carrier, related the story, as it was known to the village, of Scaife's marriage, goings-on and slow decline; and afterwards, walking down to the crossroads, with the strange thin smell of frost in his nostrils and each field and tree spellbound in the moonshine, Guy began to wonder whether it wasn't in that tale of 'far off unhappy things' that he would find the solution to his mystery. A man like Scaife went through life and left a snail's trail behind him. Country people had long memories. A bastard son, coming to man's estate, might take it into his head to avenge the wrong done to his mother. Or didn't that happen? thought Guy, quickening his step as he heard the common-sense chug of a motor engine.

No, it didn't happen, he thought, waiting for the bus, no longer influenced by frost and moonshine; men killed and swung, but not to avenge their mothers. Besides, as far as he knew there had been no by-blows of Scaife's in the lounge of The Dog that night, only two sons with a derelict farm to inherit, and one of those a decent fellow and the other uncouth, perhaps, but no more uncouth than his father and only a suspect because of his sudden excursion into gentility. Funny, that; but men have moods, thought Guy, taking his seat under the queer blue lights that suggested some fantastic trip beyond the grave, or it was possible that Mark had forsaken the public bar at the suggestion of his more conventional brother. Then the others. . .

The Hardwick woman, theoretically lawless, had had notice to quit her cottage. She had given Mrs. Hennisty a look that said, keep your mouth shut; it was possible that she had said, "I'd like to murder Scaife," but that didn't mean she had murdered him . . . rather the reverse . . . she was, surely, too hard-boiled to embark on the mug's game of murder. But was it always a mug's game? Well, not always, and, if this looked like being the perfect crime, then, Guy thought, he'd begin to suspect Crescy. As for Valentine Day . . . well, he'd been taken in before by blue eyes and helplessness . . . only, as far as he knew yet, she had no possible motive. Adam Day was an uncontrolled sort of a fellow, threw a tankard of beer at a man and thought about it afterwards, but where was his motive? Frankland was a mild little man, who might turn nasty, and there was a suspicion of Lady Macbeth about his wife; but their lives and Scaife's seemed utterly unconnected. There was only one thing to do, Guy thought, and that was to concentrate on the crime itself: who had nicotine in his possession: how had it been introduced into the neck of a man sitting upright against a wall in a room full of people. . . . ?

CHAPTER IV
TUESDAY

THE CHIEF CONSTABLE, in Harris tweeds and his regimental tie, appeared to have suffered the same change of heart as the Superintendent. "Northeast!" he roared. "Ha, ha! A favorable wind for Melchester!" Damn you, thought Guy, and, producing a hearty but mirthless laugh, he said he hoped so. "That's right, my boy," said Carruthers. "Success comes to those who expect it." Guy doubted that and said so. Three years ago, he had had less self-confidence; intimidated by the bellowing, he had forced his big, slow body and quiet, persevering mind to keep step with the Chief Constable's quite ineffective bustling, but this time he wasn't going to be pushed along; he was going to be himself; he was going to set the pace and do the talking.

"Call it luck if you like," said the Chief Constable indulgently. "You'll certainly need some luck if you're going to catch a fellow who's got the nerve to commit murder under the eyes of a half-a-dozen people. I don't know this pub except from the outside. This modern craze for spending the evenings in pubs isn't in my line for country. But Dawes tells me that the corner seat that the old man occupied is in full view of the bar there. Where's that plan of yours, Super?"

Dawes produced a sheet of paper. He explained to Guy, "I sent a constable up on Sunday afternoon after I'd been there. Good idea. Questions crop up that can be settled straight away if you've something like this in front of you. Here you are. Here's the lounge. The corner seat's marked X, the shove ha'penny board S, and there's the door into the lobby. As you can see, sir," he pointed out to the Chief Constable, "the people standing round the shove ha'penny board were near enough to him, and everybody who went to and from the lobby passed his table."

Guy said, "The game of shove ha'penny was played after he was dead—if we can attach any importance to Mrs. Hennisty's statement that, when she came from seeing about the lights, he wasn't breathing."

"But can we?" said Dawes. "She only says that she didn't notice he was breathing. In any case, I'm not sure what importance we can attach to any of these statements. As I told you last night, Northeast, these

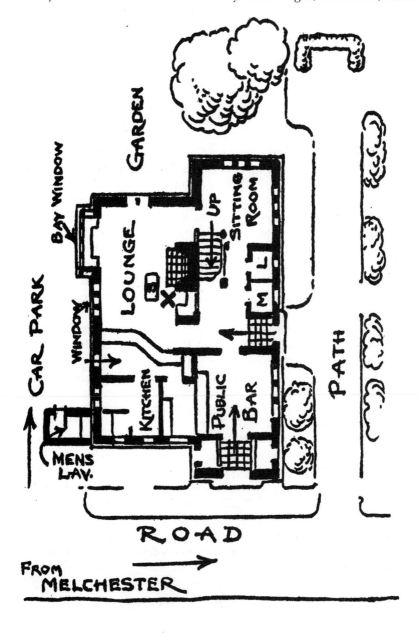

people are all in a little click together. The lady novelist . . . well, it's obvious that she's out not to help but to hinder. The others may be the same but cleverer, clever enough to give an appearance of frankness to their statements."

"Who," asked the Chief Constable, "is this Hennisty woman?"

"Well, sir," said Dawes, "she keeps a pub, but she seems to think she's a lady."

"Pukka sahibs," said Carruthers, "do these things nowadays. Have to."

"I think," said Guy, "we can call them 'pukka sahibs,' but, if you'll excuse my saying so, sir, that's no reason for taking their statements as gospel. I must say, though, Mrs. Hennisty struck me as being reliable and so did her brother—a play-the-game kind of a fellow."

"I don't know any of 'em," said Carruthers. "Queer lot, I should think. Dawes seems rather to fancy this lady novelist. Queer lot, novelists. Drink like fish. I've heard what goes on at their parties."

"I've seen the lady, sir. I went out to Witheridge Green last night and had a look at the party. From their conversation I gather they fancy Mark Scaife, but it's early days to be fancying anybody."

"I quite agree," said Dawes. "Let's stick to facts. The bits I set down in my notes were just my first impressions."

"I know, sir," said Guy. "Very useful. But I wish I could get at the method. A jab in the neck. . . . All very easy if anyone had been alone in the room with him."

"There's a host of witnesses to prove that no one was alone with him. I suppose," suggested the Chief Constable, "that the Hennisty woman couldn't have done it before anyone else came into the bar. There's no corroboration of her statement that she heard him breathing."

"But you're forgetting, sir, he spoke to Mrs. Hardwick and his son Edward."

"Of course, of course. Well, let's concentrate on these people who went in and out. What did they go in and out for?"

"Their explanations seem quite feasible, sir. They went out to the lavatories or, when the constable turned up to complain about the lights, to see what was going on. No," said Guy putting down the plan, "I think we shall have to tackle this from quite a different angle." He turned to Dawes. "Have you had the confirmation from the analyst?"

"Yes. They rang up late last night and confirmed it this morning in writing. It was nicotine."

"Hell! That's easily obtainable."

"Not so very. You have to sign for it in the poison book," said Dawes.

"Yes," Guy admitted, "but anyone with a fair knowledge of chemistry can distill it for themselves from cigars, or a pound of shag, besides which, it's the sort of thing that lies about farms and where there are keen gardeners. Mrs. Frankland's a farmer, and the Scaifes. And there's a big garden at The Dog, isn't there?"

"Yes," said Dawes, "and it's down in black and white in the lady novelist's statement that she's done a lot to her garden. Potters about and writes it up afterwards, I expect. Namby-pamby stuff. What I like is a good Western."

"Well, there we are," said Guy gloomily. "A trip round these farms and gardens seems indicated. What's the betting that I find a tin of nicotine at every one of them?"

"Cheer up, man," said the Chief Constable. "You've got a bit more to go on than that. There's something juicy for you in the confirmation we got this morning." He rapidly untidied the heap of papers on the desk as he rummaged. "Here we are. *Nicotine . . .* Hum, ha . . . . *Exhibit A. The small fragment of absorbent material proved after microscopical examination to be sponge and, when compared with commercial samples obtained locally, it was found to approximate to the coarse type sold for cleaning cars rather than to the toilet variety.* Hum, ha . . . *Exhibit A was soaked in a small quantity of distilled water and the liquor then tested and identified as nicotine. A fine sediment was left in the test tube, which has not yet been satisfactorily identified.*"

"That's better," said Guy. "Nicotine and a car sponge. That narrows things down a bit. Well, sir, I'll be off on my treasure hunt."

"I'm afraid," said the Chief Constable, "we can't put a car at your disposal. There's a war on."

Guy said he would hire a push-bike and, after a little more conversation, he repaired to a cycle shop recommended by the Superintendent, only to find that neither here nor anywhere else in the town was any machine, however decrepit, available. He went back to the police station, practically commandeered a bicycle belonging to an intimidated young constable, and set off, wobbling, up the long hill out of Melchester. Half an hour later he passed The Dog and, after enquiring the way of two strangers to the district, a stone-deaf roadman and an Austrian refugee with no English, he discovered by the wayside Sidney Smallbone, sitting reflectively on his bicycle, occupied, no doubt, by delicious daydreams of darts matches. Smallbone said that he was on his way to the Hall with the meat for dinner, and he piloted Guy through a pair of wrought iron gates, rusty and apparently permanently open, and up a grass-grown drive, darkened by overhanging trees and narrowed by encroaching bushes. "Front door or back?" asked Smallbone, and Guy said he thought the front; to which Smallbone replied that if he went to the front he wouldn't get any answer. "Bell's bust," he said. "Been bust ever since I can remember. It used to be enough of a job to get an answer from the back—that there Mrs. Binfield's as deaf as a post, or else she finds it 'andy to be so. But since Mrs. Edward's been 'ere, she sometimes answers." With a sudden appearance of briskness, he leapt off his bicycle and shouted, "Butcher!"

The door opened, giving a view of a wide, stone-flagged passage, but, before Guy had time to take in anything, a large black dog of doubtful parentage came hurtling out and bit him. "Blast!" he cried, and Smallbone, who had handed in his parcel of meat, said, "Got you, did 'e? 'E's a devil and no mistake. Ought to be destroyed, 'e ought. Dangerous, that's what 'e is. You'd better come back with me to the doctor's and 'ave it cauterized."

"Rot," said Guy, who was a dog-lover. He rubbed his leg and grinned at the dark, intelligent-looking young woman who stood in the doorway. She had caught hold of the dog and was sturdily hanging on to its collar. "It's humiliating, that's all. Dogs are supposed to know who likes them."

"Tom isn't a very nice dog," replied the dark young woman. "None of the dogs here are. They belonged to my father-in-law, and I believe he encouraged them to go for people. Would you like to come in and bathe your leg?"

"Good lord, no," said Guy. "My leg won't hurt, but I'd be awfully obliged if you could lend me a needle and thread." Tom's teeth had ripped a triangular tear in his almost new gray flannel trousers.

Dragging the dog, the young woman walked back along the passage and Guy followed her. She opened a door, pulled the choking animal through, slipped out and slammed the door on it. "There!" she said, dusting her hands together, and, opening the opposite door, she ushered Guy into a square room, with tall, barred windows, obscured by a laurel hedge. The room was plainly furnished with a large table, covered by an old-fashioned cloth of red serge, a set of Windsor chairs, a decrepit wicker armchair, an ambiguous kind of sideboard, a sewing machine, a bamboo occasional table and a gramophone with a horn. Judging by the position and furnishing of the room, Guy decided that it had been the servants' hall.

The dark young woman went to the sideboard, brought out a workbox and threaded a needle with gray cotton. Guy said he could sew and took it from her and began to draw together the edges of the tear. The young woman stood watching him. Presently she said, "You didn't tell me what you came for. I hope you're not selling anything, because we've just had a death in the family and we're all in a muddle."

Guy, intent on his needlework, answered, "No. I'm not selling anything. I wanted to see Mr. Edward Scaife. I'm a Detective-Inspector from Scotland Yard."

"Oh! Well, I'm Mrs. Edward Scaife. Perhaps I could help you?"

"Perhaps you could," said Guy finishing off and taking the scissors she handed him. "Only you weren't at The Dog that evening."

"No," said Janet. "I was in Melchester at the cinema. One must get a change sometimes. I came out by the last bus—for the moment, for the first time in my life, I'm without a car."

"Didn't your father-in-law keep one?"

"No. He was quite unbelievably old-fashioned. He said that the world hadn't been fit to live in since the introduction of the combustion engine."

"I see. Well, it's lucky you're on a bus route. Then you went to The Dog to collect your husband?"

"No. Actually my husband had promised to meet me at the bus stop. He was a few minutes late, but I waited, and when he came he told me about my father-in-law. We went to The Dog and stayed till the ambulance men had taken the body away."

Janet spoke very quietly. She had a calm, flat voice. In her dark green woolen dress, with her hair parted in the middle and drawn back into a knot, she seemed a timeless creature, and this impression was heightened by the fact that in speaking she used no modern slang or turn of phrases. A dull woman, Guy thought, and suddenly he thought of Cressy Hardwick. You mightn't approve of Cressy; you might dislike her; but she wasn't dull. . . .

Straightening up and handing back the needle and scissors, he said, "I see. Who was in the place then—Mrs. Hennisty, of course, and Conway?"

"Yes, and the doctor and Waller, our local constable—rather a slack man. And Cressy Hardwick. I don't know why she stayed."

"Isn't she a great friend of Mrs. Hennisty?"

"Well," said Janet with a level little laugh, "I believe it's really Peter Conway whom she's friends with. Rather silly. I mean, she's not a young woman. I should think she's many years older than he is. And she's divorced."

To his surprise, Guy felt annoyed. He changed the subject. "Can you tell me of anyone who had a particular grudge against your father-in-law?"

"Many people hated him," said Janet. "Since I've been living here I've realized that he had a lot of good points, but they didn't prevent him from doing a lot of harm."

"What were his good points?"

"He had the courage of his convictions. He was much more intelligent than anyone believed, only his mind ran on the wrong lines—that was the tragedy."

Guy said, "You're the only person I've met who's had a good word to say for him."

"That's only because I'm able to see both sides of the question. I don't take any credit for it. I was an Oxford girl. My father was a professor. I got a very sound education at the Oxford High School before I went to the Agricultural College, where I met my husband."

"I see," said Guy, rather impressed, for he had left his local grammar school at sixteen. "Well, that being so, you've probably got ideas of your own. Who do you think killed your father-in-law?"

"I've been puzzling over it. Are the police quite certain that he was killed?"

"Quite certain."

Janet thought before she spoke.

"Well, frankly, I should have said one of the village people. You see, even up to the end, he was dreadful about women and girls. But none of the village people were in the lounge bar."

"And the people who were in the lounge bar—with the exception of your husband and his brother, had any of them had any dealings with your father-in-law?"

"Mrs. Hardwick was his tenant and my husband says he overheard her telling Mr. Day that my father-in-law had given her notice to quit. She seemed very upset over it. Mrs. Frankland brought a cow here once, but it was Mark, my brother-in-law, whom she saw. As a matter of fact, I think she had been here before, because Mrs. Binfield, the housekeeper, made rather a curious remark."

"What did she say?"

"Well, it wasn't a very nice remark," said Janet, fiddling with her workbox. "You know what country people are."

"I do, and I'm hardened," said Guy.

"Well, Mrs. Binfield compared her to a bitch in spring. The point is that she said, 'Here she comes *again.*' And, when she saw Mark talking to her, she said, 'After the young one, this time.'"

Guy said, "That's odd. I can't imagine Mrs. Frankland . . ." and Janet said, "It's not a very nice subject, but her husband's rather a milk and water little man." Guy said, "Quite," and then he asked if Edward Scaife were on the premises. Janet said she believed he was over at the farm with the builder, and offered to show the way. Guy followed her along the passage to a tattered green baize door and into a large hall, stone-flagged, out of which a magnificent stone staircase ascended, curving gracefully, to the upper floor.

"What a lovely house this is!"

"It's quite unsuited to modern conditions," said Janet coldly. "It's not only the length of the passages, but the impossible size of the rooms. Look at this!" She opened a double door of mahogany and Guy looked over her shoulder at one of the most beautifully proportioned rooms he had ever seen. It was a long room with six high windows looking out on the drive and the ruin of the park beyond. Slender white pillars supported the painted ceiling; at either end was a fireplace of Italian marble, furnished with basket grates, now rusty and hung with cobwebs. The furniture had been stacked in the middle of the room and covered with dust-sheets, gray with grime. "A lovely room," Guy said, and thought that, if he'd been the owner of the house, he'd sooner have sat here with chattering teeth than in the sordid and depressing atmosphere of the servants' hall.

Janet, shutting the door, sniffed. "It's quite impractical. The only thing to do with these great white elephants of houses is to pull them down."

"Oh, *no,*" said Guy.

In silence, then, she led him across the hall and out through the front door. Before the white pillared portico, the drive swept into a circle, but a narrow path led on, three hundred yards or so, to farm buildings, damply screened by trees. They passed a stable built on three sides of a square. There was a clock tower and the clock lacked hands and the stable doors were off their hinges and the broken panes of the windows were cobweb-hung. "That ought to be pulled down too," said Janet. "Nobody nowadays wants hunter stabling for twelve." Beyond the stable was the farmyard and here two men were standing, looking about them. Janet called.

One of the men came forward. Janet said, "This is my husband. Edward, this is a detective from Scotland Yard." Through his tight mouth Edward ejaculated, "Good morning. You're enquiring about my father's death, I presume?"

Guy said yes; he had a few routine questions to ask Edward and his brother, and Edward suggested that Janet should find Mark and tell him that he was wanted, while he and Guy returned to the house. "And ask Mr. Cox to go on looking round," he called after Janet and he explained to Guy, "I've got Cox in to see if we can make anything of the farm buildings. As I expect you can see for yourself, my father let the place down terribly."

"Yes," said Guy. "It's a pity. I suppose you inherit?"

"Yes," said Edward, and he added bitterly, "A fine inheritance, what with mortgages and rabbits and nettles and a great ruddy house to keep the roof on."

"I believe," said Guy, "that there *are* people who can make farming pay. My brother farms in Wiltshire and he seems pretty prosperous."

"I'm a trained agriculturist," said Edward. "Given a fair start, I'd guarantee to show a profit. But look what I'm up against! This land's been starved for years and two-thirds of it are as dirty as hell. Look at the stock! My father's idea was to turn everything out haphazard and let nature have its way. He would never spend a penny on stud fees."

They had reached the front of the beautiful, melancholy house and Edward led the way round to the back door. "My father," he said, "lived in the kitchen, but when I came here, six months ago, I insisted on making one room habitable, and my wife and I have been using the old servants' hall. We had a job to get him even to allow that—he grudged the firewood, though, God knows, there's plenty of it lying about." He walked across the room and kicked up the slow, smoking fire. "Chimneys need sweeping," he announced in dissatisfied tones.

Guy thought, and wondered if he were intended to think, that there wasn't much motive for murder in the inheritance of Witheridge Hall. He said, "Can't you sell the place?" and Edward said, "Who'd buy it in the state it's in? Besides, no one wants these big houses. You'd get a better price for a bungalow."

That was true. Rather desperately Guy said, "About your father's finances? I suppose he was genuinely in low water? I mean there are men who won't spend a penny to keep a place up, but have plenty tucked away somewhere."

"He wasn't like that," said Edward. "He was fond of the land. If he had had any money, he would have spent it. He wasn't a hoarder. No, he was just beaten by conditions, plus his own obstinacy."

"Well, now," said Guy, getting out his notebook, "what about Thursday night? I'm rather counting on what you can tell me, because I believe you arrived early and spent the whole evening in the lounge bar."

Edward seemed disposed to be helpful. Yes, he had heard Mrs. Hardwick telling Mr. Day that she'd had notice to quit; her voice had been low, but he had caught abusive phrases; she had alluded to his father as a dirty devil and a nasty old man. Asked if he now intended to turn Cressy out of her cottage, Edward said, no. She had been a good tenant; she had improved the property; and he believed that you didn't lose by treating people decently. He had no idea why his brother had suddenly taken it into his head to spend the evening in the lounge bar. He hadn't himself suggested it. His brother had been brought up differently from himself—very unfair, of course—and had always seemed to prefer the society of farm laborers. He had noticed Mrs. Hennisty, Mrs. Hardwick and Mr. Frankland going out and he had seen his brother go. He thought he would have noticed if any of them had paused beside his father for an appreciable length of time. He couldn't say anything about Mr. Day coming back, because he had been concentrating on the game of shove ha'penny. Well, he was a comparative newcomer; he wasn't really *in* with these people, but he had always had the impression that Adam Day and Mrs. Hardwick were great friends.

"And who do you think killed your father?" Guy asked finally, but all he got was a reiteration of Janet's idea.

"I'll see your brother now," he said, and, while he waited, wrote at the foot of his notes: "A decent fellow, careful about money, perhaps even mean. Owing to the state of the place, no particular motive. Any value as building land?"

There was the sound of nailed soles on the stone flags of the passage and Mark Scaife came in. He walked slowly and clumsily, like one long accustomed to tread heavy soil. He came in without a word, shut the door behind him and stood glowering across the table at Guy.

Guy said, "Morning. I wanted to ask you a few questions. You're the deceased man's younger son?"

In a hoarse, defiant tone, Mark corrected him. He said, "His bastard son."

Guy said, "Oh . . . !" and remembered thinking, supposing there were a bastard . . . and, men kill and swing, but not to avenge their mothers. "I see," he said, doodling in his notebook. "Is your mother alive?"

"No," said Mark, his tone of voice unchanged. "She died three months ago."

"I'm sorry to ask these questions—who was she?"

"A servant," said Mark.

"And you weren't brought up here?"

"No. I was sent here when I was fourteen. There was no more money. . . ."

"I'm told," said Guy, "that it was your custom to spend your evenings at The Dog in the public bar. On Thursday night, for the first time in your life, you went into the lounge bar. Why?"

"Why the hell shouldn't I?" said Mark. "My father and my brother went in there."

"There's no reason on earth why you shouldn't, but you never did. What was the idea?"

Mark swallowed. "My half-brother and his wife had been on at me. Said I was no better than a beast. Reckoned I'd show them. . . ."

Coming from a man so illiterate and probably without imagination, that rang true. Edward hadn't said anything about it; did that show a want of frankness or merely the usual ignorance of what goes on in other people's minds? "I understand," he said. "Now, when you left the room, you passed quite close to your father. Was he alive?"

But Mark hadn't noticed. With a sudden flashing smile he explained that he had been in a hurry—there had been treating and he had put away two pints of beer. "But you left for good then?" said Guy. Mark replied, "I should say I did," and his face changed and glowering he added, "I've got an alibi, if that's what you want to know."

"I do want to know," Guy admitted, "but it's purely a matter of routine. Where were you?"

"I walked down the road and caught the bus into Melchester."

"And when you got to Melchester?"

"I went to see a young lady."

"Can you give me her name and address?"

"I could if I liked," said Mark.

"Well, you'd better like," Guy told him. "If you don't it'll cause us both a lot of trouble and I can promise you I shall find out in the end."

"How would you like your private affairs nosed into?"

"Not at all. But, on the whole, I'd prefer it to hanging."

Mark thought for a moment.

"All right. Miss Winnie Goddard, 52 Camden Street."

Guy wrote it down.

"And I suppose you came back on the last bus?"

"No. I missed it. I walked out."

"What was the time then?"

"A quarter to six," said Mark sheepishly.

"I see. Well, I suppose Miss Goddard would confirm that." Guy then supposed that the estate would pass to Edward, and Mark replied that it would, and volunteered that Edward had got a nasty shock when he had discovered that the old man had left Mark a legacy of two hundred pounds. "Will there be enough to pay that out?" Guy wondered, and Mark said there'd have to be; legacies, he knew, were the first claim on an estate and he wasn't going to consider any arrangement: he believed in doing as you'd been done by. Guy then asked whom he'd back as the murderer, and Mark said, some fool who didn't mind if he swung. Guy said that no cold-blooded murderer ever thought there was a chance of swinging; they were conceited men; and Mark said it was no use giving him a dirty look; he wasn't conceited and, if he had been, Edward and his wife, in the last six months, would have seen to that. By asking what Edward had against Mark, Guy returned to the subject of Mark's mother.

Had Scaife treated her fairly? he asked, to which Mark replied without apparent rancor, that there wasn't such a thing as fairness in the world. He admitted that his mother had died in extreme poverty, but that didn't seem to worry him; during the whole interview, it was his dislike for Edward and Janet which seemed most clearly defined. Then Guy shut up his notebook and asked if Edward were still about? As a matter of routine he had got to check up on what poisons were kept on the farm.

Mark said that six months ago he could have given the answer and it would have been none, except for sheep dip. His father didn't hold with a lot of chemical muck and quite right too, but Edward had been trained at a college and a lot of damned nonsense Mark considered it; either a man had farming in his blood or else he hadn't; and Edward was mad keen on fertilizers and weed-killers and, in an effort to convince his father, he had thrown money away buying the muck and trying it out with results which Mark described with scorn and blasphemy. Guy asked where Edward kept his supplies and Mark said over at the stable, in the old harness room, in the dry. He didn't know if the room was kept locked, but, if Guy had finished with him and liked to come along, they could try. Guy said he would like to get Edward's permission, so Mark went out into the passage and yelled, "Oi!" Edward came from the kitchen. Guy said, "Sorry to bother you again, Mr. Scaife, but purely as a matter of routine I've got to check up on the poisons kept here."

"Well, there aren't very many," said Edward. "My father was all against scientific farming. It's heartbreaking to think of all the research that goes on and then these obstinate old men won't take advantage of it. There's some sheep dip, isn't there, Mark, over at the farm?"

"You know there's some sheep dip," said Mark sullenly, "but there's some more . . ."

Edward gave him a cold look and quickly said, "There are a few things I've been experimenting with. I hoped to convert my father, but it was like running one's head against a stone wall. At my own expense I bought some small quantities of weed-killers and insecticides and so on. If you want to see them, we must go back to the stable. They're in the harness room."

"It's rather a waste of time," said Guy, who liked to keep on the right side of people, "but, if I don't do it, I shall only get hauled over the coals and sent back to worry you again. Do you keep the place locked?" he asked, as he went out with Edward, Mark following behind.

"I did to begin with, but I'm afraid I've got slack about it lately. Everyone combined to discourage me, and it's infectious—the general slackness of the place."

They walked in silence across the stable yard and Edward opened one of the few doors which remained upon its hinges. "I made this place into a sort of little office," he explained. "Thought I'd keep what accounts I could and so on, but I couldn't get any cooperation from anyone. They'd sooner see the place sold up than alter their ways." This was apparently intended for Mark, but he made no reply.

In spite of the worn and rusty state of the harness, the room smelt of leather and Edwardian prosperity. The stove had been recently used. The place was tidy and the air felt dry. On a deal table was a pot of ink, pens, catalogues of agricultural implements and ledgers containing Edward's abortive attempts at accountancy. "I don't know what you're looking for," said Edward, "but that's all I have." He indicated a shelf, which held a neat array of tins.

"Lot of muck," said Mark from the doorway, and Edward rounded on him. "What are you hanging about for? What do you know about it? Your ideas on farming went out when the corn laws came in."

Mark spat nonchalantly. "I can get things to grow and I can cut down weeds without buying a lot of chemicals and getting myself suspected of murder," he said with a grin.

"Nobody here is suspected of murder," said Guy before Edward could speak. He had seen all he wanted on the shelf . . . arsenic by the pound, but no nicotine. "As you say, Mr. Scaife, there isn't much here. But I ought to know about this door being locked. Can you remember when you gave up locking it?"

"During the first month I locked it regularly. Then I began to leave it open during the day and only to lock it when I packed up and went in. Lately—for three weeks or a month I should say— I haven't bothered. Well, nobody else on the place bothered about locking up anything."

"It must have been very disheartening," said Guy, "but now things will be very different, I daresay."

He apologized for wasting Edward's time, took his leave and walked meditatively round to the back door, where a greasy old woman was shaking a mat and letting the dust fly over his bicycle. Assuming her to be the deaf Mrs. Binfield, he yelled out, "Good morning!" and got, through toothless gums, an inaudible reply.

"You're the late Mr. Scaife's housekeeper, aren't you?"

"Eh?"

"You're the late Mr. Scaife's housekeeper, aren't you?"

"Ar."

"I'm a detective from Scotland Yard."

"Eh?"

"I'm a policeman."

"Ar."

Excusably, Guy went straight to the point.

"Who do you think killed Mr. Scaife?"

"One of them 'e done 'arm to. Elsie Chandler. Bert Saunders. Bob Brewer. That there little feller over at Cold 'Arbour farm. You can take your pick on 'em, policeman. And then there be plenty more."

"Cold Harbour Farm—you mean Mr. Frankland?"

"Ar."

"Why should he kill Scaife?"

The old woman shook the mat and the dust flew over Guy.

"Couldn't stop 'is wife runnin' round 'ere." She added the canine comparison to which Janet had referred.

"And who's Elsie Chandler?"

"Works at The Dog. She 'ad a girl. Brewer, 'e 'ad a sister. Bert Saunders, 'e 'ad notice to turn out."

All quite wild and unfounded accusations, Guy thought, as he bicycled down the drive; to begin with, only one of the people whom the revolting old woman had mentioned had spent Thursday evening in the lounge. All the same, it might be worth while investigating this Elsie Chandler; if she worked at The Dog, her movements might have escaped notice. At the gates, he turned towards the inn; he had intended to get lunch there and it was now half-past twelve.

He went into the lounge bar. Eve came from the kitchen quarters, greeted him cheerfully and served him with sausage rolls and beer. He asked her about Mrs. Chandler and she told him what she knew of the old story, but she was certain that at no time on Thursday evening had Mrs. Chandler left the public bar. The same applied to Bert Saunders. She knew that he had been given notice to quit. She had heard him going on about it—oh, he'd only said what you'd expect—the usual thing about bloody landlords. Bob Brewer hadn't been in the place for weeks. He was a Territorial and had been called up at the beginning of the war. Guy lit a cigarette and remarked that he had heard some gossip about Mrs. Frankland. It seemed incredible, but her name had been coupled with Scaife's. What on earth would people say next? Eve asked angrily. Who had been saying such an unbelievable thing? She hoped Guy knew what village people were.

Guy said that he did and asked the way to Cold Harbour Farm. Eve directed him and he paid his bill and went off up the highroad till he reached a white gate leading to a rough drive, which ascended through windswept pastures, wire-fenced, to a grim-looking farmhouse, built of flint and rubble and whitewashed.

Mr. or Mrs. Frankland seemed to have a fancy for whitewash; all the outhouses were whitewashed and the dog kennel and the coping of the garden wall. The effect was grimly clean.

Guinea-fowl announced Guy's arrival. He knocked on the open front door. The passage, carpeted with linoleum, smelt of Lysol. A garden door at the other end of the passage was open and the easterly wind blew briskly through.

There was no answer from the house, but, after a moment, Bridget Frankland appeared from the farmyard. She wore a jersey, corduroy trousers and gum boots. "If you're selling anything, I don't want it," she announced firmly.

"I'm not selling anything. I'm a detective from Scotland Yard, inquiring into the death of Mathew Scaife," Guy said, with equal firmness.

"Oh," said Bridget, "so that's why you were at the pub last night is it? I wondered who you were. You don't look much like a detective, do you? I don't know that I've ever seen one, but I've always imagined them as little ferrety men. You're over six feet, aren't you? And you're not exactly ferrety." From his head to his heels her dark blue eyes ran over him.

Guy said stiffly, "You're Mrs. Frankland, I believe? I want to ask you and Mr. Frankland a few questions. . . ."

"Oh, yes. Well, come indoors. My husband's at home today. He goes to London two days a week but the rest of the time he works here. He's on a paper—a weekly digest, and he writes a lot for it himself. He won't thank you for disturbing him, but he'll have to put up with that. Won't you have a drink, Mr. . . . ?"

"Northeast. No, thank you." He took the chair she indicated and briskly opened his notebook; ladies who looked you over with dark blue eyes must be kept severely to the point. He snapped out a string of baldly official questions about Thursday evening, but at the end of them had scarcely an addition to make to the Superintendent's notes. Then he said, "You knew Mr. Scaife before, I believe?" and Bridget replied, "Not socially. I'd been to the farm to buy eggs and so on, and when I kept goats I used to take them there for service."

"Did you ever go into the house?"

"He took me in once and showed me over. But that was about five years ago. He hadn't gone so much to pieces then."

"He hadn't a very good reputation, had he? I mean," Guy said awkwardly, "wasn't it rather rash of you to go in?"

"My dear child," said Bridget, "I'm not a young girl. I'm perfectly capable of coping with nasty old men."

Guy thought she was. Going into the house with Scaife would have been enough to set tongues wagging. Probably she was just one of those people who like playing with fire. He doodled. Bridget observed, "The police *have* got dirty minds, haven't they?" Guy looked up to protest and saw David Frankland standing at the door.

David, finding himself observed, straightened a face avid with curiosity, and advanced, rubber-soled, into the room. "What, another policeman?" he exclaimed. "From Scotland Yard," Bridget told him, and David said, "Oh," and to Guy, "I'm sorry to hear you've got a dirty mind." Embarrassed, Guy replied, "I was asking a few questions about the late Mr. Scaife. I understand he was rather an unpleasant character."

David shrugged his narrow shoulders. "I don't know anything about him. My wife farms, and on various occasions she has taken her beasts to the Hall. I suppose old Scaife was about the place, but he wasn't a man you could get into conversation with. Or was he, dear?" The look in his gooseberry-colored eyes must mean something, Guy felt sure. A weak little man with a wife he didn't trust . . . an insanely jealous, a dangerous little man? . . .

Bridget said, "All the conversation Scaife had was grumbles about the government. Have you finished with me, Mr. Northeast, because I'm rather busy? I've got some stock to move." Guy let her go and began to question her husband, concentrating on the time on Thursday night when he had left the lounge bar. He had gone to the men's lavatory, he said, and when he had come out, he had stood in the passage, because the others had gone out into the garden to see about the lights and he had been mildly curious to know whether Waller meant to make trouble. As it had transpired, only Conway and Mrs. Hardwick had been in the garden: Waller had gone and Eve Hennisty had come in. Yes, he had overheard the conversation between Conway and Mrs. Hardwick. Mrs. Hardwick had mentioned the smell of the chrysanthemums. David had got the impression that Conway was endeavoring to turn the conversation to more personal matters, but he hadn't succeeded. Cressy Hardwick was a brilliant woman, but as hard as iron. Yes, he kept a car, good God, yes. Even with one, living in the country was bloody; without one, it would be impossible. He was a Thinking Man. He'd go stark staring mad, stuck down here among cows and morons. Yes; on the days when he went to town he drove himself into Melchester and garaged the car. No, he said, staring; he didn't have it cleaned at the garage. The garden boy cleaned it. No, they didn't go in for flowers much; he loathed gardening and his wife, like all farmers, couldn't be bothered with flowers. Roses? Oh, well, yes; there were a few ramblers, but they were left to their own devices. Green fly? What was it? Oh well, if the roses had it, they had it. Even before the war, with the world in the state it had been in since the Treaty of Versailles, no Thinking Person could have wasted time pottering about, spraying roses. . . .

Guy had taken a dislike to David. He was inquisitive, snooped, over-heard things and was obliged to prove his virility by growing a beard. The weak, in Guy's considered opinion, were ultimately the dangerous ones. If there were any truth in the gossip about Bridget, he wouldn't put it past David to take the poisoner's sneaking way. But, though Bridget might be sex-starved, he doubted whether, even five years ago when Scaife had been less of a wreck, she would have embarked on an in-trigue with such an elderly and unattractive man. Mark Scaife, perhaps . . . but Mark had no grouse against his father, only against Edward. . . . Oh, thought Guy, cautiously freewheeling down the drive, oh for some good hard facts to build upon!

David had directed him to the Days' house, an elegant little ex-ample of Regency building, on the Green. A maid in a sprigged print dress told him that Mr. Day was at his office in Melchester, but Mrs. Day was at home, and he was ushered into a period parlor at the back of the house. Valentine, charming in pale blue, welcomed him. "Ooo," she said, "now I suppose all our poor little secrets will be revealed."

Guy felt brutal as he opened his notebook, but Valentine wanted to help, though of course she wasn't clever, like darling Cressy, or obser-vant, like men. As it turned out, she added little to his meager supply of facts, but she gossiped freely and with relish. Bridget Frankland was a dear in some ways, but farming, in Valentine's opinion, made women coarse, and David was an intellectual and not exactly a he-man, and it was a dreadful thing to say, but Bridget did rather run after men. Any particular man? No, that was the worst of it. Valentine wasn't intolerant. She meant that when two people really did love one another . . . But Bridget wasn't fastidious; anything in trousers . . . People were so differ-ent. Cressy Hardwick wasn't like Bridget. She didn't run after men, but, though she must be well over forty, poor dear, she sort of collected them.

Guy asked if Valentine had known Cressy long, and Valentine said, "We met her soon after she came here. I was sorry for her. I'm broad-minded and I thought that people might look askance at her because of that knife-throwing affair."

Guy sat up.

"What knife-throwing affair?"

Valentine said, "Ooo. Don't you remember it? It was awful. It was all in the newspapers—great headlines. It happened at a party in London. Cressy was there and her husband—they weren't divorced then—and the girl that Hugo Hardwick's married to now. They had an argument and Cressy got into a rage and threw a knife—she said afterwards, quite openly, that it was intended for her husband, but anyhow it hit the girl and a policeman heard her screaming and went in and everyone tried to invent excuses, but the girl blurted everything out, though afterwards she behaved very nobly—much more nobly than I should have behaved—and tried to withdraw the charge. Crescy was fined and bound over, but it was rather awful, especially the headlines—*Authoress Attacks Rival* and that kind of thing. So I thought I'd be kind to Cresy and, though I'm not a bit clever, we've always been great friends."

"I see," said Guy thinking: a fine friend. "That was nice of you, Mrs. Day." He got to his feet and walked towards the window. "Charming garden. You've still got a marvelous show of roses."

"Aren't they lovely? It hasn't been a very good year for them, though."

"Not enough sun, I suppose? And too much green fly."

"There wasn't so much green fly as usual. I think I only sprayed the roses once this year."

"What do you use for them?"

"Nicotine. It's much the best thing."

"The garden must keep you busy, and then, I suppose, there's all the housekeeping as well?" Guy gave what he hoped was a look of admiration for the busy little woman. "And then there are all the jobs that men ought to do themselves, but don't, so their wives do them—mending fuses . . . cleaning the car."

"Well, there are a lot of odd jobs," Valentine admitted, "but I'm a silly, helpless person I'm afraid. I can't mend fuses and I simply draw the line at cleaning the car. My husband started off by doing it regularly on Sunday mornings, but of course that didn't last long. But I was firm. I insisted it should be cleaned at the garage. I'm only vain about one thing—these . . ." She stretched out for his inspection a pair of soft white hands.

He checked an instinctive recoil.

"I see. Well . . . er . . . I don't wonder. I really must be getting along."

Valentine rose too. "I expect you're very busy. Who do you think murdered that poor old man?"

Guy said, "We don't think, Mrs. Day. We wait until we know," and Valentine said, "How grim! Most people think it was Mark Scaife, but I don't. I've got quite a different idea." Guy asked what her idea was and Valentine, prettily dithering, said that she wasn't a detective or anything clever; she had absolutely nothing to go upon; it was only an idea. Irritated, Guy snapped, "That sort of idea's no use I to anyone," and with that he went out, wondering if it were possible for any human being to be so foolish as the exquisite Valentine. Yet why should she put on an act? According to her own account, she had never done more than nod good-morning or good-evening to any of the Scaifes. Her husband was a more promising subject. He had stood arm-in-arm with Cresy Hardwick. It was because of Cresy Hardwick that he had thrown a tankard of beer at Conway. Cresy Hardwick had thrown a knife at a girl at a party and she had a grudge against Scaife. A call on Cresy Hardwick seemed to be indicated.

To get to Little Bottom Cottage you went down a lane behind the church and that led you into the Bottom and then you could see the cottage—so children coming out of school explained to him. He plunged down a precipitous cart road, jolted over flints till he thought it prudent to dismount, and wheeled his bicycle down into the silence of a great beech wood. Half a mile brought him to the end of the wood and there were pastures rising on each side of the valley and, looking southwards, a small thatched cottage, from the chimney of which a spiral of smoke rose blue against the background of October trees. A path, doubling back, led to the cottage, and from the road you could look down into an apple orchard, where a brown pony was grazing. Guy leaned his bicycle against a tree and walked up the path. Dogs bayed. Three cats jumped like streaks of lightning off a window sill.

He knocked on the door and Cresy opened it.

She was wearing black trousers and a black and yellow checked shirt. Her nails and lips were scarlet. She had a straw in her hair and a smudge of black across her small nose. She appeared to be in high spirits. She said, "Ha! Detective-Inspector Northeast from the Yard."

Guy said, "Sorry to worry you again, Mrs. Hardwick, but there are just one or two questions . . ."

"Come in," said Cresy. "Look, this is my sitting-room. The Borzois are Olivia and Victoria. I've been toasting crumpets. You're just in time for tea."

"We're not allowed to accept drinks and eats when we're on duty," said Guy.

"Don't be silly," said Cresy. "No one," she added characteristically, "will know."

Guy could smell the crumpets. He gave a noncommittal laugh.

"I'll get them," said Cresy. "You make friends with the dogs," and she went away.

Guy, stroking the Borzois' sentimental heads, looked round the room. It was a low room; he had had to bend his head to pass under the lintel of the door. Between the black oak beams the walls were painted white and the only pictures were two old mezzotints, Mercury and Cupid in the Character of a Link Boy, published in the year 1777. Cresy hadn't furnished to period. There was a French marqueterie bureau, a Queen Anne writing-table, white bookcases, Persian rugs on the brick floor, a Victorian sofa with curved ends of mahogany and two modern armchairs. On the wide hearth a fire of apple logs was burning and a black kettle was precariously balanced over it. The room was dim, and the firelight gleamed in the old gilt frames of the pictures and the gold lettering on the backs of the books.

Cresey came in, bringing a brown teapot and a plate piled with crumpets. She set them down on the hearth, went out again and reappeared with a silver sugar basin, a jug of milk, two cups and saucers and plates and knives on a tray. She kicked the logs together and the kettle began to sing. Then she broke the queer companionable silence, saying, "Do sit down."

Guy sank into one of the armchairs. He got out his notebook and fountain pen. "I've forgotten what I was going to ask you," he said and pulled himself up, remembering that Cresey Hardwick had thrown a knife at a girl at a party and had a motive—a weak motive, but how can one tell what matters most to other people?—for the murder of Scaife.

"Just a minute," said Cresey. "The kettle's boiling. I'll make the tea."

She poured the water into the teapot. The apple logs shifted, flared and filled the room with a nostalgic smell of summer. Guy was a small boy again, climbing trees that were ships and castles and Mount Everest, in the orchard at Thorn End.

"A crumpet?"

"Thank you."

"Sugar?"

"Two."

"Milk?"

"Please."

Cresey sat down on a stool, her teacup on the floor beside her. "It's frosty outside," she remarked. "Summer's over. But I like the winter in the country, don't you?"

"Yes," said Guy. "Hunting, and everything looking different. In towns there's no particular difference, except that the streets are wet and you're cold."

"I hate being cold," said Cresey, "except as a prelude to getting warm again. This is a very warm cottage. Except for the kitchen and the bathroom, which I built on, there are only two rooms, so I can't ask anyone to stay with me, thank God."

"Don't you like people?"

"Not much. They're all right outside your life, but once you let them in, they start telling you what to do."

"You needn't do it."

"I always do do it. They shout and argue. Perhaps in a previous life I was an obedient dog. Another crumpet?"

Guy took another crumpet. As he stretched out a hand, his notebook fell off his knee and it came into his mind that he wasn't investigating the murder of Mathew Scaife; he was having tea with Cresy Hardwick and that wouldn't do. He picked up the notebook and said, "Well, now, what about all this? I'm afraid I've been hearing some gossip. I believe you've had dealings with the police before."

Cresy said, "Gosh! Who told you?"

"You mustn't ask that. It was in London, wasn't it?"

"Yes," said Cresy. "It was in London. I thought it was all buried and forgotten. Cor lumme, how one's sins do find one out. Another crumpet?"

"Please. I'm afraid I'm being very greedy," said Guy.

"Why not? 'It is not long the time of wine' and crumpets." She sat down again and stared into the fire, her thin arms round her knees.

Guy glanced at her. He didn't feel brutal, as he had felt questioning the dainty Valentine, but he felt that this business about Scaife wasn't important; that there were many more important things to talk about, sitting with Cresy Hardwick in this quiet firelit room. He said, "You seem to take a very abstract view of things."

"Some people," said Cresy, "hear the hum of eternity. Others don't."

"I don't," said Guy. "I'm a beastly busybody." He couldn't imagine why he had said that; normally he congratulated himself on being one of the world's workers and despised dreamers and those who told their fancies. There must, he thought, be some ancient magic loose in this cottage. He said, "That being so, I'd better get busy. You were bound over, weren't you, for throwing a knife at a girl?"

"A Miss Worthington," said Cresy in scornful tones. "Actually, I aimed at my husband, but I've never been able to hit anything with anything. Rather ironically, that was one of the things that wrecked my married life—Hugo despised me dreadfully because I couldn't hit balls. Miss Worthington screamed like an air-raid warning and a copper came in. Otherwise we might have hushed it up, only Miss Worthington had to have six stitches in her arm."

"And why," Guy asked, "did you throw a knife at your husband?"

Cresy said slowly, "There was an argument. It was about an artist. Hugo, backed up by Miss Worthington, took his usual sane, smug view. Of course, it had been blowing up for a long time. I felt murderous about him anyway, and his remarks about Marie Laurencin were the last straw."

"And did you," Guy asked, "feel murderous about Scaife?"

There was silence. The room reproached him. Either the crumpets he had eaten weighed heavily on his stomach, or else his heart was crying out on him for what he had said.

Crescy turned and faced him. "Yes, I felt very murderous about Scaife. But I didn't murder him. I may throw knives at people, but I'm not a poisoner. No. Definitely not."

"I've got to ask these questions," he said wearily. "Do you keep a car?"

"Yes. Bouncing Bertha. A Baby Austin of immense age."

"Clean her yourself?"

"In theory, yes."

"Anyhow, you've got a cleaning outfit?"

"Well, not exactly an outfit—a few rags and a tin of polish and a sponge."

"I see," said Guy in a tone of resignation. "And do you keep nicotine in any form in this house?"

"Cigarettes, of course. And on my fingers. And I've got a tin for spraying the roses. Why? Was Scaife poisoned with nicotine?"

"You mustn't ask that. The tinned stuff—I suppose you've used some of it. Is there any left?"

"Quite a bit," said Crescy. "Oh hell! Does that put me in a spot? Or is it *on* a spot? Anyhow, am I a suspect?"

"Not more than anyone else. But I wish you'd cast your mind back to Thursday night and remember seeing someone pause beside Scaife."

"I can't."

"And, if you could, you wouldn't."

"Quite."

"Stupid of you."

"I've always been contrary," said Crescy. "I daresay that in a previous life I was a mule."

"I thought it was an obedient dog."

"Both, perhaps. I daresay I've had several lives and that's why I'm so damned sick of it all."

"Are you damned sick of it?"

"Mostly."

"That's night starvation. Look here, I didn't come to talk like this. Have you ever studied chemistry?"

"No."

"Good. Got any books on the subject?" he asked, glancing at the shelves.

"No," said Crescy.

"Can I look?"

"Yes, do."

He got up and cast an eye over Crescy's poets. In the shelf below were taller books, learned books: *The Dialogues of Plato,* Aristotle's *Theory of Poetry,* Mendel's *Principles of Heredity,* and *Forensic Medicine and Toxicology,* by Dixon Mann and William A. Brend. . . . His heart sank incomprehensibly. "Why have you got Dixon Mann's *Forensic Medicine?*" he asked.

"Oh, that! I was writing a detective novel. . . ."

"Can I see it?" asked Guy.

"No, I'm afraid you can't," said Crescy. "I got in a rage with it and I tore it all up and threw it in the fire."

Guy sat down on the arm of his chair. The hounds, who had been watching him a little suspiciously, dropped their heads again on their paws.

"When did you buy the book, Mrs. Hardwick?"

"Ages ago. I think it was April or May. I wanted to verify a clue, and it was wrong. Hugo always used to prove that I was wrong by looking things up in books—he'd even get up from meals to do it—so, naturally, I got enraged."

"It's all very unfortunate," said Guy.

"There seems to be a lot of circumstantial evidence against me," said Crescy. "I'm always unlucky. My God, it's a wonder I didn't stop near Scaife to pull up my stockings!"

Guy looked down at her and found himself saying consolingly, "You know, you're going too far ahead. At present I'm only . . . well, sort of casting for a line. If you had stopped near Scaife, it wouldn't have proved anything. We should still have needed a whole lot more."

"Thank you," said Crescy. "You're nice, aren't you? There's someone," she said, and there was a bang on the door and it opened and there stood Adam Day.

"Oh, sorry, Crescy," said Adam. "I thought you were alone."

"No," said Crescy, "I'm not. I'm being closely questioned by the arm of the law."

"That's quite all right," said Guy. "As a matter of fact, I wanted a word with Mr. Day."

"I'll get some drinks," said Crescy and disappeared.

Guy said, "I called at your place this afternoon, sir, but you were in Melchester. I saw your wife. She couldn't add anything to what she had told the Superintendent. Can you?"

"Not a thing."

"When I was in the bar on Monday evening, you were all talking about Mark Scaife—"

"We shouldn't have," said Adam, "if we had known who you were. Nasty job it must be snooping round."

"It is," said Guy. "Actually, Scaife's given me what I regard as a perfectly good explanation of his presence in the lounge bar. But from the way you talked I gathered that most of the money was on him. Why?"

"Simply because of the fact for which he gave you a perfectly good explanation. That's absolutely all. Isn't it, Crescy?"

Crescy, bringing a decanter and glasses, had returned.

"It is," said Crescy. "Sherry, everyone?"

"I won't have anything to drink. I must be off now," said Guy.

"One for the road?" suggested Adam.

"No, thank you."

"He's not allowed to drink when on duty," said Crescy, going with Guy towards the door. "Shall we see you at The Dog tonight?"

"I don't think so. I'm going back to Melchester and then I think I'll call it a day." He went off down the path and turned once to wave to Crescy, who was still standing at the open door. She or Adam had switched the light on and Guy could see into the room, and it looked like a refuge from the darkness that was folding down on the valley and the frost that cut the air. One day, Guy thought, he'd have a cottage and a room with white walls and a fire of apple logs and a woman . . . only you didn't meet women like Crescy, only girls, whose ideal was a smart little house in the suburbs, a house with a lounge and a braying wireless and electric fires. There was a girl he took out sometimes—Pam Driver; she was pretty and smart and she always had plenty to say for herself, but you couldn't imagine her living in a thatched cottage, keeping a one-eyed pony in an orchard, stepping over a pair of dogs only suited to Imperial Russia, every time she crossed her lounge. Guy had been thinking seriously about proposing to Pam Driver and now, getting on his bicycle and pedaling off uphill, he couldn't see why an official visit to a middle-aged woman, who was one of his most hopeful suspects in a murder case, should have put him so completely off the idea. Perhaps he had been right when he had thought that there was magic loose in the cottage, or perhaps it was Crescy who had done something to him . . . perhaps she had been born fifteen years too early, or he, fifteen years too late. . . .

This wouldn't do. . . . He got off his bicycle and wheeled it up the hill. Now he must concentrate. Adam Day had come to Crescy's cottage and the dogs hadn't barked; therefore, Adam Day frequently came to Crescy's cottage, probably every evening at the same hour. Adam Day was attracted by, or enamored of, Crescy though what Crescy could see in him, God only knew; and Valentine, poor girl, suspected something, enough to make her eager to blurt out the story of Crescy's murderous but cockeyed assault on Miss Worthington. When Adam Day came back from playing darts he might have killed Scaife because Scaife had given

Crescy notice to quit and Adam couldn't bear the thought of losing her. He had, after all, thrown a tankard of beer at Conway, and that showed him up as quite as violent a character as Crescy, the only difference being that, purely by chance, she had had a knife and he had had a tankard in his hand. How was that? Very poor, Guy's common sense told him. He himself had once thrown a turnip at his brother, Roger. You didn't murder a man because he was turning the woman you loved out of her cottage. You found her another cottage, that was all.

But you didn't throw knives at people because they made remarks about Marie Laurencin.

And you didn't throw turnips at people because they said, probably with truth, that your efforts at plowing had mucked up the whole field.

Oh, damn. . . .

The only thing to do, he thought, was to go back to the pub, take a drink to pull himself together, and try to clarify the situation by setting all this nebulous stuff down on paper. Accordingly, he mounted his bicycle and rode across the Green to The Dog, where he found the lounge bar empty. He ordered a sherry, which Eve brought him, and then he established himself in a chair by the fire and opened his notebook, and she withdrew. He had great faith in putting things down on paper. You could turn things over in your mind for ever, but there was nothing like analysis for catching out sentiment and the preferences you couldn't help forming. So now for it. . . . In large capital letters he wrote MOTIVE and beneath that the name of everyone who had been in the lounge bar on the night of the crime. Edward Scaife's name came first, and that Guy underlined three times, for, in one way or another, acquisition was behind most trouble and Edward was Scaife's heir: protest though he might over the poorness of his inheritance, he was at least, now, master of all he surveyed; a trained agriculturalist and an apparently self-confident character, he might well cherish hopes of eventually running his estate at a profit.

Next came Mark Scaife, and Guy underlined his name also three times. Mark was a tough and, though revenge as a motive is out of date—with cloak and sword, it has become a theatrical property—there was his legacy; two hundred pounds wasn't much, but it was enough to enable Mark to marry his Winnie, or to snap his fingers at Edward and clear off to Canada. Crescy received one underline, but, after a moment's hesitation, Guy added another: Scaife's death might mean that Crescy stayed in her cottage and, though a cottage didn't seem much of a motive, she was an unaccountable woman; probably her sense of proportion was different from the average person's; she might, he felt, have regarded Scaife simply as 'one insect the more.' And Little Bottom Cottage . . . He

pulled himself up. Adam Day . . . Well, Adam Day had no motive except
that he was devoted to Crescy. If she left her cottage, there would be no
more calls on his way home from Melchester—and a good thing too,
Guy thought; Adam had a wife of his own and should stick to her. Crescy
might have incited Adam to kill Scaife, but that didn't seem like Crescy;
she might run her own head into a noose, but not someone else's. Adam
escaped an underline and so did his wife. She had an adequate reason
for murdering Crescy, but no earthly connection with Scaife. It was just
conceivable that Bridget's indiscretions had provided her with a motive,
while David might be mistakenly, or with reason, jealous. Rather half-
heartedly, Guy provided them both with an underline. Then Eve and
Conway. Neither had a motive of any sort. With Scaife's death they had,
indeed, lost a good customer.

He turned over a page and wrote, again in capitals, OPPORTUNITY. If
he could believe what all these people had told him, no one had ap-
proached within an arm's length of the murdered man. Could he believe it? Well, for psychological reasons he doubted Crescy, Mark Scaife
and Adam Day; he doubted Edward because of the strength of his motive; but the information, or rather the lack of information, had been
unanimous, and apart from that, he trusted Eve Hennisty. Conway, he
felt, was equally reliable, but his unfortunate absences from the lounge
made his statement less useful. So far as the act of killing was concerned,
everybody then had equal opportunity, but under this heading he must
also include the opportunity of obtaining the poison. Crescy and Valentine had owned up to the possession of nicotine, but, until it came to
search warrants, he couldn't conscientiously write off the others. Then
the sponge. . . . Crescy had one and in all probability the Franklands.
The Scaifes had no car. The Days' car was cleaned in Melchester. Damn
it, OPPORTUNITY wasn't getting on at all, and Dawes would have something to say about that; he had a mania for facts and would dismiss as
mere speculation all that already stood under the heading of MOTIVE.
OPPORTUNITY. . . . How could anyone in this room have stabbed the old
man in the neck without approaching him? He had been sitting in that
corner. Upright, too, and with a table in front of him. Guy got up, crossed
the room and sat, like Scaife, upright in the cozy corner.

Nothing occurred to him. Well, now, people had gone out and come
back: was there anything in that? He went out and groped his way across
the dark lobby. At the garden door he turned and stood for a moment,
desperately imagining that he wanted to murder Scaife, who was sitting
in the lounge bar, in the cozy corner. It was then that he noticed a thin
shaft of light, to the right of the lounge door, in the partition between
the lounge and the lobby.

He walked up to the partition and felt it over with his hands. It was made of wood—stout matchboarding, and the narrow crack between two of the boards was roughly equidistant between floor and ceiling. He took out his fountain pen, but that was too thick to be inserted; he had a short, thin pencil, which he had picked up somewhere, in his breast pocket, the unsatisfactory sort of pencil provided with diaries. He found it, and with a little forcing it went through. Was he on to something? With a racing heart he hurried into the lounge.

The room, thank heaven, was still empty, and there, in the boarding behind the corner seat, was the point of his pencil. He sat down and could feel it . . . damn . . . between his shoulders . . . no, higher than that, against the fourth or fifth vertebra. Was Scaife a smaller man, or one of those people whose length is all in their legs? Well, that was easy to find out. He had only to ring the mortuary.

He went to the bar and knocked on it, and Eve came, saying, "I hope I haven't neglected you, but I thought you would rather be left alone with your little notebook. More sherry?" "No, thank you," said Guy, trying to keep excitement out of his voice, "but may I telephone?" "Of course," said Eve. "Come into the sitting-room."

She showed him the telephone and left him. He spoke to the mortuary attendant and asked that Scaife's body should be measured, as if in a sitting position, from the puncture in the neck to the buttocks. While he waited for the man to ring back, he occupied himself by looking over his notes and those of the Superintendent, for this new discovery, if it meant anything, must focus suspicion on anyone who had left the lounge after Eve had gone out to Waller, while it cleared those who had remained inside. Edward Scaife could no longer figure as chief suspect; Bridget Frankland and Valentine Day were ruled out, too; Crescy had followed Eve immediately and returned in the company of Conway, but David Frankland had stood about in the lobby; Adam Day could have lingered there on returning from his game of darts, Eve on her way upstairs and Mark Scaife as he left the room. It flashed into Guy's mind then, that his field had widened; anyone who had spent the evening in the public bar must now be considered, besides a whole world of outsiders; in the dark of the blackout anyone could have sneaked up the garden path and entered the lobby. Hell, that tore it! No, not completely. The murderer must have had a pretty accurate knowledge of Scaife's habits, must have known where the old man sat, must either have taken a chance or had the opportunity to observe the old man's exact position. And that brought him back again to the people who had been in the lounge bar.

The telephone bell shrilled in his ear. It was Tadley, the mortuary attendant, speaking. In a sitting position, from the puncture in the neck to the buttocks, Scaife's body measured thirty-four inches. Guy replaced the receiver, pulled out the folding footrule he always carried, and went back into the bar. Eve was there. She said, "Did you get through all right." Guy said absently, "Yes, thank you," and, "I hope you'll excuse my somewhat mysterious activities." He unfolded his footrule and measured the boarding. It was thirty-four inches from the point of his pencil to the cushioned seat.

"Now," he said to Eve, "I've made some progress. The same again, please, Mrs. Hennisty, and I'm going to bother you for the names of everyone who was in the public bar on Thursday evening after nine."

"The public bar?" said Eve, and then nobly remembered to mind her own business. "I wasn't there after nine o'clock. At least, not until after Scaife was dead, when Peter tactfully cleared the lounge. But he'll tell you, and what he can't, Mrs. Chandler will."

She called Peter and he came from the public bar. Nine o'clock hadn't meant much to him on Thursday evening, but he thought he could remember who was there at the time that Waller came, if that would do. Guy said it would do very well, and Peter thought for a moment. Then he said, "Bert Saunders and Sidney Smallbone. Smallbone's the young fellow you played darts with, and Saunders is the tall man you talked to. Janes, the carrier—the bloke who joined in when Saunders was telling you about old times at the Hall—he was in early, too, and he didn't leave until just before Eve fetched me to tell me about Scaife. Bligh, the postman, was here, but he'd got a committee meeting of the Bowls Club and he left well before Waller came. Old Tom Farraway had gone—he always goes to bed at half-past eight, anyway, and Albert and Percy Tew had gone—they're our bakers and they rise at an unearthly hour. I think I can swear that by the time Waller showed up, only Saunders, Smallbone and Janes were in the bar."

"And Mrs. Chandler."

"Yes, of course. I'd forgotten her."

"And did any of them leave the room—by any door?"

"Not while I was there," said Peter. "And, from a few moments after Waller left till Eve fetched me, I was there the whole time. Wait a minute. . . . There was a gap of about two seconds when I put my head through the door and asked if anyone wanted to play darts."

"And you didn't happen at any time to see anyone hanging about outside? In the garden or car park?"

"No," said Peter, looking interested. "Does that mean there's a possibility that it was an outside job after all?"

"I can't say yet," Guy told him. "Can I see Mrs. Chandler now?"

Peter suggested that he should make use of the sitting-room, and, after a few moments, Mrs. Chandler joined him there. Of course she remembered who had been in the bar on Thursday evening. She had a very good memory. She wasn't like some—ignorant as that there wall. When Mr. Waller had come about the lights, he had come to the door of the public bar and Mr. Conway had told him to go round to the garden door, and had himself gone through into the lounge bar. Bert Saunders, Mr. Janes and that bit of a boy, Sidney Smallbone, had then been in the bar. Mr. Janes had left before Mrs. Hennisty had called Mr. Conway to see the body, but Bert Saunders and that Sidney had stayed on till Mr. Waller came in and reminded Mrs. Hennisty to close the bar. While Mr. Conway had been out of the room seeing after the lights, Bert Saunders had also left it. He had gone to the gentlemen's cloakroom; no, not the one in the lobby; it was the outside one what was used by them in the public bar. How long had he been absent? Well, as long as you'd expect. Yes, he had come back before Mr. Conway—several minutes before. Had she herself gone out at any time? Certainly not. She had her work to do.

Guy then asked her some more general questions. Had she ever had anything to do with Scaife? "No," said Mrs. Chandler. Guy said that surprised him because he had heard some gossip, an old story that he was sorry to bring up, but it was his duty to investigate everything that came along. If he meant Edna, Mrs. Chandler said, her pale face flushing, that was years ago and he must be hard up for clues if that was the sort of thing he'd got to go upon. She supposed that she needn't tell him the story—there was plenty who'd be only too pleased to do that; all she'd got to say was that you didn't get to her age without coming to know that it was no use creating: what would be, would be. Guy was not unfamiliar with this philosophy. It was common among those accustomed to see the fruits of their labor nonchalantly destroyed by a night's frost, a gate left open, or a week of rain. He didn't for a moment suspect the woman. Her ignorance of chemistry was in itself enough.

With a few reassuring words he sent her back to her work and presently followed her into the public bar. He wanted to speak to Saunders, but Saunders had not yet turned up. He ordered a pint of beer and stood for a few minutes listening to the talk, which was mainly concerned with Edward and the changes he was likely to make. The general feeling seemed to be that no good ever came of any change. Two young men were playing darts and Guy toyed with the idea of giving dinner at the Red Lion a miss, getting a snack at The Dog and playing a return game with Sidney Smallbone when he came in. Scaife's murder was likely to be the one subject of conversation and he might hear something, or would confusion be only the worse confounded by the irresponsible gossip of the villagers? Probably, he thought, but, against that, he would like to take his revenge on Smallbone . . . he'd been preoccupied last night . . . he'd put up a perfectly deplorable show. . . . At that point in his reflections, with a sort of click, the memory of an apparently insignificant incident fitted itself into the working machinery of his mind. The machinery whirred. He got up. The darts match ended with a double six and cheers. As unobtrusively as possible he went to the shelf and turned the darts over. What meaning could he read into the fact that only twelve perfectly ordinary three-flighters were there?

CHAPTER V
WEDNESDAY

GUY HADN'T, AFTER all, remained at The Dog on Tuesday evening. At seven o'clock he had started to bicycle back to Melchester, but before he had reached the crossroads, he had been stopped by Waller: the battery of his rear light had failed. He had taken the opportunity to talk things over with Waller. Though Guy didn't know it, the constable's view was characteristic; he provided everyone in Witheridge Green with a stainless character and expressed his opinion that the crime had been committed by an evacuee or a gang of toughs from London. Guy said, "But, my dear fellow, what connection had Scaife with London?" to which Waller replied, "You never know, sir, but I should say that there was something in that old man's past that would give you a line on it." "The people round here had a lot against him, you know," said Guy. "What about this Saunders fellow?" "Oh, sir," said Waller in a shocked voice, "he's a most honest, hard-working man. The father of a family too, real nice boys and girls, all of them. He may talk a bit big in the bar—I've heard he does—but you mustn't take any notice of that—we all talk some times, don't we? Oh, no, believe me, sir, Bert Saunders is quite above suspicion." In spite of a certain irritation, Guy had not been able to help chuckling, as he had ridden away from the Christ-like constable.

He had devoted the evening to his report and nine o'clock on Wednesday morning found him at Melchester Police Station. Dawes was already in his office and Guy was hanging up his hat when the Chief Constable appeared, hearty, red-faced and exhaling a strong odor of germicide.

Quickly disposing of Guy's remarks about the weather, he snapped out, "Well, Northeast? Got something for us, I hope?"

"I'm not quite ready for a warrant yet," said Guy, smiling. "But I've sorted all these people out and I've got plenty of interesting information."

92

"I've got a piece of very interesting information," chipped in Dawes. "Came by post this morning. The sediment from the fragment of sponge is powdered pumice."

"Powdered pumice, sir?"

"Yes. That should be a help to you. You want to use your imagination. The moment I read it, I got a picture in my mind of a shelf in some garage and a car sponge lying in proximity to a bag or a tin of powdered pumice."

The words had given Guy a mental picture too. It was a picture of a brown pony grazing under apple trees. He said, "Powdered pumice is chiefly kept for cleaning steel bits and stirrups, but I believe it's also used for rubbing up old pewter and so on. There are horses at the farm, of course, and," he said reluctantly, "Mrs. Hardwick keeps a pony."

"Does she keep a car?"

"Yes, sir. And she admitted quite frankly to having a car sponge. I should imagine most of these people have one, but, unless you're lucky, it's a job to get a chance of snooping round."

"You want to be tactful," said the Superintendent, who seemed keen on teaching Guy his job this morning. "Well, Mrs. Hardwick keeps a car and a pony. Does anyone else?"

"I'd better take you through them," said Guy, pulling out his notebook. "At the Hall, there's no car; there's weed-killers and so forth, but no nicotine, and now I must add that there are horses. At the Franklands' there's a car, which is cleaned by the garden boy, so one can assume they've a sponge, but as far as I know they've no horses and they don't seem the kind of people who would rub up antiques. Again, no nicotine. They've neither time nor inclination for gardening. The Days have a car, but it's cleaned in Melchester; they've nicotine, but no horses. I should think they were just the people to clean up pewter—no, I wouldn't though: they've a Regency house and it's furnished strictly to period. I've no suspicions against Conway or Mrs. Hennisty. Mrs. Hardwick, I'm afraid, keeps a car sponge, a pony and nicotine."

"Looks like full marks for Mrs. Hardwick," said the Chief Constable.

"Possibly," said Guy, "but, after going the round of these people, I went back to the scene of the crime and I made a discovery which rather alters things." He asked for the plan of the ground floor at The Dog, told them about the crack in the boarding behind the cozy corner, and, without allowing them time for comment, went on quickly. "This definitely clears the people who remained for the whole evening in the lounge and focuses suspicion on Mark Scaife, Day and Frankland."

Dawes said, "I seem to remember that the lady novelist went out too."

"She went out immediately behind Mrs. Hennisty, sir. I admit that she came back alone."

"Weren't there other people in the place?" asked the Chief Constable. "According to this plan of yours, there's a door from the lobby into the public bar."

"Yes, sir, and there's one from the lobby into the garden. But the point is that only the people in the lounge knew exactly how Scaife was sitting. It wouldn't have been much use shoving the weapon through the crack unless you knew that. You might have shoved it into his clothes, merely, or into thin air."

"Yes, quite," admitted Carruthers. "But what about the windows?"

"The windows are blacked out, sir. A very efficient arrangement of paper and laths. The constable was round that night about a light, which was showing from an upper window on the garden side, so he would certainly have noticed if there was a chink in the lounge windows—they look out on the car park and it's open to the road. And though half the village seems to have had a motive for murder, you at once come up against the fact that some knowledge of chemistry was needed."

"I don't see that. Everyone knows that nicotine's a poison," said Dawes.

"Yes, sir, but what I mean is, the murderer evidently had some idea of the strength and the probable effect on the victim."

"It might be worth while putting a man on to check purchases at the local seedsmen," suggested the Chief Constable.

"Yes. That might bring some other suspects into the limelight," said Guy.

"I'll have that done," Dawes agreed. "And, Northeast, you might find out tactfully who among that lounge bar click has any training in chemistry."

"I've already done that," said Guy with pardonable irritation. "Edward Scaife was trained at an agricultural college, apart from the knowledge he may have acquired at school. Mark left school at fourteen and doesn't hold with scientific farming. Frankland, I suppose, had a good education, but political history seems to be more in his line. Day—well, I imagine he's public school, but they don't take you far in chemistry, do they?" He appealed to the Chief Constable. "All Greek and Latin, isn't it, sir?"

"Not," said the Chief Constable, "if you're on the modern side. But Day's an architect. His firm—Bolney, Bolney and Day—built my gardener's cottage, and built it damn well too. I shouldn't say he'd done much in the way of stinks, but I don't know."

"And what about the lady novelist?" asked Dawes.

"I asked her—tactfully," said Guy. "No knowledge of chemistry, but"—Damn, he thought, how everything piles up against her—"when I was down at Little Bottom Cottage I found Dixon Mann's *Forensic Medicine and Toxicology* there."

"By Jove!" roared Carruthers.

"But it's not so damning," Guy went on, "as it sounds. To begin with, no attempt had been made to conceal it—it was staring me in the face. To go on with, she had a perfectly good explanation—she'd been writing a detective novel . . ."

The Superintendent laughed. "We've heard that story before. It's been used as an excuse for a lot of things."

"I know, sir. But, after all, she is a novelist."

"Hmm. Has the tale been printed?" asked Dawes.

"No, sir. It was never finished. I asked to see the manuscript, but it wasn't available. Her explanation was that the story hadn't worked out and she'd torn it up in a temper."

"By Jove!" said the Chief Constable again.

"The trouble is," said Guy, "that I can't find her an adequate motive."

"I seem to remember that she'd had notice to quit her cottage," said Dawes.

"But can you call that an adequate motive—for murder, sir?" said Guy.

"Hardly," replied Carruthers. "It's not as though the place had been in her family for centuries. That, though it may seem odd to you fellers, would be a perfectly adequate motive for any crime. What's bred in the bone, what? But who *has* got an adequate motive? The Scaifes? That place is practically derelict and mortgaged up to the hilt, so they say."

"Edward Scaife told me that, sir. He rather harped on it, I thought. Is there any possibility that he could do well for himself selling it as building land?"

"I shouldn't say so. Melchester isn't spreading much, thank God. It's clay soil there, too."

Dawes added, "All the building that's being done is out towards Marley. Gravel soil there."

"Nothing in that, then. Still, Edward's a trained farmer and rather a conceited fellow, I should say. He may hope to pull the place together, and there's a lot in being one's own master. Personally, I think he had the strongest motive of anyone, but, as far as I've been able to ascertain, he's got no nicotine and no car sponge. The same applies equally to Mark Scaife. Under his father's will he inherits two hundred pounds, and though that may not seem much to you gentlemen, I should say it meant a great deal to him. Edward, as I expect you remember, didn't leave the lounge all the evening, but Mark only stayed for a short time. However, he's produced an alibi which sounds O.K. Perhaps you'd be so good as to have it checked?" he said to Dawes. "Bus into Melchester— that must have been just before nine o'clock—and then, Miss Winnie Goddard, 52 Camden Street. He spent the night there and walked out in the early morning."

"Look here," said the Chief Constable, who had been studying the plan while Dawes noted down the name and address. "What about this for a suggestion: I know Mark Scaife went out before Mrs. Hennisty and when she went out Scaife was still alive. But this lobby's quite a big place and then there are the lavatories. Couldn't he have lurked there?"

"No point in that, sir. He couldn't have known that Waller was coming about the lights."

"I suppose not," groaned Carruthers. "Well, what about Frankland? He left the lounge. Any motive there?"

"Well, there's his wife, sir. She's got rather a reputation for running after men, and there's a vague piece of gossip, emanating from Scaife's very old and doddering housekeeper, to the effect that she ran after Scaife. I really can't believe that. He seems to have been a particularly repulsive old man."

"I shouldn't altogether discount it. It's incredible what women will do," said Dawes.

"And Day?"

"Pretty hopeless. He's a friend of Mrs. Hardwick's, that's all."

"What, Anthony and Cleopatra?" asked Carruthers.

"Hardly," said Guy. "And, anyhow, Mrs. Hardwick's motive is a pretty feeble one."

"This motive business doesn't seem to be getting us anywhere," said the Superintendent. "I suggest that we go back to facts. What about the weapon?"

"Well, sir, *vide* the medical report, it wasn't a hypodermic syringe. It was just a sharp instrument, and I've got rather a wild suggestion to make. Could it have been a dart?" He spoke diffidently, because last night he had looked on the shelf and found nothing but twelve perfectly ordinary darts.

"A dart?" said the Superintendent. "Good God, no. You put a bit of sponge on the end of a dart and shove it into something and you'll see—the sponge won't penetrate; it'll merely slide up the shaft."

Guy said, "What put it into my mind was that on Monday evening I played a game of darts—camouflage," he was careful to explain, "while I was listening to the gossip in the public bar. When I had had my first throw and went to pull the darts out of the board, I found that one had stuck. I wrenched it out, and though I didn't think anything of it at the time and just threw it back on the shelf and picked up another, I'm conscious that there was something phony about it—in fact, I remarked to the fellow I was playing with that it wasn't much of a dart. It was a homemade sort of affair with a hole—an eye—at the end. Like a bodkin. Last night the incident came back to me. I looked on the shelf for the dud and it had gone. I think that's rather significant."

The Superintendent's strong fingers drummed on the table.

"Rather farfetched, isn't it? There are dud darts in most pubs."

"It's worth enquiring into I think. I'm going back to The Dog now. Then I shall have to get round again after this powdered pumice business."

"I shouldn't be at all surprised," Dawes said, "if you locate it at the lady novelist's place."

"Your money's on her, sir?"

"Definitely. Poison's a woman's weapon."

"Not exclusively," Guy said. "And there was the jab in the neck. It seems curious to me," he went on, thinking aloud, "that, if the crime was committed by one of the people in the lounge, he—or she— didn't drop the poison in Scaife's glass. It would have been comparatively easy. The fact that it wasn't done points to an outsider, but then you come up against the point I made before—that an outsider had no means of ascertaining Scaife's position."

The Chief Constable suggested, "What about the keyhole? Or the door being ajar?"

"No good, sir. The door opens inwards and towards the cozy corner. To catch even a glimpse of Scaife it would have been necessary to come right in."

"Well," said the Chief Constable, "it's no use talking round and round. It's a puzzling case, but you've got the powdered pumice to go on with now. I must say, I agree with Dawes about this dart idea. Much more likely it was trodden on and thrown out. However, you can but enquire. It would be a help to find the weapon, and there might be fingerprints, though it's not likely nowadays."

"Too many damn silly tales written about crime," said Dawes. "It beats me. Why can't they stick to clean adventure for us men and love for the women?"

Neither Guy nor the Chief Constable could answer that, and the conference broke up. Once again Guy took the long hill out of Melchester. He was becoming accustomed to his iron steed, and this morning he reached The Dog in twenty-five minutes. Peter, who was toiling in the garden, took him indoors and Guy walked straight to the shelf where the darts lay and satisfied himself that there was no dud among them. He said to Peter, who was drawing their beer, "Have you thrown out any darts in the last few days?"

"No," said Peter, preoccupied.

"When I was playing on Monday night there was a dud one. Stuck in the board and seemed as if it had been either trodden on, or tampered with. It's not here now."

"How many are there?"

"Twelve."

"That's right. Of course from time to time they do get bust or bent and we renew them. But that lot have gone on for some time now. The experts bring their own, though—perhaps the one you're talking about was left behind by someone. Was it a four flighter?"

"No. A three. If somebody left it behind because it was bust, why has it since been collected?"

"Someone other than myself may have thrown it away," suggested Peter. "I'll ask my sister and Mrs. Chandler. But it's quite on the cards that any player, finding a dud, might have chucked it out—into the fire or somewhere. Eve!" he called, and Eve came in holding a glass cloth and a tumbler, which she was polishing. Guy was conscious that in rather an awed way he admired her intensely. On whatever homely task she engaged, she did not lose her air of dignified sophistication.

In reply to his enquiry, she assured him that she had not thrown away a dart since she and Peter had gone through them just before August Bank Holiday. It was Mrs. Chandler, however, who dusted the public bar, so Mrs. Chandler was called from washing the floor of the lounge. No, she hadn't thrown away no dart; it wasn't her place to. Yes, she had dusted the shelf on Tuesday morning—she wasn't like some, who did the middle and left the corners. She hadn't noticed the number of darts: when she dusted the shelf, she lifted them up in a bundle in one hand, like so, and dusted under them. Then she gave them a flick with the duster, like so, because the feathers gathered the dust. If there had been half a dozen extra, she might have noticed the unusual size of the bundle, but one extra wouldn't make much difference. No, she couldn't have swept up a dart; she wasn't blind and she couldn't have been off seeing it in her dustpan. No, she hadn't heard anyone, except Guy himself, pass any remark about there being a dud. She suggested that if Guy wanted to know anything about the darts, he should ask young Sid Smallbone: from the way that he went on, anyone would think that the whole darts outfit belonged to him.

In a thoughtful silence Guy drank his beer. He was wondering if it would be a sheer waste of time to pursue this line further. If the dart meant anything, there was enormous significance in the fact that it had been removed: to discover the person who had removed it might be to discover the murderer. But Dawes and the Chief Constable agreed that it was much more likely that the dart had been trodden on and thrown away; Peter, unbiased, had made the same suggestion. All the same, one must, in the jargon, 'explore every avenue.' "Can you give me a list," he said to Peter, "of everyone who came into this room between the time I left it on Monday night till the time I came into it again on Tuesday evening?"

"Good God," said Peter.

"Take your time. I expect you'll find it easier if you sit down with a pencil and paper. I've things to do, so I'll get off now and be back at lunch time."

Peter promised to do his best and Guy set off on his search for powdered pumice. His mood was hopeful. Nicotine had been a different matter. All along he had felt that anyone who had used it for a criminal purpose would have been at pains to keep it concealed, and in his own mind Crescy had acquired merit when she had admitted that she possessed it. Where the Days were concerned, that didn't follow. If Adam had used it, he would not have been able to conceal it without arousing Valentine's suspicions, and *vice versa*. This let out the Franklands and the Scaifes too, but on the other hand, even though nicotine was not normally kept in a household, it could have been specially purchased and hidden by any one person. There was also the possibility that the poison had been distilled from cigars. Again, someone—Cresc y was clever enough—might be trying the double bluff, readily admitting to the possession of the poison, thinking that he'd think the murderer would never be so frank about it. The hopeful thing about the powdered pumice was that the murderer could have had no idea that particles were to be found in the fragment of sponge, so that, in all probability, there would be no attempt at concealment and no double-bluffing. Guy remembered dealings with powdered pumice, remembered cleaning old Snowball's bit in the scullery at home before he went hunting and the row there had been afterwards; minute particles of the pumice had got everywhere, even into the rabbit pie, and he had heard about it when he came in from hunting. It wasn't even necessary for the sponge and the pumice to lie, as Dawes had imagined, on a shelf together. The damned stuff was bewitched and would get anywhere . . .

He went first to the Hall and was again received by Janet, who quite understood, she said, that fresh questions kept cropping up: no, he wasn't disturbing her; she was only darning socks. The tone of her voice as she

spoke of darning socks was scornful, giving him to understand that, as a
highly educated woman, she was wasting her abilities on so domesti-
cated an occupation, and he compared her unfavorably with Eve Hennisty, who could polish a glass as though it were a sophisticated occupation. Expressing surprise that she could stay indoors on so fine a morning, he brought the conversation round to the weather and, after com-
paring the present abundance of grass feed with the scarcity last season,
asked, casually, how many horses were kept at the Hall farm. She replied
that there were seven, but they would soon be replaced, she hoped, by
tractors, and Guy allowed her to deliver a lecture on the advantages of
mechanized farming: although, on account of her timely expedition to
The Four Feathers, she was outside his suspicions, he wanted to get her
talking; living at the Hall, she must surely be acquainted with undercur-
rents in the life of the murdered squire. But was this, he asked, a suit-
able time to switch over to tractors? Horses, of course, were fetching a
good price, but what about the shortage of petrol? Janet touched on the
immense saving of labor, and Guy mentioned the cleaning of harness.
Yes, she told him; all the harness at the farm was old-fashioned stuff; she
was going to poke round one day and see what she could find in the way
of horse brasses. Guy expressed an interest in horse brasses, gave details
of a mythical collection, to which he was anxious to make additions, and
presently they were walking up to the stables in search of brasses. The
harness-room door was locked, and Janet volunteered to get the key
from her husband. She went off, walking sturdily across the newly plowed
pasture, and Guy seized the opportunity to investigate the stables. He
passed quickly from one empty and evil-smelling stall to another, and
finally came to a loose box, occupied by a cart mare, obviously suffering
from grease. This was evidently the part of the stables which was used
now; beyond the box was a forage room and through the open door he
caught a glimpse of a tangle of harness, carelessly thrown across a corn
bin. He hurried in. The place was untidy and smelt of mice. On the
shelves were rusty currycombs, bald dandy brushes, stained, half-empty
bottles of colic drinks and tins of skin remedies with the lids off and a
film of dust over the dried-up contents—no wonder skin remedies were
needed in Scaife's stables, Guy thought, turning over the harness, the
hard twisted traces and the moth-eaten saddle, strewing moldy stuffing.
At the bottom of the pile he found the bridle—a steel bit, of course, and
if it was ever cleaned, surely in this old-fashioned establishment there
must be powdered pumice. He peered about. Up on the window ledge
he found it, damply oozing from a rotted paper bag.
    Now then . . . The Scaifes had no car, but there was a sponge in most
stables . . . but not, so far as he could see, in the Scaifes' stable . . . not on

the window ledge . . . not on the shelf among the bottles. Footsteps in the yard warned him of Janet's return. He went out of the forage-room door and walked to meet her.

"I've just been talking to your sick mare."

"Oh yes, grease," said Janet uninterested.

"I don't wonder. It's cheek to say so, perhaps, but your father-in-law's horseman doesn't seem to have spent much time on grooming."

"I don't suppose he had much time to spend on it. My father-in-law had about half the men he needed to run the place by his old-fashioned methods. They're a slack lot too, in Loamshire."

"It's bad economy," Guy remarked, "to neglect horses. Or harness. But you can't expect to keep horses as they should be kept with a couple of rusty currycombs and almost bald dandy brushes. I was brought up with horses myself. That poor devil of a mare—her eyes need sponging out. I'd have done it myself, but I couldn't find anything to do it with."

Janet, fitting the key into the harness-room door, said, "You wouldn't find such a luxury as a sponge in these stables. Of course, it's disgraceful, the way the horses have been kept, but, as we've practically decided to get rid of them, we're not replacing anything. Now, we ought to find the brasses here, I think. It's only what's actually in use that's kept in the forage room."

Guy spent about ten minutes looking at horse brasses, in which he was not the least interested; then he recommended Janet to clean up the few which they had discovered and have them valued, and she promised to let him know the price she would take for them. "Now I really mustn't waste any more of the ratepayers' time," he said jocularly. "About these routine questions . . ." he just remembered, and enquired the exact hour at which the murdered man had dined and left for The Dog on Thursday evening. Janet, wrinkling her high brow, replied with careful precision, and, as he rode away, he congratulated himself that she would never guess how, in the middle of their casual chat, she had given him the only answer he had come for.

Powdered pumice at the Hall, but no sponge. At Cold Harbour Farm a sponge, but was there powdered pumice? In answer to his remark that he had been down at the Hall and Mrs. Scaife had told him that they were switching over to tractors Bridget said that she had no arable land; she had thought once of getting a cob to cart round the chickens' food, but it was unnecessary now that she had battery hen houses. Guy described the state of the Hall stables—the fearsome mess in the forage room, spilt powdered pumice all over the place, even in the fodder. Awful stuff, wasn't it? Bridget asked what it was used for. Cleaning steel bits, Guy told her, and rubbing up old stuff like pewter. Hadn't she ever used it? No, Bridget said; as a child she'd had a pony, but she supposed the bit was plated because she had always cleaned it with Brasso. Well, now, Guy said, to get down to what he'd come about . . . and he asked her the exact time that she had entered the lounge at The Dog on Thursday night and left it.

Bridget was, quite naturally, unable to give more than approximate times and she looked worried. He reassured her: these were merely routine questions; and he bicycled away cursing. A sponge, but no powdered pumice at Cold Harbour Farm. Never the powdered pumice and the sponge and the nicotine all together. . .

He went back across the Green. It was one o'clock, so he decided to repair to The Dog for lunch before calling on the Days or at Little Bottom Cottage. As he entered by the garden door, he could see through the half-open door of the lounge, an emerald green back and a head of honey-colored curls, that could only be Crescy's. Good. That would save him the damnable long hill to and from the Bottom. He turned, however, into the public bar. There were several customers there. Peter, on the other side of the bar, nodded to him and waved a folded sheet of paper. "There's a snack ready for you in the other room," he said, "and here's what you wanted." Guy took the paper with a word of thanks and went through into the lounge.

"Hullo," said Crescy.

"Hullo," said Guy, wishing that she didn't always make you feel so instantly at home and friendly. "I didn't see a car outside? How did you get here?"

"Walked."

"What energy. All uphill, too. I wonder you don't ride or drive your pony."

"One-Eye's retired. He's very old. He was at least twenty-five when I bought him."

"Still, he'd carry you."

"I don't know if he's ever been ridden. When I bought him, he was in a cart. At least, he was being sold complete with harness. Oh, God!" said Crescy, "he did look old, standing in a corner of the market waiting to be sold and to go on working for ever and ever."

Eve had come in. She brought a plateful of scrambled eggs on toast, which she hoped was the sort of thing Guy wanted. She said, "You've got too much imagination, Crescy."

Guy said, "Did you buy the harness?"

"I had to," said Crescy. "I didn't mean to work him, but someone else was bidding for him, and they wanted him complete. It must be awful to be sold with your harness. . . ."

"It's awful," said Eve, "how sentimental people get about horses."

"One must be allowed one soft spot," said Crescy.

Guy, experiencing one of those moments when he hated his job, quite unreasonably because he had felt nothing of the kind when catching out Janet Scaife in much the same fashion, said, "You can get a very good price now for pony harness. Why don't you advertise it? I suppose you've never cleaned it and it's gone to glory?"

"No, it hasn't. I've cleaned it up occasionally."

"What did you use? Probably you've done more harm than good with Brasso and boot polish."

"No, I've been most professional. I was brought up with ponies. I've used saddle soap and powdered pumice. So there!" said Crescy.

Damn and blast! Guy said wearily, "I hate powdered pumice. It's bewitched. It gets everywhere."

Crescy said, "Mine's nearly disappeared. I think the chickens eat it."

"They would if they could get at it. Where do you keep it?"

"Here, there and everywhere. I wish I had a place for everything and everything in its place, like Eve has."

"It's so much less trouble," Eve told her.

"But it's present trouble. I mean, if you're a person who lives for the present, you *can't* be tidy. And it's a Good Thing to live in the present. *Take no thought for the morrow* . . ."

"I refuse to argue with you," Eve said. "You always floor me with quotations and I can't remember any." They talked on about Crescy and Guy got off his stool and went to the chair by the fire to read the list that Peter had given him.

It was lamentably long. It was headed, *Public Bar,* and under the subheading, *Monday Night,* were the names: Saunders; Janes; Bligh; P. Conway; E. Hennisty; Mrs. Chandler. *Tuesday Morning* gave him: Brewers' vanman; Mrs. Chandler; E. Hennisty and P. Conway: *Tuesday Noon,* T. Farraway; D. Brown; H. Prior; C. Hardwick, after which name came a note in brackets: *Had snack in lounge but went into public bar afterwards to play darts with self,* and Mrs. E. Scaife, who also earned a note: *brought back empty cider bottles and stayed for a few minutes watching the game. Tuesday Evening before Arrival of Detective-Inspector Northeast* yielded the mixed bag: A. Day *(for a bottle of sherry);* D. Brown; H. Prior; T. Farraway; three strangers, probably commercial travelers; Militiaman with Flossie; M. Scaife.

Guy pulled out his notebook and jotted down: P. Conway; E. Hennisty; Mrs. Chandler; C. Hardwick; A. Day. Then he asked for Peter, and Crescy said she must go before she was thrown out, and slipped down from her stool. "No routine questions this morning?" she asked Guy.

For a moment he considered asking her if she had noticed a dud dart during her game with Peter, but he remembered how, earlier in the day, he had complained to himself: never the sponge and the nicotine and the silver sand all together, and now he had found one place where they were all together—at Little Bottom Cottage—at Cresy's home. He looked down at her, his heart like lead. "No," he said. "No routine questions."

Cresy went out, taking, it seemed to him, his pleasure in the day along with her, and he turned to Peter. "I've been over your list. Now, when you were playing darts with Mrs. Hardwick, did you notice the dud one?"

"No," said Peter, "but actually. . . well, I was finishing up—wiping the bar over or something— and Cresy collected the darts and handed me mine."

"Without any remark about a dud?"

"She didn't say anything. Would you like to ask her? She hasn't been gone a minute. Shall I go after her?"

"No," said Guy. "I want this kept quiet. It's only hunch I've got."

"I suppose I ought not to ask, but I imagine you think the dud dart was used as the weapon—Good God! . . ."

"Remembered something?"

"My God, I have! I deserve to be crucified. Call myself a policeman! On Thursday night, after everyone had gone I was seeing Cresy out and we found a dart in the lobby."

"Whereabouts?"

"Well, Cresy was behind me and she kicked it and it went tinkling across the lobby. She said, 'Have you dropped anything?' and I said, 'No, I don't think so.' We looked and Cresy picked something up and said, 'Look, it's a dart,' and I said, 'How damned careless people are,' or words to that effect. Cresy went into the public bar and put the dart on the shelf and that was that. I never thought any more about it."

"Well, that rather clinches it," said Guy. "And it's good for Cresy— Mrs. Hardwick. If she'd had anything to do with the murder, she could have taken the dart away then and destroyed it." Or— wait; this needed thinking out—Peter knew she'd found the dart . . . if she'd made off with it and later the police had tumbled to the idea that a dart had been used, as far as Peter was concerned, she'd have been for it. . . .

His thoughts were interrupted by Peter's voice with an edge to it.

"You don't imagine that Cresy had anything to do with the murder?"

Guy said, "You know enough about police work to understand that in the early stages of a case we suspect everybody."

"You don't appear to suspect me," said Peter.

"No, I don't suspect you. You had no earthly motive."

"Nor had Crescy."

His voice was a challenge, and Guy thought it prudent to change the subject. "I'll just run through these names with you. Mrs. Chandler; Mr. Day; Mark Scaife. Had any of those three an opportunity of removing the dart without your noticing?"

"Mrs. Chandler had. But you don't suspect her, surely?"

"I don't," said Guy a little impatiently. "She was never in the lounge, anyway. But I've got to get everything cut and dried. Mrs. Chandler: yes. Now what about Scaife and Day?"

"Adam only came in for his sherry. I went to get it. Mrs. Chandler was serving beer. I suppose he could have grabbed a dart off the shelf. There were other people in the bar . . . they may be able to tell you."

Guy turned to Peter's list. "D. Brown; H. Prior; T. Farraway; three strangers, probably commercial travelers; Militiaman with Flossie; M. Scaife."

"I'm wrong," said Peter. "As you were. Adam came in before any of those others. Mrs. Chandler was doing something for Eve. There was only me in the bar."

"A. Day: yes."

"But you can't, surely, suspect old Adam. . . "

"Now for M. Scaife."

"Well, he came in and threw back a pint and went out again. I was surprised that he didn't stay longer, but it crossed my mind that it might be only natural—I mean, I suppose that he's technically in mourning."

"And who was in the bar then?"

"The whole boiling—except, of course, for Adam."

"You didn't see him go near the shelf?"

"No, I didn't. You know, it's frightfully difficult to remember this kind of thing, but I should say that he came straight up to the bar, stood there, threw back his drink and made a beeline for the door. That's my impression, but I don't know that I'd swear to it."

"Mark Scaife: yes." Guy waited a moment. "I notice you don't say, 'Surely you can't suspect old Mark.' "

"Well," said Peter, "you see, I don't know so much about him."

"That's the way of it. Any stranger or comparative stranger is capable of murder, but never one's own friends or employees. Yet the murderer's not a type—just someone like ourselves, who's been driven too far."

"I shouldn't say that," retorted Peter. "I can't imagine myself committing a murder."

"No. You'd take some other way out. If you were hard up, you wouldn't murder your rich uncle—you'd simply go through with the unpleasantness of the bankruptcy court. If you had a nagging wife, you'd leave her. If you'd got a girl into trouble and couldn't provide for her, you'd tell her to go to hell. It is incredible how many people go to the gallows rather than face a spot of trouble that would blow over in a month or two anyway." And, as the words came out, he remembered, "It's present trouble . . ."

"Well, you're the expert," said Peter. "But I can't help thinking there's a flaw somewhere in the murderer's mind."

"Anyhow," said Guy, "it's no use standing here and generalizing. You might just show me whereabouts in the lobby Mrs. Hardwick was when she kicked the dart and where she found it."

Peter led the way into the lobby. Crescy had been behind him, but he thought she must have kicked the dart immediately after shutting the lounge door. They had found it outside the men's lavatory. Guy, saying he might be back later, took his leave and wheeled his bicycle across the Green to the Grove.

Valentine Day, in a bright overall and gloves, was gardening. She was one of those women who garden prettily, with a raffia basket and neat untangled balls of twine. But she was only pottering, she said, and Guy wasn't in the least disturbing her. She led him this time into a little room at the front of the house where a fire was burning cheerily.

Guy had been wrong about the period furnishing at the Grove. This room was furnished in the heavy fashion designed to support conventional masculinity. He admired the pewter candlesticks and mugs on the mantelpiece. Valentine said she didn't care for them. They didn't suit the house. It was her husband who had misguidedly collected them in his Oxford days.

"They must be a nuisance to clean," Guy sympathized, and he invented a pewter mug, which he had bought at a junk shop. He had spent hours cleaning it, he grumbled, with elbow grease and powdered pumice.

Valentine didn't use powdered pumice. She used elbow grease and plate polish. Was powdered pumice good? She might try it next time she had the energy to clean the beastly things.

Guy said what he had really come for was to ask a few routine questions. Could she cast her mind back to Thursday evening and tell him what length of time had elapsed between the moment when her husband had come back from the public bar and the moment when Mrs. Hardwick had joined him at the shove ha'penny board?

The mention of Crescy's name brought a gleam to Valentine's eyes. But she couldn't say for certain. Two or three minutes, perhaps.

"And how long would you say the darts game lasted?"

Valentine really didn't know.

"Not long, I should think," Guy said, getting nearer to his point. "Your husband's an expert, isn't he? I wish I was. It's a game that fascinates me. I suppose one really ought to buy a darts board and play at home."

"We've got a board," Valentine said with admirable frankness. "But I wouldn't have it indoors because of the walls. It's out in the garage. We don't often use it, because it's tiresome moving the car out, but it comes in handy when we've got people staying for the weekend and there's a wet day."

A visit to the garage seemed indicated. Guy wondered if you could get a decent board under a guinea. The Days' board had cost twenty-five shillings. Was it a decent one? It seemed all right. While he was here, could he see it? Yes, certainly.

The Days' garage was the old coach house. The car was out. The darts board was hanging on the far wall. "That's just the kind I want," said Guy, looking round for the darts and locating them in a cardboard box without a lid, on a shelf. "I must just see if I can get a double one," he tried to say boyishly.

Valentine laughed. "And I always imagined that detectives were stiff, official kind of men!"

"We're only human," said Guy looking through the darts and finding eight all perfectly ordinary ones. "Did you have to buy the darts separately, or were they thrown in?"

"They're extra, but they're quite cheap and they last for ages. These are the original ones."

Guy threw three times and got the double one at last. "There! Now I really must get on." He put the darts back in their box. Nicotine, but no powdered pumice. Darts, but it hadn't been necessary to replace one. No sponge, or . . . wait a minute, had he slipped up there? In the first fine rapture of housekeeping, Adam Day had cleaned his car. "That's right. Must be tidy," he burbled. "I only wish I could keep my garage as neat as yours."

"Well, you're a man. I'm very tidy myself. I think a woman ought to be. But I don't like tidy men. It doesn't seem natural somehow."

Guy's powers of invention failed him. He blurted out, "When I was here before, you told me that your husband used to clean your car. Have you still got the sponge he used?"

"I expect it's still knocking round the place. Why?"

"Just another routine question."

Valentine stood silent, looking a little scared. Guy said, "Where would it be? Perhaps in that cupboard." He went to the cupboard in the corner and opened it. He found dusters, a tin of polish and a dried-up sponge.

He felt the sponge. There was no gritty feel to it, but, as he replaced it with his back to Valentine, he tore off a large fragment and held it in his clenched hand. An instant later, the fragment was transferred to his pocket. He straightened up. Valentine said, "There isn't anything awful, is there, about our having a sponge?"

Guy felt sorry for her. He said, "No, not a bit. A car sponge is a very ordinary household article. Nearly everyone has one. I'm just checking up on them."

"Crescy Hardwick's got one. Once, when I went to see her, she was cleaning her car."

"I know," said Guy. "Nearly everybody's got one. Why do you mention Mrs. Hardwick particularly, Mrs. Day?"

"Crescy's queer, isn't she? I mean, she's got a funny moral standard. . . ."

"You mean that if I asked you straight out who you thought was the murderer, you'd say Mrs. Hardwick?"

"I suppose I should."

"Do you know anything definite, or would it be only a guess?"

"Well," said Valentine, looking down at her shoes, "it wouldn't be a guess exactly—there's such a thing as feminine intuition, isn't there?"

"Not in a murder case. There's only evidence. You're sure you didn't see anything to support this theory of yours?"

"No. I didn't see anything," said Valentine, regretfully.

Guy, bicycling back to Melchester, again felt sorry for her. She was a spiteful little creature, but it must be hard for her to guess or know that she was losing her man, and losing him in a way that must puzzle her, for she would never understand how her youth and loveliness simply didn't count when she was up against Crescy Hardwick's personality. There were Valentines by the dozen, Guy thought, freewheeling down to the crossroads, but there was only one Crescy: if you loved her, you'd love her passionately, spiritually, quite exclusively and forever. How did he love Pamela Driver? She was, to sum it up in one vulgar word, bed-worthy, and she was a good companion, but she couldn't make or mar your life for you; she didn't in any way affect your hope of heaven; it would be very nice to be married to her, and that was all. While Crescy. . . . He pulled himself up. The Days had no powdered pumice. Their darts were in order. Only Crescy possessed sponge, powdered pumice and nicotine and had had the opportunity of removing the dart she had doctored.

But why had she replaced the dart on the shelf? Why hadn't she put it in her bag, taken it home and destroyed it?

Because Peter had heard it tinkle across the lobby. When she had followed him out, she had meant to wrench it from the boards or to pick it up if it had fallen, but inadvertently she had kicked it. Then, as they were groping for it, Peter had seen it as soon as she had. She had not had time to conceal it and pretend that she had dropped a penny.

There didn't seem to be much hope for Crescy. No hope at all, said Dawes, when Guy dropped in on him. "But look here," said Guy, "we haven't a thing to go on. This is all absolutely circumstantial evidence."

"I'm not," said Dawes, "suggesting a warrant. But you know now where to look for your direct evidence. Find the dart. Get hold of her car sponge. And warn her and damn well put her through it."

"The dart," Guy objected, "is probably in Little Bottom Wood somewhere. Talk about looking for a needle in a haystack! Still, as you say, I'd better go down there tomorrow and get a statement. I'll get the car sponge too. In the meantime, I've pinched a piece of the Days' car sponge. You might have it tested."

"I will," said Dawes, "but I think it's a waste of time. Everything points to the lady novelist."

Guy felt his heart sink, as though in a lift. "It does, I know. But, all the same, I don't feel happy about it. These things that point to her— they're all the kind of things that might pile up . . . well, in fact, as I said just now, they're all circumstantial. Why did she admit to possessing nicotine? Why didn't she conceal the book on toxicology?"

"Double bluff," said the Superintendent.

Guy remembered that he, too, had thought of that. With a sigh he said, "Well, we must see what tomorrow will bring forth. I'll push off now," and he left the police station with a scowl on his face and no pleasant word for anybody.

He went back to the Red Lion and his usual indigestible imported dinner. A glass of sherry and two double whiskeys did nothing to dispel the cloud of depression which hung over him. What was the matter with him? Years ago he had had it out with himself: murder was murder, and to sympathize with the criminal was sheer sentimentality. You had to think of the victim, of the victim's relatives, of society in general. But he couldn't help thinking of Little Bottom Cottage, smelling of oak and apple logs, of the one-eyed pony in the orchard, the cats on the window sill and the white hounds of Imperial Russia, of Crescy, the only Cresy, of how he'd feel when he'd got it out—Mrs. Hardwick, I've some questions to ask you, and it's my duty to warn you that anything you say may be taken down and used in evidence against you. . . .

CHAPTER VI

WEDNESDAY EVENING

CRESCY HAD WASHED and polished her liqueur glasses. She arranged them on a tray and carried them into the sitting-room and set them down on the Queen Anne table beside the bottles of *creme de menthe* and Benedictine. Four quart bottles of draft beer and her white Copenhagen mugs stood on the flap of the marqueterie bureau, which she had cleared by her usual method of gathering everything up and transferring it to the larder: and on the top of the white bookcase was a tray of coffee cups, so now she had nothing to do but to make the coffee. Crescy adored entertaining, not as Hugo Hardwick had liked entertaining, with long dull dinner parties, at which everyone wore party faces and made party conversation, but in this informal, intimate way, and, in spite of being suspected of murder, she was in high spirits and she realized that, and thought how unreasonable and indestructible a thing is happiness, and wondered whether it was in the bounds of possibility to wake up in tearing good spirits on the morning when you were to be hanged. It was possible, she concluded. Circumstances made no difference to that queer activity of the spirit. She had been rich and miserable; ecstatically happy when broke; she had been glum at gay parties and bursting with the joy of living in the dentist's chair. Tomorrow she might be arrested, but tonight she was giving a party: Edward and Janet Scaife, the Franklands, the Days and poor old Peter, if there was nothing in particular doing at The Dog and he found that he could get away.

Edward Scaife had more or less invited himself. Winston Churchill was to broadcast after the nine o'clock news; there was no wireless at the Hall and the battery of Eve's portable had unexpectedly died on her. Eve had announced this, at cocktail time, at The Dog, and presently Edward had come up to Crescy and wondered if she would be at home that evening and whether it would be a terrible infliction if he and his wife dropped in to hear the speech.

"Oh, do come," Cresy had cried enthusiastically. "I'd love you to. Come in early for coffee and liqueurs and we'll make an evening of it," but afterwards she had thought that making an evening of it with Janet and Edward might be too much of a good thing, so she had invited Peter, and later she had summoned the Franklands and the Days by telephone.

In spite of the blackout and having to walk, everyone was pleased to come. The Days gave little dinner parties, at which Adam strove to talk amusingly, but there was always a blight over them: the obvious display of the best dinner mats and the best wine glasses and the best dinner service was dispiriting, and more dispiriting still was Valentine, mute and anxiously awaiting some culinary disaster. The Franklands invited you to come in after dinner. There was always a slight but depressing shortage of alcohol, the chairs were hard and either the fire was low or Bridget threw the windows open, declaring that the room was unbearably stuffy. But at Cresy's place you were warm; you sprawled; the room was blue with smoke; you drank a little too much and, even though you were normally a dull dog, you found yourself talking brilliantly. Under some benign influence away flew care. You thanked heaven for things that as a rule you cursed; you even thanked heaven that you possessed no costive wealth nor soul-destroying regular job. A sort of virtue attached itself to the old clothes that you were wearing; dreadfully smug you would have looked in the dress you'd hankered after in Melchester only yesterday. As for your husband or wife, well, if you quarreled it kept you awake; it was better, you decided, than sinking soporifically into a slough of domestic felicity.

The Scaifes arrived first. Edward wore a mackintosh and wanted to hang it up, so Cresy directed him to her ubiquitous larder and she took Janet up to her bedroom to dispose of her coat and hat—Janet was apt to wear a hat, and although her clothes were in better repair than most people's, she looked, in consequence, a trifle old-fashioned.

"I see you like old things," said Janet, casting a glance at Cresy's big Regency bed with curved ends, the elegant little dressing-table, littered with a wildly luxurious array of cosmetics, the frilled white muslin curtains, the faded French carpet with its romantic garland of roses and the bow-fronted walnut chest of drawers, where an open drawer revealed a silky muddle. "I don't. I know it's a low taste, but I like modern things. I love their efficiency."

"I don't call that a low taste," said Cresy, sitting on the bed. "I think it's a very worthy one. Besides, why shouldn't you like what you like? But what are you going to do with all the old stuff at the Hall? It's lovely, isn't it?"

"I don't mean to go on living there," said Janet. "In the last six months I've absolutely worn myself out trying to keep even the few rooms we live in tidy and clean. That dreadful big kitchen—the miles I've walked in it! And the range and that great stone sink! I want Edward to shut the place up and build us a labor-saving bungalow."

"Will he?"

"Oh yes, when things get better. They soon will, too. Farming's all right if only you're trained and efficient. We've ordered a couple of tractors and I'm going to take over the dairying. We've started rebuilding the cow sheds; I'm going to have all the milking done by electricity."

"Ugh!" said Crescy.

"But why?" said Janet. "You get your milk from us. You'd never have done so if you'd seen the state of the cowsheds. Surely you prefer clean food."

" 'A bit of dirt won't 'urt,' " said Crescy. "But milking by electricity seems unnatural. I hate anything unnatural. Sets my teeth on edge. Help yourself to some powder, Janet."

"I don't use it," said Janet.

"Worthy woman," said Crescy. "Come on then. Let's go down."

Edward was standing by the fire. Tall and straight, he wasn't, Crescy, thought, unattractive; it was only when you looked at his tight, ungenerous mouth that you couldn't feel any affection for him. And he seemed incapable of making himself at home. He never sat down uninvited or took a cigarette unless it was offered to him. He wasn't even making friends with the dogs. Probably the result of a chilly boyhood, she thought, saying, "Sit down and help yourselves to gaspers while I make the coffee." She went through into the kitchen.

Janet said in a low voice to her husband, "It's tiresome about Mark. I'm not sorry to lose him, but we could have done with his two hundred pounds."

"We could," said Edward, "but, even if he'd stayed, I doubt whether he would have invested it in the farm."

"He'd have blued it most likely," said Janet. "Men like him—" She broke off as Crescy came back with the coffeepot. She poured out and put the coffee and the milk down on the hearth to keep warm. Then there were voices outside and she went to the door. The Franklands had arrived and a yell of, "Hi! Don't shut us out," announced the Days. A few moments later Valentine and Bridget had returned from upstairs and everyone had been supplied with coffee, cigarettes and liqueurs and was comfortably seated in the deep armchairs or on cushions on the floor.

Adam, who was sitting on cushions and had his back against Crescy's chair, asked, "Has everyone besides Valentine had their dose of routine questions today?"

"I have," said Janet, "but it developed into a talk about horse brasses. I don't think he's very efficient, that man."

"He's very good-looking," said Valentine.

"In a stolid way," said Bridget. "It's not a type that appeals to me. Not easily stirred. Sentimental but sexually moribund, I should say."

"I don't know anything about his sex life, but I should think he's pretty deadly at his job," Crescy said.

"Oh, do you?" said Bridget. "I don't. I agree with Janet. We had a pleasant chat about horses too."

"There you are," said Cresc y. "He talked horsey to both of you. He wanted to know something about horses." She put her fantastically tipped fingers to her forehead. "What the hell could it have been?"

"There's no horses in the case," said Bridget.

"Wait a minute," said Cresc y. "I met him in The Dog at lunchtime, and he told me he'd no questions to ask. . . . But we'd been talking. . . . We'd been talking about One-Eye. There you are—horses."

"Hoofmarks," cried Adam. "Perhaps he found hoofmarks outside The Dog. You're for it, Cresc y. You're the only one of us who can ride."

"I can ride," said Bridget, "but I haven't got a pony. Still, I suppose I could have borrowed one, or stolen One-Eye."

"You're mad, Adam," said Cresc y. "No one with criminal intentions would draw attention to themselves by riding about. Hullo, that sounds like Peter. Let him in, David. I can't move for Adam . . ."

David had difficulty in moving because of everybody and the dogs, but he picked his way to the door and Peter came in. Cresc y said, "We need you, Peter. The sleuth's gone all horsey and we want to know why."

Peter, pouring out his coffee and a Benedictine, said, "Must we discuss the murder?"

Adam said, "Of course we must. If we don't we'll get repressions and we'll all be in the loony bin by the time the sleuth makes up his mind."

Peter, standing with his back to the fire, looked down at Adam. Blast the fellow, sitting like that, with his head against Cresc y's knees. "If you'd move," he said, "I could sit down somewhere," but Adam only replied, "Step over me."

Peter controlled a desire to step *on* him, stepped over him and sat down beside David on the floor. Cresc y said, "Why has the sleuth gone horsey, Peter dear?"

"I didn't know he had," said Peter unhelpfully.

"He talked to us all about horses this morning," Cresc y said.

"Not to me," said Valentine. "He talked to me about the price of darts boards. Oh yes, and he told me straight out that he's checking up on people's car sponges."

"Car sponges?" said everyone.

"Yes. But it doesn't matter frightfully if you've got one, because nearly everyone in the case *has* got one."

"Valentine seems to have gleaned a lot," said Adam.

"Ah!" said Bridget. "That's because she's got blue eyes."

"So have you," said Crescy.

"But I've got black hair," said Bridget. "I'm not the type. Valentine's just the one he'd fall for. You know all about psychology, Crescy. Don't you see?

Crescy said, handsomely, "Any man in his senses would fall for Valentine." The line between her eyebrows deepened as she looked down at Adam's dark head against her knees.

"Can't we get at this?" said David. "Horses. What can the connection be?"

"Traces of horse dung on the floor near the body." This suggestion came from Bridget.

"No good," said Crescy. "Anyone might have picked it up coming along the road."

"Well, let's talk about something else," said Peter.

"Peter," said Crescy, "it strikes me that you're going all policified."

"He is," said Adam. "Peter's the sort of man whose Job Would Come First."

Peter said smoothly, "This isn't my job. But I don't know any more than anyone else what's in Northeast's mind."

"You could hazard a guess," said Crescy.

"It's no use guessing," said Peter, "and anyhow, when you think that we're all suspects, it's a pretty beastly thing. . . ."

"I don't see that," said Crescy, passing her liqueur glass to be refilled. "Even if one of us had murdered the squire—and I suppose one of us did—it wouldn't stop our being friends."

"Nonsense," said Peter.

"Crescy's absolutely right," said Adam.

"I don't know," said Valentine. "I should be scared."

"Why should you be scared?" asked Crescy. "Supposing I'd done it, I shouldn't be different. I should still be the same person as before."

"You wouldn't," said Valentine, "be the person we'd thought you were."

"Why not?" said Crescy. "It's circumstances that push people into things."

"A murderer is someone who has run amok," said Bridget. "A mad dog. If Victoria or Olivia went mad, no matter how much you'd cared for them, you'd keep out of their way until you could knock them over the head. Wouldn't you?"

"But I don't think a murderer is like a mad dog," said Crescy.

"You never do think what anybody else thinks," said Peter irritably.

"And thank God for that," said Adam and stared at Peter.

Peter stared back. "Crescy's attitude—I mean, being pro-murderer and antipolice—it's so damned silly. It doesn't do her any good with Northeast."

Adam sat up.

"Are you insinuating that she needs to ingratiate herself with Northeast?"

"Shut up, Adam," said Crescy, annoying Peter still further by placing her hands on Adam's shoulders and pulling him back to rest again against her knees. "Of course Peter wasn't insinuating anything. Everybody knows that I'm Suspect Number One."

"Nobody knows anything of the sort," said Peter.

"You sound as if you'd got inside information," said Adam. "If you have, why don't you spill it? As Crescy said, one of us may be a murderer, but we're all friends."

"What about Winston Churchill?" said Crescy hastily.

"It's only a quarter to nine," said Edward, looking at his wristwatch.

"It takes time to warm up, though," said Crescy, "and we'd better hear the news. Peter, you might tinker. You're so good."

"A bloody sight too good," muttered Adam.

"What did you say?" asked Peter, turning knobs.

Adam said, "It was intended for Crescy's ear."

"Well, I didn't hear it," said Crescy, getting up, stepping over David and the hounds and standing beside Peter. "Oh, gosh, an organ! Throttle it down, ducky. We shall be warned by the merry peal of bells."

Peter and Crescy stayed beside the wireless and the others began to talk about the war. David expounded theories on the Balkans and Valentine thought that everything was terrible, while Bridget reminded everyone that nature was one long, inexorable war. Adam held forth on the foolishness of calling up twenty-year-olds before older, steadier men, and Edward contributed a few remarks to the effect that agriculture, efficiently organized, would win the war. Presently the bells rang out; the one o'clock and four o'clock news bulletins were repeated and then Winston Churchill spoke. Afterwards, getting down to beer, they discussed him, only Valentine and David disapproving: a little cheap, said David; too bloodthirsty, said Valentine. That discussion petered out. Inevitably, the conversation drifted back to the murder. Cresy had sat down in her former place. Edward and Peter had dispensed the beer and were standing by the table arguing the respective merits of mild and bitter. Bridget said that the one good thing about the murder was that it took one's mind off the war, and Janet said how could she say that, and Bridget said sorry, but she was congenitally tactless. David said that his interest in the murder was academic; what really interested him was the way the detective was working. Of course it was obvious why he had asked everyone about nicotine, but there was a clue about car sponges and a clue about horses, and here were eight suspects all completely in the dark as to what those clues portended. Edward, who had left Peter, and was wandering about looking at Cresy's books and pictures, chipped in. "But there may be nothing in it. In spite of what Mrs. Hardwick says, I don't think Northeast's very intelligent. He's probably after some mare's nest. Hullo!" he exclaimed, pulling a book out of a shelf. "Here's a nice book to have about the house! Really, Mrs. Hardwick! *Forensic Medicine and Toxicology!*"

Cresy turned her head and said sleepily, "Oh that! That's another of Northeast's clues. That's what elevated me to the proud position of Suspect Number One. He found it."

"Good lord," said Peter.

"Why didn't you put it away?" said Janet.

"I never thought of it," said Cresy. "I bought it when I tried to write a detective novel. The novel died on me and I tore it up in a rage. Pity, because when I told that to Northeast he asked to see the manuscript."

"Oh, Cresy!" groaned Peter.

"Ugh!" said Edward, deep in the book and not listening. "Here's a picture of a bloke after five months' immersion in sea water. I must say it would cure me of any desire to go sailing." He turned the pages and exclaimed again, this time incoherently. "Conway," he said, "look here . . ." and Peter went to him.

"What's up now?" asked Cresy.

Peter said hoarsely, "The corner of a page has been turned down. It's the page on poisoning by nicotine."

"Cor lumme!" said Cresy.

"Cresy," said Peter, "do be serious. Supposing Northeast saw that "

"I daresay he did. He said it was all very unfortunate."

Everyone was looking at Cresy. Edward said, "Why did you mark that place, Mrs. Hardwick?"

"I didn't." Cresy stubbed out her cigarette. "As I think you all know, I lend my books to people."

Peter snapped out, "Have you lent this one lately?"

"Yes," said Crescy.

"Who to?"

There was a dead silence.

"I've forgotten," said Crescy.

"Crescy, don't be absurd. You *can't* have forgotten," said Peter.

"I have," said Crescy. "Very unfortunate, isn't it?"

"It is," said Peter in a grim voice. "Even if you don't get yourself hanged, you're withholding information.

"Don't be silly," said Crescy. "You can't withhold information you haven't got."

"But you *have* got it," said Peter.

Adam said, "Look here, Conway, we all know you're a policeman. But you're not employed on this case. There's no reason for you to do Northeast's job for him."

"I'm not doing Northeast's job," Peter denied indignantly. "I'm trying to make Crescy see sense. She hasn't forgotten whom she lent that book to. She's simply acting up—if you can call it up—to her insane ideas."

"Well then, leave her alone. It's none of your bloody business," said Adam.

"Oh, God!" cried Crescy. "Do stop arguing about me. I can look after myself. Turn on the wireless! Let's have some dance music!"

She leaped out of her chair, skipped over the dogs and turned on the wireless. A military band blared forth, full blast, and silenced everybody.

"For God's sake," said David.

Bridget got up and turned a knob. *There'll always be an England,* the band played more reasonably. Valentine got up too. Looking scared, she said that she and Adam must go.

Adam sat where he was.

Edward explained that he rose at six, and Janet, Bridget, and Valentine went to get their things. Bridget and David were the first to leave the cottage. Then Janet and Edward went. Valentine said, "Come along, Adam." Adam didn't move.

Peter said pointedly, "Shall I see Valentine home?"

Adam hadn't meant to leave till Peter did, but now he had to get up. He stood for a moment scowling at the fire, vainly trying to think of an excuse for staying on. Finally he said, "Coming, Conway?" and Peter, with an irritating grin on his face, answered, "Not just yet." But Crescy said, "Go along with them, Peter. This party's dead."

Peter's grin vanished. He said, "Can't I stay for a minute? I want to talk to you."

"But I don't want to be talked to," said Crescy. "Sorry, Peter, my dear, but I've got an attack of temperament coming on."

Peter stood looking down at her. He loved her. . . . She was impossible. . . . He shrugged his shoulders and went out behind the Days without a word of thanks or a good-night.

Crescy, tired to death, left the room as it was, and went upstairs to bed. Her great white hounds followed her, bounding up the steep, narrow stairs; they slept in her bedroom on the sheepskin hearth rug. Thinking of Peter, proper and possessive, and Adam, who belonged to somebody else, she undressed, washed and got into emerald green pajamas. Dispirited, she sat on the edge of her bed with her nightly glass of milk in her hand. Why, she wondered, had she gone into a flat spin when Scaife had given her notice to quit the cottage: it wouldn't be long, anyhow, before Peter and Adam between them drove her from the district. At one time she had thought that it would be comparatively easy to cope with Peter; she could turn him down and they could remain good friends, but it hadn't worked out that way: distrusting her friendship with Adam, Peter was standing by, wary, miserable and damned interfering. As for Adam . . .well, she didn't want Adam . . . she didn't want anyone . . . but she was fond of him: he had charm . . . and she was human; one of these evenings he'd stay too long and there'd be something else to regret forever and ever. It'll be just as well if they hang me, thought Crescy, taking a gulp of milk and setting the glass down, remembering that she had already drunk three glasses of *creme de menthe* and two pints of beer and would have to keep getting up all night anyhow; and she got into bed and shook into her hand the veronal tablet, which she really must get out of the habit of taking. It stuck in her throat; she took another sip of milk to speed it on its way, and lay down remembering how the blood from the knife wound had seeped slowly across the silver tissue of Patricia Worthington's dress, and her face, chalk-white and terrified, and her mouth, open, screaming. Damn Peter and Adam. Why couldn't they see that she, whose memories were such that she couldn't sleep undrugged, was no good—no earthly good—to any man?

CHAPTER VII

THURSDAY

IT WAS A fine mild morning. Over the gold of the Little Bottom beeches, angelic clouds were sailing; now the sun sparkled on the rain-washed pastures; now flying shadows swept them and were gone. But Detective-Inspector Northeast, wheeling his bicycle once again over the abominable surface of the roadway, felt no pleasure in the morning. The bright weather merely intensified his distaste for the job before him.

Of course, he told himself, murder's a dastardly crime and murder by poison is the meanest form of it. The work that he had chosen was fine work—confounding rogues, keeping the world fit for honest folk to live in. But the fact was that this morning he wished he had never chosen it. He wished he was sweeping streets, hewing coal in the dark, lying in a trench full of dead Germans—anything rather than making his way down to Little Bottom Cottage to bully an admission from a woman for whom he felt . . . well, damn it, what? . . . something at any rate that he had never felt for any other woman. . . .

He tried to harden his heart, which, in spite of being only a muscle, was doing queer things sinking down into his stomach and resuming its normal position only to contract painfully when he thought of Cresy and her crumpets, Cresy and her great fire of apple logs, Cresy and One-Eye. It was all planned, he made himself remember; it was a premeditated crime, cunningly and secretly contrived: keep your pity, he told himself, for those who, in honest rage, strike down their tormentors. So, arguing with himself, he came to the foot of the hill and the beech hedge, over which he could see the orchard and the brown pony drowsing under the apple trees.

Though it was half-past nine, there was no smoke rising from the cottage. If Cresy were in bed, she'd have to get up, he determined. He left his bicycle at the gate and walked up the path between the leaf-

119

buried and evidently rather unsuccessful attempts at herbaceous bor-
ders.

The door was shut. The three cats were on the window sill, but again
they streaked off like greased lightning. From the hen house in the
orchard came a subdued but indignant cackling. Evidently the mistress
of Little Bottom Cottage still slept. Well, she must wake and take what
was coming to her.

Feeling like fate and not enjoying it, Guy hammered hard upon the
door.

The hounds bayed. Good. However soundly she was sleeping, that
would wake her. But after a few moments the baying ceased. Except for
the cackle from the hen house, there was silence.

Damn her, Guy thought; she's foxing. Nerve racked after a practically sleepless night, he hammered, this time loud enough, he thought,
to rouse the village.

With equal fury the hounds replied to him. Upstairs a window—her
bedroom window, he assumed—was a little open and he could hear the
hounds moving about, scratching at the door, pacing in circles. Had she
made off? The garage door was shut. She might have fled on foot for
lack of petrol.

He walked round the cottage. There was no back door and blue
check curtains were drawn across the windows. He came back to the
front and tried the door. It opened.

Guy walked into the aftermath of Crescy's party. There were cushions on the floor and beer mugs. The fire was out, a mountain of white
ashes. The room smelt of beer. There were coffee cups and liqueur glasses
on every available ledge and table. On the writing-bureau there was also
a milk can and beside it a pencilled note, asking for 'Two pints, please,'
on a ragged corner of paper.

Guy, standing amidst the confusion, shouted, "Mrs. Hardwick." The
hounds barked once and then scratched on the door, whining. He considered his position. He had no search warrant. If he went upstairs and
she had gone, nothing need be said about it, but if she were hiding
under the bed, he'd be for it. He remembered the stillness of another
house and a dog whining. Taking two steps in his stride, he was up the
stairs.

He knocked on the bedroom door. The only answer came from the
dogs, something between a growl and a whine, half threat and half welcome. He opened the door an inch or two, spoke to them, opened it
wider. They stalked out and stood beside him, licking his hands.

He said, "Mrs. Hardwick?" and went into the room. Cresscy hadn't
fled and she wasn't foxing. She was lying in bed, one thin, bare arm

thrown out over the green coverlet. That she wasn't sleeping naturally he knew at once from her heavy breathing.

He went to the bed and laid a hand on her forehead. It was cold and clammy. He felt her pulse. It was faint and slow. Well, everything was obvious.

On the bedside table, among poetry books and beside a tumbler of milk, was a glass bottle of tablets—'The Tablets. One only to be taken on retiring.' So Dawes was right. His 'lady novelist' was guilty, but she hadn't waited for the bungling justice of the society of men. Characteristic, Guy thought, dashing down the stairs to the telephone, because, God knew why, it was his duty to save her from the death she'd chosen, to bring her back from the peace she'd found, to fear and shame and the gallows.

He glanced round the dissipated room. The telephone stood on the bookcase with the directory beside it. Badcock . . . Baines . . . Baker. Dr. Baker answered the phone himself. Tch, tch. Yes, yes. He knew the way to Little Bottom Cottage and would be there in ten minutes. Hold on—keep her warm and get some water boiling.

Guy put down the telephone, let the dogs out and went into the kitchen. On a porcelain-topped table by the window were a couple of primus stoves; he shook them, found them fullish, lit them and filled a kettle and a saucepan with water. He pumped up the stoves, put on the kettle and saucepan and went back upstairs carrying blankets, which he had found in the airing cupboard above the copper hot water tank. Cresy had not stirred. He took her flaccid, clammy arm, placed it under the bedclothes and spread the blankets over her. Then, in search of hot water bottles, he found his way to the bathroom, a luxuriously fitted little room across the landing, furnished in green even to the frilled muslin curtains. He found a hot water bottle hanging on the towel rail. He took it downstairs and while he waited for the kettle to boil, occupied himself by making up the somnolent hot water stove. And all this, he thought bitterly, to bring back to life and a second and much more horrible death, one already blissfully past the hour of fear and hesitation, far down the road to the kindly frontier and freedom from the harsh rule of mankind.

The kettle boiled. He filled the hot water bottle, took it upstairs and pushed it in under the bedclothes to Cresy's icy feet. Then there was nothing to do but to take the opportunity to snoop round. He didn't snoop round. He went to the window, shut it and stood there, looking down the path to the road, wishing that Baker would come and wishing that he wouldn't, wondering through what process of events and reactions Cresy's brilliant life had moved to this bedraggled end. He had argued that a murderer's like any of us, but he couldn't, even now, see Cresy, as he knew her, as the poisoner of Scaife. Perhaps he had been mistaken in his view of her. He went to the bed and stood looking down at her, searching the colorless face for some fault that vivacity had concealed. It was a delicate face, but it wasn't a weak one; the mouth was generous; the small, pointed chin denied irresolution, suggesting rather the strength of a Toledo blade. Guy distrusted alike weak and strong, heavy faces; there was a cheap bombastic strength, which, up against things, cracked like cast iron, but these finely made people didn't crack: mentally, morally and physically, they outlasted your magnificent specimen. The sound of a car, descending the hill in second gear, took him back to the window, still puzzled. All he knew now was that in spite of the common-sense evidence before him, he couldn't fit a poisoner's cap on those honey-colored curls.

Baker came trotting up the path, followed by a woman in the depressing uniform of a district nurse. Guy met them at the door. "I've brought Nurse to help me. Yes, yes. Sleeping tablets, you said. Well, make me plenty of black coffee—the stronger the better. I suppose there's coffee in the house?"

He skipped upstairs, still chattering. "Brilliant woman, Nurse. Brilliant woman. Highly strung, of course. . . ."

Guy made coffee. The nurse came down for hot water. "Any hope?" he asked. "I haven't much experience of these cases," Nurse said coldly. "My patients are hard-working women, who don't need to take sleeping drugs. But Doctor said—more to himself than me—that he thought we might pull her round. We shall know more when the stomach has been washed out. Are you a relative?"

"No."

The nurse, who had cold gray eyes and a tight mouth and looked much more like a murderess than Cresy, took the coffee and hot water and Guy lit a cigarette and waited beside his stoves. Of course, what he ought to do, besides snooping round, was to telephone to Dawes, but he couldn't bear the thought of Dawes at Little Bottom Cottage, hoping against hope that Baker would restore to him his victim, gloating over this evidence of his own perspicacity. So he waited and in about half an hour the nurse came down again. "The patient has vomited," she announced without enthusiasm.

"I suppose that's a good thing?"

"Yes. Doctor's given strychnine hypodermically, and also the coffee. Do you know where there's some kindling wood? I want to get a fire going in the bedroom."

Guy found kindling wood—apple twigs—in a basket behind the door and an excursion to the shed alongside the garage yielded some small ash blocks. The nurse took them. Shortly afterwards Baker himself came down.

"Well, well. That's that. Yes, yes. Well, Northeast, ruling out an unexpected collapse, we'll pull her round."

Guy said nothing.

"Dreadful thing," said Baker. "Tch, tch. Thpp. Well, well. Attempt at suicide, undoubtedly. Lucky thing you found her." His darting glance rested for a moment on Guy.

Guy explained, "I came down to ask her a few questions. She was in the pub, you know, the night that Scaife was done in."

"Yes, yes. Well, I'm glad it's not my affair. Charming woman—I've met her—unstable of course, like all these writers. Well, even if things go as they should, you can't ask her any questions for at least twelve hours."

"As soon as that?"

"Oh, yes, yes. I don't imagine that she took a lot of the stuff. Rather a halfhearted attempt, I should say."

"Have you considered the possibility that it wasn't suicide?" asked Guy. "She may have found she couldn't sleep and taken an extra tablet or two. Or she may have been—well, she may have had one over the eight—there's evidence of a slightly alcoholic party here."

"Of course all that will have to be thrashed out," said Baker vaguely.

"Yes. I wonder. . .There's a tumbler of milk by her bed, Doctor. We'll keep that. I'd like to have it analyzed."

"I shouldn't imagine that she dissolved the tablets," said Baker. "She would just pop them into her mouth and use the milk, perhaps, to wash them down. But I'll tell Nurse to set it aside."

"I might as well take it along with me," Guy told him. "I shall be going back to the police station before long." He found an empty medicine bottle on a shelf in the larder, rinsed it, and took it upstairs. "Wrap the tumbler in a towel before you touch it," he told the nurse, and he took the tumbler, as well as the bottle of milk, away with him.

As he pushed his bicycle once again up the hill, an idea came to him. He knew that the Chief Constable lived at a village called Lesser Pocklington, about three miles across country from Witheridge Green; he would ring up and find out if Carruthers were at home: he was, Guy considered, an easier man to influence than Dawes.

The point was that the moment Dawes heard of Crescy's attempt at suicide, he would press for a warrant, and Guy, desperately and without reason, wanted time. Time for what? Even to himself, he couldn't answer that question; how much less could he hope to produce an argument that would restrain the vigorous Dawes?

He had to enquire the way to Lesser Pocklington; his stomach was empty; somebody ought to be sent down to Little Bottom Cottage to see to Crescy's animals, so, with the idea of killing three birds with one stone, he went into The Dog and found himself alone in the lounge bar with Eve. He cut short her pleasant greeting. "Mrs. Hardwick's ill!"

"Ill? What's the matter?"

"I want you to keep this to yourself," he told her. "How or why, I've no idea, but she took an overdose of her sleeping tablets and I found her unconscious this morning. Baker and the district nurse are with her and she's going to be all right. But someone ought to go down there and see to things."

"I'll go at once," Eve said. "Of course, there are the dogs and everything. Poor Crescy! How did it happen?"

"I haven't an idea," Guy repeated a little impatiently. "I believe there was something of a party there last night. Were you there?"

"No, but Peter was."

"Well, I won't bother him just now. Can I have a small whiskey and a sausage roll? And how do I get to Lesser Pocklington?"

Eve supplied him with food and drink and while he ate and drank she rang up Pocklington Grange and ascertained that the Chief Constable was available. Ten minutes later he was cycling along a pleasant but uninteresting country road. It ran in a southwesterly direction, and from an inconsiderable hill just above the village of Lesser Pocklington, he could see across country Marley Clump, a green mound, topped by beeches, rising from the checkered plain. Shortly afterwards, he discovered the white gate that Eve had described, and a drive between paddocks brought him to Pocklington Grange.

He was admitted to a hall decorated with horns, heads and hides, and thence to a small, official-looking sanctum at the back of the house. Carruthers was waiting for him. "Well, Northeast, what's this? Got your man?"

"Afraid not, sir," Guy said firmly. "Only a new ramification, but I thought I'd let you know. Mrs. Hardwick—the novelist—has taken an overdose of sleeping tablets. Baker's still with her, but he thinks he has pulled her round."

"Ha!" said Carruthers. "One up for Dawes."

"I'm not at all sure of that, sir. If we don't want to put our feet into it we shall have to go very carefully, very carefully indeed. If it was suicide, it was, according to Baker, a very halfhearted attempt. It may have been an accident."

"Accident?" boomed Carruthers. "People in their right minds don't take overdoses of sleeping drugs by accident—they know what it means."

"Well, you see, sir, there'd been a bit of a party the evening before. The room had been left as it was—a lot of empty bottles and so on. Mrs. Hardwick may have been in a confused state of mind."

"Disgustin'," said Carruthers, "the way these women drink. In my young days mem-sahibs didn't go beyond a sip of white wine with the fish and a glass of port with the dessert, but now nothing comes amiss to them—beer, whiskey, gin. Well, I suppose it's reasonable to consider that she may have been half seas over—a fast little woman, according to Dawes. Can't anyone who was at the party tell you what state she was in?"

"I'll see some of them this afternoon," Guy promised. "My point is, sir, I definitely don't want to rush things."

"I saw the Super this morning," said Carruthers. "He's made up his mind against this Hardwick woman, and I must say I think he's right. He was hoping you'd get something out of her. You know, Northeast, considering the circumstances, it's only logical to conclude that this sleeping drug business was an attempt at suicide. Your explanation that she was sozzled cuts that way too. If she'd been sober she'd have done the job properly, what?"

"There were plenty of tablets left in the bottle, sir. I should have imagined that someone who was lit up would have taken the whole boiling—recklessly."

"She might," suggested Carruthers, "have fallen into a drunken stupor halfway through."

"I shouldn't imagine she'd be as drunk as that, sir. She's accustomed to alcohol."

"Disgustin'," repeated Carruthers. "Well, Northeast, I gather that you want us to hold our horses for a day or two?"

"Yes, sir. She can't run away."

"The Super will be disappointed. He fully expected that you would come sprinting back for a warrant this afternoon."

"Better to be safe than sorry, sir."

"But shall we be safe? We don't want her to give us the slip. She's tried this suicide stunt—she may do it again."

"The district nurse is with her and she's a dragon. And I daresay Baker will be there most of the day. He mentioned the possibility of a collapse. He also said that if all went well I could question her in twelve hours' time. That brings it to about ten o'clock tonight. If he allows it, I'll certainly question her then. In any case, she can't be charged in the state she's in."

"That's true," said Carruthers. "Well, you'd better get in touch with me after you've seen her. Maybe you'll want a warrant then. By the way,

Dawes reports that she's the only one of our suspects who had bought nicotine locally. She signed the poison book at Hanley's a couple of months ago."

"Not much in that, sir," Guy said promptly. "A couple of months ago is just about the time you'd begin to get fed up with the green fly on your roses." He remembered Valentine telling him that it hadn't been a bad year for green fly and he went on quickly, "And if it was bought for a criminal purpose, it would be madness to buy it locally."

"Murderers always do make some foolish mistake," urged the Chief Constable. "As you say, there's not much in it; but 'many a mickle makes a muckle'—a lot of truth in these old sayings, what?"

Guy agreed to that and then he took his leave—time was precious—and bicycled furiously back to Witheridge Green. He hadn't any idea what he hoped to find there; it was out of his character to trust in luck or in queer feelings; he believed that success was achieved by plodding on, putting one foot before the other—so, and not spectacularly, were mountains climbed and wars won. It was borne in upon him that he was acting against all his principles: he had to own to himself that if he hadn't liked Crescy he would have agreed with Carruthers and Dawes that the case was building itself up inexorably against her. But he consoled himself with the admirable maxim: when in doubt, do nothing. Crescy couldn't run away. This lust of the Superintendent's and the Chief Constable's for an early arrest was merely a desire to prove their ability, and Guy, with placid satisfaction, felt that his own ability no longer needed proving; his spurs were won; he was a different man from the nervous youngster with an inferiority complex who had fussed himself to death over the Marley case.

He went back to The Dog, ordered his snack and asked Mrs. Chandler if Peter were available. Peter appeared and sent Mrs. Chandler into the public bar. "My sister's not back from Little Bottom Cottage yet," he told Guy, "and my leave's up tomorrow. I hope to God you'll soon have definite news for us. I suppose you've heard the rumor that Mark Scaife's leaving?"

"No, I hadn't. Where's he going?"

"He'd hardly blazon that abroad," said Peter dryly. "But I bet it's somewhere where there's no extradition." So Peter, too, Guy thought, was desperately afraid for Crescy.

He said, lighting a cigarette, "I believe you were at Mrs. Hardwick's party last night. Can you give me an account of what happened? It doesn't matter if nothing important did happen. I want to know every silly little thing."

Peter stared gloomily out of the window. Guy got the impression that he had lost his former inclination to be helpful.

"There's a lot against Mrs. Hardwick now," he continued. "Whatever you say can't make it very much worse for her. And there might be some little thing, which you've missed, that might be helpful."

"Something did happen," Peter said, "but whether it's against Crescy, or not, depends on how you've summed her up. If you think she's truthful . . ."

"I don't," said Guy. "I think in some circumstances she'd lie like stink. I wouldn't trust her on oath. On the other hand, there are circumstances in which I'd trust her implicitly."

Guy, as he spoke of Crescy, smiled, but there was no smile on Peter's face. He loved Crescy, but he loved her against his will—disapprovingly. Supposing everything turned out all right, would Crescy marry him? Guy hoped not. He wasn't the man for her.

"Well, I hope this was one of the occasions when you'd trust her implicitly. Anyhow, I ought not to withhold information. It was like this. The Franklands, Edward Scaife and his wife, the Days and myself were invited to spend the evening at Little Bottom Cottage. Our wireless here had honked out and the Scaifes haven't got one; Edward wanted to hear Churchill and he had asked Crescy if he could drop in and listen to hers and I think she really made a party of it because the Scaifes aren't what she calls sympathetic. I was the last to arrive. I found them all chatting about the murder and wondering why you had been what Crescy called 'talking horsey.' Well, I tried to change the conversation, but without much success, and then we listened to the news and Churchill, and then, of course, the moment the wireless was switched off, back they went to the bloody murder. Scaife and I were carrying on another conversation, and, after it had petered out, he went meandering round the room, looking at the books and pictures—I expect that, like myself, he was a bit fed up with all the talk about the murder. Presently he took a book out of the shelf and remarked on it. I believe you know about it. It was Dixon Mann on Toxicology and Forensic Medicine."

"Yes. I know about it."

"Well, he started off by being funny. Then he called me over to him. He'd found a dog-eared page—the page on nicotine poisoning."

"My God," cried Guy, "I missed that. I never looked—I know the book. I knew it included a paragraph on nicotine. Did he say anything—to the others, I mean—about it?"

"I did."

"And what did they say?"

"Crescy said, 'Cor lumme.' Nobody else said anything. I begged Crescy to be serious and Edward asked her why she had marked that place. This is where I want you to believe her. She said that she hadn't marked it and that she often lent her books to other people."

"I see. Did you ask her—"

"Yes," Peter interrupted. "I asked her to whom she'd lent it. She said she had forgotten."

Guy said, "You don't expect me to believe that?"

"I don't believe it myself," said Peter. "I told her so. We argued, and then Day had to chip in. God blast him, he told me to mind my own bloody business."

"And then, I suppose," said Guy grinning, "the beer mugs flew through the air?"

"Not quite. They might have done, only Cresy shrieked out that she could look after herself and told us to stop arguing over her. She jumped up and turned the wireless on full blast—of course, she's very temperamental. Bridget Frankland very courageously turned it down to normal and then the party broke up. I intended to stay on and try to get some sense out of Cresy, but she said she didn't want to talk and threw me out with the Day family."

"That's all very interesting, but, being of a cautious nature, I won't say more till I've thought it over. Tell me this, though. When Mrs. Hardwick said she'd lent the book, were there any dirty looks from anybody?"

"I didn't notice. I suppose I was looking at Cresy."

"There's another thing," said Guy, "and it's important. I could see this morning that alcohol had been flowing. How much drink had Mrs. Hardwick taken?"

"I should say a couple of liqueurs and two half-pints of beer. But, as I told you, the party was in full swing by the time I got there."

"When you left—was she at all under the influence?"

"Technically, no. She was . . . well, perhaps just slightly illuminated."

"She isn't the sort of person who might have gone on drinking when the party was over?"

"By herself? Good lord, no. Cresy does drink far too much, but it's convivial drinking. When she does take a meal at home, she drinks water. I know that, because she gets all her stuff from us, and she only buys it when she throws a party."

"I asked," Guy said, "because I thought that if she'd been really tight, she might have made a mistake over the number of tablets—taken one and then forgotten that she'd taken it and taken another. Or found she couldn't sleep and swallowed several in exasperation."

"She might have done that, anyhow. She's a very absentminded person and she's also very easily exasperated. And reckless."

"Conway, from your knowledge of her, can you fit in suicide?"

"That," said Peter, throwing down a cigarette end and stamping hard on it, "hardly applies in the present circumstances. Obviously one infers that, if she attempted suicide, it was because she had something to do with the murder, and I'm sure she hadn't, so, logically, I can only put the whole thing down to accident."

He spoke loudly but defiantly and there was no certainty in his face; he looked worried to death, and with complacent contempt Guy thought, what a lover! He said, "I see," and, after a long and thoughtful silence, he got down from his stool, saying, "Since I'm here, I'm going to snoop round a bit. Don't take any notice of me." He felt pretty desperate. He had absolutely nothing to support his increasing belief in Crescy's innocence, but when, two days ago, he had seemed to be quite at the end of things, a snoop round The Dog had put him wise to the crack in the boarding.

He walked into the lobby, bent down and put his eye to the crack. He could see nothing. "Conway," he called, "shove up the shutters and turn the lights on and sit down as Scaife sat, will you?" Peter obeyed, sat down with a thump which shook the partition, but all that happened was that the streak of light was blotted out; you couldn't distinguish shoulders, head or collar. Straightening his back, Guy said, "No bloody good, but stay where you are for a minute." He went into the lounge past Peter and came out again; he stood near the shove ha'penny board; he got Peter to bring a torch and searched the boarding for a spy hole; he went into the public bar and took a glance through the door. "Nothing?" said Peter. "Damn all," said Guy. He switched off the lamp on the bar and, while Peter took down the blackout shutter of the window behind the bar, went to take down the other. Then he cried, "Wait a minute, Conway," and went out, hurrying through the public bar and round into the car park.

Peter had opened one section of the long window and stuck his head out. He saw Guy stoop down, shut one eye and peer apparently at the window. There was no crack in the blackout shutter, he knew; Waller would have noticed it and moreover he himself was fussy about the blackout and only last night he had looked the shutters over. "What is it?" he couldn't help asking, and Guy said, "Come and look," still peering.

Peter went out to him. There was the window, one section completely blacked-out by the shutter, the other by the panel of plywood, in which the fan was set. Guy pointed to the cap of the fan and Peter put his eye to it. Through the blades of the stationary fan he could see dimly into the room.

"Go and turn all the lights on again," said Guy.

Peter went in and again switched on the lights and put up the shutter. After a few moments, Guy joined him.

"When the lights are on I can see into the cozy corner," he said. "If it was dark outside, I could see even better. You know what this means, Conway?"

"Well," said Peter, anxious not to make a fool of himself, "it means that someone could have looked in. . . ."

"It means that the murder could have been done by someone who didn't spend the evening, or any part of the evening, in the lounge. All along that's held me up—how anyone else could have known that Scaife was in the corner seat, much less the position he was in. Supposing he had been leaning forward—even slightly—what would have been the use of shoving the dart through the wall? The murderer *had* to know. Curse and blast and damn, the fan's sufficiently obvious. Why didn't this occur to me before?"

"When you inspected the windows it was late in the evening. I expect the fan was working."

"Of course," said Guy, and then a horrid thought occurred to him. "Thursday night—was it turned on then?"

"I shall have to ask Eve," said Peter. "We don't turn it on, this weather, until the room gets smoky. Sometimes people—our regulars—turn it on themselves."

"And are there," Guy asked, "usually two bricks in the car park, up against the wall, directly under the cap of the fan?"

"Not that I know of. No, I think definitely not. My God, I wouldn't make much of a detective. I didn't notice them just now."

"There are some bricks lying about by your garage. A couple could have been picked up and carried along. That's what rules out the aggressive Saunders."

"Saunders? Why?"

"Tall man," said Guy absently. "Well, let's see." He got out his notebook. "Shutters down again, please, Conway." He seated himself at the bar, lit a cigarette, opened his notebook and found a sheet of paper written over in Peter's schoolboyish hand—Peter's list of people who had the opportunity to remove the dart from the shelf in the public bar. "Thank God for this," he said. "It's going to be even more useful than I thought. Without it, everyone in the village would be equally suspect now." He read out the names: "Saunders, Janes, Bligh, P. Conway, E. Hennisty, Mrs. Chandler, Brewers' vanman, T. Farraway, D. Brown, H. Prior, C. Hardwick, Mrs. E. Scaife, A. Day, three commercial travelers, Militiaman with Flossie, M. Scaife." Turning to a clean page in his notebook, he began a new list. "Saunders," he said. "Too tall to need the bricks. No knowledge of chemistry. A passable motive that gives him one black mark. As to the rest, we'll leave it out for the moment. He works at the Hall and probably has the same access to nicotine as his employers, which appears to be nil. Now Janes. A small man—one black mark. No knowledge of chemistry and no motive, or perhaps a query. Bligh: the same. P. Conway and E. Hennisty—we'll leave them out; I've never fancied them. Mrs. Chandler: small woman—a black mark and one for motive, but none for knowledge of chemistry. Brewers' vanman: any earthly connection with Scaife?"

"Not that I know of. I imagine he's a Melchester man."

"Big?"

"Huge fellow."

"No marks. Farraway, Brown and Prior: big men?"

"Farraway isn't. He's a little old man. Brown and Prior are six footers."

"But no knowledge of chemistry?"

"Good God, no. Farm laborers. Farraway's a shepherd."

"Farraway gets a mark for being small. Motives queried. Now then, C. Hardwick. For a moment I shall rule out these lounge people—they'd no need to look through a spy hole."

"Mark Scaife," began Peter, but, as he spoke, Eve came in. Peter snapped out, "How's Cressy?" and Eve said, "Going on nicely according to the Dragon. Baker's gone away on his rounds, but he's calling back this evening. I shall go down later and give the dogs a run and shut up the hens."

Guy had continued to copy down names and mark them. A sudden snort from him brought a hopeful look from Peter, but Guy said nothing, only stared at his list and, tilting his chair back, beat a tattoo with his pencil on the bar. Then he spoke to Eve. "Cast your mind back to Thursday night, Mrs. Hennisty and think hard—it's important. Was the electric fan turned on?"

"The electric fan . . ." said Eve with her hand to her forehead. "The electric fan. . . . On Monday someone asked for it—Valentine, I think. But on Thursday . . . oh, now I remember! I turned it on early because the fire had been smoking, but Scaife complained of the draft and I turned it off again."

"Scaife complained? Good lord! That's irony." Guy shut up his notebook, leaned his arms on the bar and buried his face in them.

"Would a drink help?" asked Eve.

"Not," said Guy in a muffled voice, "in the middle of the afternoon." Then suddenly he looked up. "Smallbone . . ." he said, "wasn't it Smallbone who had his bicycle stolen and it was his sister's bicycle and she created something awful and he had to walk home?"

Eve said, "Yes. I remember it. He complained to Waller. Waller was rather heartless. He said we had got a corpse here and Sidney would probably find his bike where he left it. I never heard whether it had been found."

Guy got off his stool. "May I telephone?"

"Certainly." Peter led the way into the sitting-room. "I gather," he said, quite unnecessarily shifting the directories into a more prominent position, "that light is breaking somewhere?"

"Don't be too hopeful," Guy warned him. "It's probably a false dawn. All I've got is an idea, and it's up against a very definite alibi."

But Peter wanted to hope. He said, "Alibis have been bust before now."

"Well, I'm going to have a shot at busting this one." Guy began dialling a Melchester number and Peter withdrew.

Eve said, "Do you think he's on to anything? I'm so worried about Crescy, Peter. Of course, *we* know that it must have been an accident—absentmindedness or something—but I can understand that it would look bad to anyone who didn't know her—coming just after Edward drawing everyone's attention to that book of hers, too."

"I wish she wouldn't take sleeping drugs," said Peter. "After this is all over, we must try to do something about it, Eve. Northeast said he had an idea, but he was up against an alibi. God knows what he means."

"Mark, probably. He must have produced an alibi for the rest of the evening and that's why Northeast has never concentrated on him. Oh, I can't help being sorry for him, Peter. He's never had a chance."

"It's no use being sentimental," said Peter. "Mark, after all, has had as much as the majority make do with—health and a pair of hands."

"Still, being a bastard's no treat," said Eve.

The conversation languished. Through the sitting-room door they could hear Guy's voice and a few words when he raised it. "Can you look up the time sheets? . . . David Noakes. . . . His evening off, is it. . . . Sometime tomorrow. . . . I say, do you realize that it's the police speaking? Between eleven-fifteen and twelve-thirty. That's better. I'll come to your garage. . . . Very well, then."

"You oughtn't to listen," said Peter, picking up a tray.

"Well, what are you doing?" retorted Eve.

Guy came back. Anxiously they scanned his face. He said, "Do you serve tea?"

"No, but you must have some with us," Eve said hospitably. "I'm going to have a cup now, before I go down to the cottage again."

Peter and Guy stood about in the lounge discussing football pools until Mrs. Chandler appeared with a tray of tea things, which she carried into the sitting-room. Eve drank a hasty cup and set off for Little

Bottom Cottage. Guy sat for an hour talking of this and that to Peter, who couldn't help wondering impatiently why the fellow didn't get on with his job. Presently Eve came back. She said that the nurse seemed pleased with Crescy, but hadn't allowed Eve to see her. Dr. Baker, she said, would be returning to the cottage at eight o'clock.

Guy remained at The Dog till half-past seven. Left alone in the sitting-room, he fell asleep and was only wakened by Peter going in to ask if he would like a snack. Rather indignantly, Peter remarked to Eve, "Mark Scaife will be halfway to America before Northeast's broken his alibi."

"Well," said Eve, almost equally nerve-racked, "it's no use getting impatient. You snubbed me when I said he wasn't much like a detective."

"What you wanted was a Wimsey or a Gethryn," retorted Peter. "I told you that in real life it's common sense and perseverance that solve crimes. But it's not common sense to sit in there snoring while Mark Scaife makes his getaway."

"Perhaps it isn't Mark Scaife," said Eve picking up her knitting. "Did you notice, when he was sitting at the bar before tea, how he suddenly said, 'Smallbone!'? Perhaps it's Smallbone, though I can't imagine why."

"Nor can I," said Peter. "I think it's much more likely that he's still after Crescy."

"Then why all the telephoning? And the chat about the fan?"

"God knows," said Peter, lighting another cigarette, and, "How different the world would be if men could knit," said Eve.

The appearance of an Air Force officer and his towheaded female companion then claimed her attention and Peter went away into the public bar. Shortly afterwards Guy emerged from the sitting-room, drank a small whiskey, bought a packet of cigarettes and said that he was off. Eve said in a low voice, "Be kind to her, won't you?" to which appeal Guy responded with a singularly ungracious grunt. He went out into a night of soft southwesterly wind and flying stars.

The lane, between hedges and then under the still leafy branches of the beech trees, seemed dark at first, but, when his eyes became accustomed to the faint starlight, he switched off his torch and was vaguely conscious of the fantastic beauty of the tall pale trunks of the beeches and the branches swaying high among the stars. A profound melancholy descended on him. Through the magic of this night he went, a policeman with a notebook . . . and down at the cottage Cresy, lying drowsily in the big mahogany bed with the curved ends, was waiting for a policeman with a notebook . . . that was all. And for that the southwest wind was blowing, the soft darkness of the woods was thick with the disturbing scent of leaves and rain. A scented night, stars . . . and a policeman. And every autumn there would be nights like this, and how long would it be before he forgot her and someone else would do?

There was a light beaming from Little Bottom Cottage—you couldn't directly blame Crescy, since she was in bed, though probably her black-out arrangements had been slap-dash in the extreme. He hurried up the path and the first thing he said to the nurse, who opened the door, was, "You're showing a lot of light from the bathroom window, Nurse. You'll have the Air Warden round."

"Oh, dear," said Nurse, "it's really been very difficult, and it's hardly fair that the blame should fall on me. Most people have made proper arrangements by now, but Mrs. Hardwick's got nothing—she tells me she 'hangs up things.' It isn't as though she was a poor person either, though I daresay she doesn't get much for her tales. They're not very exciting. I read one once. It was supposed to be a love story, but I found it very dry."

"Am I to be allowed to talk to her?"

"Yes. Doctor said it would be quite all right. These thin little shrimps of women look delicate, so they always get a lot of sympathy, but they're really as strong as horses. I'll run upstairs and turn off the bathroom light, and then, while you're talking to her, I'll take the opportunity to make a cup of tea."

Guy followed her upstairs. She went to the bathroom and he knocked on Cresy's door. Cresy's voice said, "Come in," and then, "Oh—hullo!"

She was lying propped up by frilled pillows. The shaded lamp shed a soft circle of light over the bed; elsewhere the firelight danced on the walnut furniture and the white walls. To the plain man standing in the doorway, the effect was unbelievably romantic; a scene out of a play, a French novel or a farfetched film. Feeling all hands and feet, he shut the door, collected his wits and said, "Good evening, Mrs. Hardwick. I'm sorry to bother you, but there are a few questions I must ask. . . ."

Cresy laughed. "I expect there are. Would you like a drink first? There are liqueurs and things in the kitchen cupboard."

"No, thank you," said Guy. "And I have to warn you that anything you say may be taken down and used in evidence against you."

Cresy had taken up a silver box from the bedside table.

"Cigarette?"

"No, thank you. Did you hear what I said, Mrs. Hardwick?"

"The awful warning? Yes. Would you like to bring up that chair. The doctor said I wasn't to smoke," she observed, luxuriously inhaling, "but now's my chance. I shall tell Nurse it was you, if she says anything."

"You haven't much regard for the truth, have you?" said Guy, taking out his pen and opening his notebook.

"No," agreed Cresy.

"Well, I want the truth now. I want to know how all this happened. How many extra tablets of your sleeping drug did you take last night, Mrs. Hardwick?"

"I'm sorry, Detective-Inspector Northeast, but I can't tell you."

"Why not?"

"Because I don't know. I took one as usual, but the others were given to me."

"Oh," said Guy, simulating surprise. "And what evidence have you to support that theory?"

"I don't suppose I've any real evidence. All I know is that I took one tablet as usual. I went to sleep and I woke up to find myself being as sick as a dog and the doctor and the nurse hovering. I think the tablets had been put into my glass of milk and, fortunately for me, I only drank half of it."

"And who do you suppose put the tablets into the milk?"

"I can't imagine. I had a party here last night—anyone could have done it."

"Well, we'll come back to that. Tell me: why should anyone want to get rid of you?"

"Well," Cresy said slowly, "something happened at the party—they came across that tiresome book of mine, the one you found, on toxicology."

"Who came across it?"

"Edward Scaife. He was being funny about it and then he found a page turned down—the page on nicotine poisoning."

"And then?"

"Well, everyone looked askance at me, so I said I'd lent it."

"Was that true?"

"Yes."

"And to whom did you lend it?"

"I've forgotten. I said so, but nobody believed me."

"I don't believe you either."

"That's a pity," said Cresy, "because, in that case, I suppose you don't believe that I did lend it."

Their eyes met. Cresy's face was chalk-white, but in the soft lamplight she looked young, a girl. Why did Time play these tricks? How could something that didn't exist so muck up everything? This wouldn't do. The pace of the interview was slowing down to the tempo of the dancing firelight and the shifting apple logs. He cleared his throat and said briskly, "The position is this. In my own opinion, you lent your book to someone and that person is Scaife's murderer. You haven't forgotten to whom you lent it. But that's not the view that will be taken by other people. They'll think it's a put up story."

"And why don't you?"

"I'm here to ask questions, not to answer them. Come on, Mrs. Hard-wick. Who was it?"

"I've forgotten. Honestly."

"Honestly?"

"Umhm."

"Then," said Guy, "I shall have to believe it's a put up story."

"All right," said Crescy.

"And you realize what happens to your theory that someone at-tempted to poison you? That's only feasible if someone had a motive, the motive being that you might, at any time, reveal to the police the name of the person you lent the book to."

"I don't see that. X, or Fantomas, might not have believed that I'd forgotten."

"Nobody," said Guy exasperated, "believes that you've forgotten. Well, let's go back to the milk. While your party was on, where was it stand-ing?"

"By the bed. I drink a glass of milk every night in a vain attempt to develop feminine curves and a pacific mind. I poured it out when I was getting the drinks ready for the party. I gave what was left in the jug to the cats, and Eve says they're all right, so the tablets—if it was the tab-lets—must have been put into the tumbler. You see that, don't you, my dear Watson?"

"And who had access to your bedroom?"

"Oh, everybody."

"And did anyone know that you took sleeping tablets?"

"Not as I knows of. It's not a thing you run round telling people. Most people think that not being able to sleep is exhibitionism. Or else they get hearty and tell you to take healthy exercise."

"When you poured out the milk, did you bring it upstairs at once?"

"No. I gave the cats theirs and then I pattered about for a bit. I brought it up when I came to do my face."

"No one called when the tumbler was standing—where was it?—in the kitchen?"

"Yes, it was in the kitchen. No one called—there isn't a back door and I was pottering in and out."

"Then that seems clear. Now, Mrs. Hardwick," said Guy, getting up and walking over to the fire, "this may not have occurred to you. Pro-vided your theory is correct, the person who killed Scaife is sticking at nothing. You know too much—or may remember too much. There's been one attempt on your life and there'll be another."

Crescy, in her circle of lamplight, smiled.

"Now that I know, I can keep an eye open."

"Nonsense. You don't realize how cunning a certain type of mind can be. Scaife's murder wasn't an affair of slipping poison into a drink; it was planned out to the last detail, and not only that—the poison was administered so cunningly that it would have passed unnoticed by nine out of ten doctors. And let me tell you this: if you had drunk your whole glassful of milk last night, and I had found you dead in the morning, there would have been only one possible verdict: suicide; and we should have assumed that you were Scaife's murderer and the case would have been closed. You can't fight that kind of mind by merely keeping an eye open."

Cres/ appeared to consider. He didn't look at her, but at the ornaments on the mantelshelf: a china foal, a glass pig and a Doulton group of foxes. The silence was broken at last by a sigh, too pathetic to be genuine, and she said, "It's a pity, but it's just like my luck. I've always had a rotten memory."

Guy swung round. "It might be jogged," he said sternly, "if I arrested you on a charge of withholding information."

"Frankly, I'd rather like that," said Cresscy. "It would be good, cheap publicity and I've always longed to see inside a prison. I should be safe from Fantomas too." She gave a little shiver.

"You'd be safe from everything if you'd tell me that name," said Guy, leaning on the curved end of the bed. "What's the point of withholding it? You're not a sentimentalist, are you? If it's someone you care for—well, supposing one of your dogs started to kill sheep, you'd have her shot, wouldn't you?"

"All that," said Cresscy, "but it doesn't apply." Her big green eyes with black shadows under them looked him straight in the face. "I've forgotten."

"Well," said Guy, "what shall I do with you? Shall I take you down to the police station and let the Superintendent bawl at you?"

"You can bawl at me yourself if you like," said Cresscy.

With an expressionless face, he put away his notebook. He could see what she was—a creature of taut nerves and a fantastic imagination, fire to his frost, but it's fire beats frost and not frost fire. He could see what of doubts and fears the long night held for her; he had learned that from the little shiver that had followed her remark about Fantomas, her look when he had suggested taking her to the police station and letting the Superintendent bawl. Nothing, he knew, would get the name

he wanted out of her, but she was going to have the hell of a night unless
. . . "No, nobody shall bawl at you," he said, "and as soon as I get back to
Melchester I'll have a man sent out to keep an eye on you. So you can
sleep tonight," he said, tracing the graining of the wood with his forefinger, "and . . . well perhaps, even though you won't help us, everything
will be cleared up by this time tomorrow."

"You're very kind," said Crescy.

Guy made a deprecatory noise, and shifted from one foot to another. "Well, I must get back now. I hope all this hasn't tired you?"

"Not in the least," said Crescy, looking tired to death. "Good-bye,
Detective-Inspector, and I'm sorry about my memory."

"Good-bye, Mrs. Hardwick. I hope you'll be quite fit in the morning. I suppose the dogs are all right and everything?"

"Yes. Mrs. Hennisty saw to everything. Nurse wouldn't let me see
her, but she sent up a note."

"That's all right, then. Well, I must be getting off," and this time he
did go, and Crescy, with a sigh of relief, stubbed out her cigarette and
lay back on her pillows. A kindly youth, she thought; an industrious
apprentice, and she wished him well, hoping he'd get a nice girl, if he
hadn't got one already, and a nice house with bow windows, and the
latest thing in radios, and suites for the lounge and the bedroom, hoping that all his life he would remain deaf to nightingales and blind to
the stars. Guy meanwhile went blundering down the staircase, wishing
her no good, who had led him up the garden and given him a view
through iron railings of flowers that were not for him to pick and lawns
where he must not wander. At the foot of the stairs he almost collided
with the nurse, who was emerging from the kitchen with a tray.

She said, "I was just coming up to turn you out. I don't want my
patient tired to death. . . ."

Guy ignored that. He said, "Look here, Nurse, you're under the
impression, aren't you, that this is a case of attempted suicide? Well, it
may be. But there's another possibility—attempted murder."

"Murder? My gracious! *Is* there a maniac going round?"

"Not a maniac, but a very sane person, who knows that Mrs. Hardwick is an important witness."

"Oh—then she didn't do it?"

"Have you any reason to suppose she did?"

"Well, when a person tries suicide—"

"As I told you, I'm doubtful that she did try suicide. I want you to be
sure that no one but you touches her food—or has the opportunity to
interfere with it. I shall be sending a constable out from Melchester to
keep an eye on the place. And tomorrow, don't on any account allow

anybody but Mrs. Hennisty into the cottage."

He left her standing pop-eyed at the foot of the stairs. My, she was thinking, this'll be something to tell Mother and Edna. Then suddenly she didn't like it. She was accustomed to death, but to death that was an act of God, who gave and could take away, so that it was very sad but quite in order. Death dealt in hate by man was a different thing, creepy, godless, a return to the jungle. Setting the tray down on a step of the stairs, she hurried through the sitting-room.

Guy, halfway down the garden path, heard the key turn in the door and the bolts shoot home. He walked briskly up the lane, collected his bicycle at The Dog, and, after one for the road with Peter in the otherwise deserted lounge, rode back to Melchester.

CHAPTER VIII
FRIDAY

SUPERINTENDENT DAWES, with the newspaper propped up in front of him, was eating his breakfast, and a paragraph to the effect that the German people were now breakfasting on blackberry tea and red cabbage added, to his bacon and eggs, an extra relish. He remarked on that to his wife, who was picking at her cereal, but Sylvia Dawes, once a bright little woman, but now faded and without spirit, only replied, "Poor things, I'm sorry for them."

"They've only themselves to blame," said Dawes complacently, and his wife made no reply. She considered that the German people had been misled, and she sympathized with them: she herself had been misled, when, as a bright little woman with several irons in the fire, she had chosen the fine, successful man sitting opposite her.

When Dawes had finished his toast and marmalade, he gave his orders. "I shan't be back to dinner, but you'd better have a nice hot supper in the oven for me. I expected that Witheridge Green case to finish up last night, but it seems to be hanging fire somewhere. These fellows from Scotland Yard are too damn cautious. It's always safety first with them."

"Better to be safe than sorry," said Sylvia, from sad experience.

Dawes made a scornful noise. "That's a motto for women and children, not for grown men. I've never been afraid of responsibility. . ."

Sylvia interrupted him.

"George, you've some egg on your chin."

"Nonsense," said Dawes, who reacted like that when any imperfection in his godlike portrait of himself was pointed out to him. Nevertheless he picked up his table napkin, scrubbed his chin and let the napkin fall upon the floor. "Well, I must be off. If you want anything done well, do it yourself—that's what I always say."

At a brisk walk designed to keep himself fit, he set off for the Police Station, but, on arriving, he discovered that Detective-Inspector Northeast had already been in, left a bottle of milk to be analyzed and a tumbler to be tested for fingerprints, studied the reports on Mark Scaife's alibi and the inspection of the poison registers, and gone out again, apparently to pay some calls in the town. "Oh, he did, did he?" said Dawes, and, with a slight loss of complacency, settled down to his usual routine.

At one o'clock Detective-Inspector Northeast came in. There was a smile on his face. He flung down on the table a pair of hogskin gloves, which Dawes considered most unsuitable to his position, unbuttoned his rather horsey overcoat—Dawes thought he looked more like a farmer at a race meeting than a detective—and said, "Well, now, all I want is a search warrant."

"A search warrant?" Dawes repeated. "I thought you'd already found all the doings at the cottage—nicotine, sand, a sponge. . ."

"I don't want to search Little Bottom Cottage," Guy said happily. "I want to search the Hall."

"The Hall? But, good God, man, it's obvious. The woman hammered the last nail into her coffin when she tried to do away with herself."

Guy's face hardened. "That wasn't suicide. It was attempted murder. Except as a witness for the prosecution, she's out of the case."

"I don't see how you can make that out."

"I made it out last night, and I've spent this morning busting alibis. Now I want a search warrant for the Hall and a couple of men with sieves." He glanced at his wristwatch. "And they've got some work to do before dark."

"Well," said Dawes, "it's your funeral. But with all that evidence against her . . . I suppose you're thinking of Mark Scaife now, but you've got to remember that in a murder case people who can't account satisfactorily for their movements are apt to get rattled and provide themselves with an alibi. That's human nature, that is, and it's no use plumping for Scaife just because you've bust his alibi."

Guy, who could have screamed with impatience, said, "I see what you mean, sir, but there's more to it than a bust alibi. I haven't the time to go into it now—this damned blackout will be down on us before we're through. If you could spare me a couple of men for an hour or two and, if possible, a car. . ."

"Well, it's your responsibility. . . ." With exasperating slowness the Superintendent gave his orders, and half an hour later the dark blue police car turned in at the entrance to the Hall. The beautiful autumn weather had deteriorated. The sky was gray, the air raw and cold, but the rose-red facade of the house preserved its look of elegance; the white-pillared portico invited gay sophisticated guests. It was all wrong, Guy thought; even hate in this house should have been graced with some touch of nobility, should have been settled out there on the turf under the cedar trees with rapiers or pistol shots at dawn. He recalled his wandering thoughts as the door was opened by Mrs. Binfield, straggle-haired and squalid, in a sacking apron and a stained blouse.

Guy shouted for Edward Scaife. Mrs. Binfield, sucking her remaining teeth for shreds of her midday meal, observed, "Ar. More trouble," and leaving the door open, disappeared. After a few moments, Edward came striding down the stone passage. "I'm sorry to trouble you, sir," Guy said without preamble, "but I have a warrant to search the house and grounds."

Edward went white, but his cold gray eyes stared steadily into Guy's absurd seraphic blue ones. "A search warrant? . . . You must carry on then." He stood aside.

"I want to begin," Guy said, "with the kitchen quarters. Can you tell me what happens to the ashes here?"

Edward passed his hand across his forehead.

"There are only the two fires—the one in our sitting-room and the kitchen range. . ."

"No hot water stove?"

"No. The water's heated—or it's supposed to be heated—by the range. I shall have," said Edward rather loudly, "to have a proper hot water system installed."

"And the ashes."

"Well, they're shoveled out into buckets and Mrs. Binfield empties the buckets into an old bin outside the kitchen door. On Saturdays a couple of the lads carry the bin to the hen run where they empty it. I'm getting a battery hen house, so there'll be no need to do that in future, but in the meantime I conclude they're carrying on."

"I see. Then there's nearly a week's ashes in the bin now?"

"That's right."

"Could someone show my men where the bin is?"

"With pleasure," said Edward, smiling disagreeably; "but there's no one about but Mrs. Binfield—I'll take them along."

He led the way down a path through the laurels, and Hughes and Carter, the two young constables, followed him. Guy went down the passage and into the sitting-room. On this gray day the room was dark and the small fire of sulky cherry wood did little to combat the dampness of the air.

Guy went round the room searching methodically. The drawer in the deal table yielded a white tablecloth, a few pencil stubs, scraps of paper evidently preserved for shopping lists and some neat swathes of string. The box on the bamboo table contained gramophone records of an immense age. In the built-in cupboard at the side of the fireplace was a stack of *The Farmers' Weekly*, several books on agriculture and stock breeding, a couple of flower vases, some blotting paper and a stone jar of ink. In the bowels of the sewing machine were needles, spools and reels of cotton. The ambiguous sideboard was occupied by bottles of beer, a bowl of fruit and the wickerwork box, which Janet Scaife had brought out on the occasion of his first visit to the Hall. Inside the work box, instead of the usual tangle, everything was neatly arranged. Thimble and scissors were thrust through their appropriate loops. Buttons were in a tiny box, inscribed 'Buttons.' Pins were in the pin cushion. Needles were in the needle case. The yard measure was rolled up and secured by an india-rubber ring. Methodical woman, Mrs. Scaife, Guy thought, remembering the frantic and almost ceaseless search for sewing materials at home. "*Has* anyone seen a darning needle?" "Dinah, you devil, you've had my scissors!" "Pam, you beast, I saw you with my thimble. . ." And his mother, who was just as untidy as her daughters, smugly observing, "Where you put it, there it will be."

He went out of the sitting-room and across the passage to the kitchen. Mrs. Binfield was washing up at the stone sink in the scullery. He went over to her and shouted, "I have a warrant to search the house."

"Eh?"

He repeated, "I have a warrant to search the house."

"Well, I can't 'elp it," said Mrs. Binfield, extracting a plate from the greasy water and slapping it up into the colossal plate rack. "Squire's gone and it don't concern me what goes on 'ere."

So Guy started to search the kitchen, which was a very different matter from searching the sitting-room. Mrs. Binfield did not, evidently, share her employer's passion for order, and drawers and cupboards were choc-a-bloc with relics of more prosperous times, armies of wooden spoons, metal molds, egg whisks, skewers, pestles and mortars, all muddled up with half empty tins of polish, old rags, old newspapers, bottles, corks and mousetraps, some still baited with scraps of mold, which had once been cheese. He turned it all over, but it was in the damp cupboard under the scullery sink that he found one of the objects for which he was searching—a coarse, poor-quality sponge.

"What do you use this for?" he asked Mrs. Binfield. She had finished washing up and was at the kitchen table, mincing the remains of a round of beef.

"Cleaning the winders."

"Had it long?"

"No, I ain't. Squire didn't trouble about the winders. Mrs. Edward, she gave it to me when she first come. 'Ardly got 'er 'at off before she started creating about the state of the place—said it stunk, she did. Then it was the winders. Couldn't see out. 'That's all right,' Squire told 'er 'If you can't see out, then others can't see in.' She didn't like that. Tossed 'er 'ead, she did, and no sooner was Squire's back turned than she give me that there sponge and a leather, what Mr. Edward 'ad when 'e kep' a car. 'You can 'ave these for the winders,' she says, ' 'core, at this rate, we shan't 'ave a car never no more.'"

"I see. And where did she get the sponge from? I mean, where was it kept before she gave it to you?"

"I can't tell you that, but I remember she went outside to get it. 'S matter of fack, young Edward, 'e 'ad 'is car up at the stables for a week or two. Then there was a row. 'E wanted some money and Squire said 'e wasn't giving away no money to them as could afford to run a car."

Guy, who had been feeling the sponge, said again, "I see," and then, "Well, Mrs. Binfield, I'm going to take this sponge away with me." He wrapped it in a piece of newspaper and stored it away in the pocket of his overcoat, which he had hung on a peg near the door.

"You're welcome," said Mrs. Binfield. "If they wants the winders cleaned, they should get the winder-cleaner to clean 'em. 'Taint my work." She minced furiously.

Guy looked round the kitchen. He had been through all the drawers and cupboards. He hadn't overlooked the drawer in the kitchen table or the horrid heap on the table in the scullery. Scratching his fair head, he asked, "Do they garden much—attend to the flowers and so on?"

"When they first come," said Mrs. Binfield, "they 'ad a try. Knott, 'e sees to the vegetables, but young Edward brought some plants with 'im, roses and things 'e'd 'ad in 'is garden over in Oxfordshire. Squire said 'e wasn't going to waste no ground on flowers, but all the same they cleared a border and planted their things."

"What tools did they use?"

"Some they brought with them. Knott said they *was a* lot of fiddling things. Tools to weed with, as if God 'adn't given 'em fingers and thumbs. Labels to write the names of the rose bushes on and stuff to spray 'em with. Knott, 'e says, 'I don't want no labels—I've got an 'ead to remember with, 'aven't I? And I don't need to go spraying roses,' 'e says. 'I scrapes the greenfly off with me thumbnail.' "

"Where do they keep their tools?"

"In that there little place outside the back door. Used to be for cleaning knives in the days when gentry was gentry. . ."

Guy wandered outside. He found a door leading into a little slate-roofed outhouse, where, on a stout bench, an enormous knife-cleaning machine awaited the unlikely restoration of gentility. Tools, mostly of a newfangled description, were neatly stacked in a corner, and, at one end of the bench, were trug baskets, a box of labels, neat green stakes and balls of green twine. There was also a tin of nicotine. He wrapped that in his handkerchief, carried it indoors and stored it with the sponge in his overcoat pocket. As he was doing so, Edward Scaife came into the kitchen. "Your men are sifting the cinders and making a nice mess," he said in a resentful but tightly controlled tone of voice. "I can't imagine what they expect to find."

Guy said, "We have to explore every avenue. . . I'm sorry, Mr. Scaife, but I want to look round the rooms you occupy upstairs."

Edward shrugged his shoulders and, as he led the way out of the kitchen, he said, "You're wasting your time here, you know, Inspector. I suppose something has put you on to my half-brother . . . well, we don't get on and he's clearing out tomorrow, but I can assure you he isn't the man to plan a murder—what he would do in hot blood or during a quarrel is another thing. I don't know how you've summed him up," said Edward, mounting the staircase, not turning his head but by a kind of stiffness about his shoulders and narrow head showing himself ill at ease, "but he hasn't either a brain or education. Hit a man over the head or blaze away at him with a shot gun—yes. But my father was poisoned. This is Mark's room," he said, opening a door opposite the head of the staircase.

Mark's room was small, square and lofty. The one window was directly above the portico. It was a shabby room with a threadbare carpet, and the iron bed, still unmade, looked incongruous beside Sheraton chairs and a mahogany tallboy. Guy said, "Well, I'll look round," and Edward withdrew. Guy heard him go downstairs and the baize door creak; then he went out on the landing and along the corridor, quietly opening the doors of the rooms. At the end of the corridor he found a large bedroom, evidently used by Edward and his wife. The brass double bed was made and covered by a counterpane of green linen. A ripple-cloth dressing gown hung behind the door, and, neatly arranged on the dressing-table, were silver-backed hairbrushes and a modest array of cosmetics. A pair of stockings and a woolen vest lay tidily folded on a chair.

Guy touched nothing, but made a beeline for the wardrobe. It was a substantial Victorian piece of furniture and, when he opened the double-doors, it seemed to him a little pathetic that in the generous space inside hung so few and such shabby garments—a mackintosh of poor qual-

ity, an afternoon dress of brown velveteen, horribly embellished with
wormlike embroidery in green and gold, a black coatee edged with worn
cat's fur, a green woolen dress and a green and brown checked jacket.
He took down these garments, which were neatly hung on wooden coat-
hangers, and examined the pockets. Except for a six-penny torch in the
pocket of the mackintosh, they were empty, but, nevertheless, he began
to whistle through his teeth. Now *the Day is Over* was the tune he whistled,
a childish innocuous tune, but men who had worked with him knew it
for his song of triumph, deadly as the whoop of the huntsman when
another kind of killer pays his score. . .

* * * *

A few moments later Guy, with a parcel under his arm, went down
the stairs. The house seemed deserted; already the gray day was darken-
ing at the windows; on his placid spirit melancholy descended like a
pall. When it was some rat of a gangster you had been hunting, there
was satisfaction in the kill, but he had no stomach for the job that was
before him; the picture his mind retained of Crescy Hardwick, lying
pale in the circle of lamplight, only stiffened his resolution until he
reminded himself that for all she could ever mean to him, he might as
well work himself up over the affairs of the moon. Falling back on the
supposition that one must do what one was paid for, he passed through
the green baize door and along the passage. Outside he met the constables. Carter said, "I think we've got it, sir." He opened a large and
horny hand. On the palm lay a short, flattish needle, blackened as though
by fire.

Guy picked it up and rubbed it with his handkerchief. "You can
see," said the constable, "that it's been sharpened—filed, probably—
above the eye. No sign of glue, though."

"The fire will have disposed of that," Guy told him. "Actually, I didn't
know that needles as thick as this existed. Very likely it was fitted in the
dart shaft without glue."

"That's not a needle, sir," interposed the other constable. "That's a
ribbon threader, that is. Ladies use them to thread elastic through their
knickers—I'm married, sir."

"I thought they used bodkins. Isn't this a bodkin?"

"No, sir. A bodkin can be identified by a sort of bulge on the business end. That's a ribbon threader, that is."

"Well, you're the expert. One lives and learns. Now, I want you two
to hang about while I drive into Melchester and back. I shan't be gone
longer than half an hour. Just notice who comes in and out of the house.
When I come back, I shall want to know who's indoors."

He got into the police car and drove away. "Wonder what he's gone for," said Hughes, searching in his pocket and pulling out a packet of Woodbines. " 'Ave a fag, mate. Might as well get a smoke while we can."

"No, thanks," said Carter, a more conscientious youth. "I don't want to acquire the 'abit. If you ask me, 'e's gone after a warrant for the arrest of Mr. Edward Scaife—that's where 'e's gone."

"Why Mr. Edward Scaife? My sister, what's married and lives out this way, she made sure it was the other one. 'E's a bad lot, 'e is."

Hidden by the laurels, but in a position from which they could observe the drive, they discussed the case, and saw, meanwhile, Edward Scaife, Mark Scaife and Janet Scaife come in. Edward came from the farm buildings; Mark, with his thick boots heavy with loam, across the park; Janet with a full shopping basket hurried from the direction of the road. A light sprang up in the window of the sitting-room and was quickly screened. And presently a dark blue car turned in through the gates and stopped a few yards from the back door. Hughes cast his third cigarette into the bushes, stepped smartly forward and opened the door of the car.

Guy got out. He walked past the constables without a word, but at the door he turned and said, "Hang about in the passage, will you?" "Yessir," said Hughes, with a wink at Carter, and they followed Guy indoors.

Guy went down the passage and knocked on the sitting-room door. Edward's voice said, "Come in." Guy opened the door and saw the lamps lit and the table spread for tea. Edward was cutting a loaf. Mark, with his hands in his pockets, lounged in his chair. Janet, sitting with her back to the fire, was pouring out tea. Lamplight, a white cloth and a brown earthenware teapot gave to the ugly room a look of homeliness, and in the second before Edward spoke, Guy had to remind himself that that meant nothing—there was Eden once and a serpent under the boughs.

. . .

Edward looked up from his bread-cutting. "Hullo, Inspector! Come to join us at tea?"

"I'm sorry, no. I have a warrant here." He cleared his throat and advanced towards the table. "Janet Scaife, I arrest you for the murder of Mathew Scaife and I warn you that anything you say may be taken down and used in evidence against you."

Janet set down the teapot. Her brown eyes stared at Guy across the table. Mark sat up, but said nothing. Edward stood still as a statue, the bread knife poised.

Guy began, "Well . . ." but Edward interrupted him. "What's all this about? Have you gone stark, staring mad? My wife was in Melchester at the time the murder was committed."

"I'm afraid not," said Guy keeping his eyes on Janet. "It's true your wife produced an alibi, but it was a faked one. She went into Melchester, but she didn't go by bus and she didn't go at the time she stated. She went *after* the murder, on a bicycle."

Janet placed the cozy on the teapot. A faint smile lit up her pale face. She said, "That's very interesting, but you've got to prove it." She looked at her husband. "The conductor on the seven o'clock bus should remember me."

"I expect that's where the Inspector's slipped up," said Edward, moistening his lips with his tongue and darting a savage look at Guy. "I suppose, Inspector, you've got this mad idea because the conductor on the seven o'clock bus can't swear that he saw my wife, but damn it all, that's not evidence—you can't expect a man to take in the faces of twenty or thirty passengers."

"Of course you can't," said Janet. "And there's another thing—I usually wear what I've got on now to go into Melchester, but that night I was wearing my green frock and my new jacket and hat. Men never recognize you in new clothes."

"That's right," said Edward. "I remember remarking on your new things. If that's what you're going on, Inspector, you'd better think again. If you proceed with this, you'll land yourself in a hell of a mess. I'll sue you for damages. I'll break you as sure as I stand here."

Guy felt sorry for Edward, a cold man, a mean man, but probably, in some fishlike way of his own, fond of the hard-natured, inflexibly purposed woman he had married. Throughout the investigations he had received no hint of any disagreement between these two, but, nevertheless, it was difficult to imagine them as lovers; one felt rather that they had come together because they respected one another: both intensely self-satisfied, they admired in each other the qualities which they shared. He said, "I'm sorry, sir, but all that will have to come later," and, to end the argument, he opened the door and beckoned in the constables.

"I suppose," said Janet in a voice that didn't even shake, "this means you're taking me to the police station. Well, it's no use making a fuss now, Edward—that, as the Inspector says, will come later. I suppose I'm allowed to pack some things for the night?"

Guy said, "Certainly. One of my men will go upstairs with you," and Janet got up and walked out of the room, Hughes following her. "I shall go straight to the Chief Constable," Edward announced, and then he turned to Mark and snapped, "What are you sitting there for? There's plenty to be done, isn't there?"

"I haven't had my tea yet," said Mark, and he took the cozy off the teapot and poured himself out a cupful. "And keep a civil tongue in your head," he went on. "I may be a bastard; I may stink of stables; I mayn't be fit to sit at meals with the gentry, but, after all, you see, it wasn't I who murdered the poor old man; it was your bitch of a wife. So put that in your pipe and smoke it."

Edward opened his mouth to answer, and Guy, leaving them to it, walked out of the room and joined Carter at the door. They stood in silence. Presently Janet, dogged by Hughes, came down the passage. She was carrying a small suitcase and wore her brown hat pulled down over her forehead. A faint smile was on her face, but in her eyes, usually hard as pebbles, fire smoldered, a sullen, dangerous fire.

Edward came from the sitting-room. He said, "We'll soon get this put right," and he glared at Guy and said, "I wouldn't care to be in your shoes then." Without replying, Guy shepherded the party along the passage. "Carter, you drive, and, Hughes, sit in the back with Mrs. Scaife."

Janet in silence entered the car. When she was seated and Hughes had taken his place beside her, she said, "I don't know how you'll manage, Edward. You'd better get hold of Mrs. Farraway—she can milk after a fashion, and I daresay I shall be back soon." Guy, getting in beside Carter, could feel her eyes on him as she added, "And Inspector Northeast, who thinks himself so clever, I wonder where he'll be?"

Then Carter, who had the engine ticking over, released the brake, let in the clutch, and down the drive between the dark laurel hedges they drove away.

CHAPTER IX
NEW YEAR'S EVE

"I THINK HE'LL COME," said Crescy.

"I'm sure he won't," said Peter. "It was a mad kind of invitation. I can't think how you and Eve had the neck to send it. He's not the sort of fellow to come traipsing down here in the blackout for a glass of mulled ale."

Cresy was drinking whiskey. Reflectively, she turned the glass in her hand.

"He isn't so painfully sane as you make out, Peter. You should have seen him eating crumpets and discussing life with me."

Peter said, "Oh, well, Cresy, you ought to be segregated. Your madness is an infectious kind."

Adam opened his mouth to say to Peter, I've never noticed that it infects you, but somehow, now that he was in uniform, his attitude had changed: why on earth should he take a crack at good old Peter, exasperatingly honest and decent and play-the-game and all that, but, still, a true friend. He shut his mouth, took a drink and from a new fount of benevolence said, "If I hadn't been so frightened of Northeast, I'd have liked him, I think. I hope he comes."

Bridget said, "Well, I agree with Peter. He won't. Darling Cresy, of course, can always get something out of everyone, but I found him dull."

"I don't think I want him to come," said Valentine. "I don't want to be reminded. You've all got over it, but I'm so absurdly sensitive. I still have dreams."

"If he does come, I want to get him talking about the murder," said David. "It's always interesting to hear how other people's jobs are done."

Adam said, "I wonder how he did do it? I mean, what first put him on to Janet. Of course, when you know whom you're after it must be quite easy to collect evidence."

"I believe I know what my mistake was now," said Crescy. "I mean, in my detective novel. I tried to make my detective a brilliant kind of person—like Dr. Priestley, only young and attractive. Northeast isn't in the least brilliant. . ."

"He certainly isn't," said David. "And I should say practically no education. Grammar school, perhaps. If you ask me, I should say he was lucky."

"Education!" said Crescy. "Education's all very well for dining-out on, but it can't make fools wise. A wise lad, Northeast, and wisdom is common sense lit by imagination."

"What funny words you use, Crescy," said Valentine.

"Well, the proof of the pudding was in the eating," said Peter, pouring himself out a glass of bitter, and Eve, glancing at the clock, said, "We'll allow him a quarter of an hour's grace and then we'll really have to give him up and bring the posset in." As she finished speaking there were heavy footsteps in the lobby, the door opened and Guy stood blinking under the mistletoe.

Everyone cheered.

"This is nice," said Eve. "We've just been talking about you and hoping so much that you'd come."

Guy, struggling out of his overcoat, said, "How could I resist such an attractive invitation? I've never tried mulled ale, but it sounds lovely."

"I hope it will be good now you've come so far for it," said Peter diffidently.

Crescy said, "It's not only the mulled ale he's come for. There's the pleasure of our company. In spite of suspecting us all, you quite took to us, didn't you, Inspector?"

Their eyes met. Damn and blast, thought Crescy. You poor young thing, I didn't mean to do that to you.

Eve said, "I'll get the posset," and she went out. Adam said, "I warn you, Northeast, we're going to make you talk shop. We've been arguing about your methods. Some people say you are wise, some that you were lucky."

Guy said, "Congratulations on the uniform, Mr. Day. You're the lucky one. As for my methods, well, I expect you were all terribly disappointed. You probably expected brilliant deductions and that kind of thing. But detectives aren't any more brilliant than anyone else. They've experience in putting jigsaw puzzles together, that's all."

Eve came back bringing the mulled ale in a Delft bowl. She served it with a silver ladle into glass tankards. Everyone found it delicious except Valentine, who said it tasted funny and was it very intoxicating, please? Everyone else said they hoped so, but it wasn't, and throughout the evening an unusual sobriety obtained.

It was David who brought the conversation back from trivialities to the murder. He said, "I know it's selfish of us to ask you to talk shop, Inspector, but I don't suppose we shall any of us be suspects in a murder case again. Do tell us how it all worked out. I'd like to see how a real-life case compares with the detective stories one reads."

Guy said, "Well, I'd better begin at the beginning for, as I said just now, a detective's work is like putting a jigsaw puzzle together, and I've never handled a case that was more like a jigsaw than this one. You realize, I suppose, who's the hero of the story—that little police surgeon of yours. For sheer thoroughness, he beats the band and, if ever I have a mysterious pain, I shall come down here and get him to look me over. Nine out of ten doctors would have missed the tiny puncture at the back of Scaife's neck. You see, death occurred instantaneously, so it hadn't time to inflame."

"Ugh!" shuddered Valentine.

"It was well thought out," said Guy, "and that, in itself, was enough to give me a line. I knew at once that I had got to look for someone with a good brain, educated enough to know something about chemistry and, or, medicine. I don't know if it struck any of you at the time that even later on, in fact after I had discovered that the murder was done from outside the room, I never really concentrated on any of the crowd in the public bar. Actually this was one of the factors which turned my attention to our novelist: she denied any knowledge of chemistry, but she could have acquired any knowledge she wanted from books. Yet in spite of that and other things that kept piling up against her, I never fancied Cres—Mrs. Hardwick—as a poisoner, though I can say now that all along she was the Superintendent's favorite, and I can't blame him. Your obstructive tactics," he said to Cresy, "were enough to mislead anyone."

Cresy said, "I couldn't help it. Informing sticks in my throat, like lies in other people's. And I'm always on the side of the hunted. . ."

"That silly story about forgetting who'd borrowed your book . . ." Guy began, but Valentine wasn't going to let the conversation develop into a tete-a-tete, and she broke in, "Do tell me, Inspector—did you suspect me? You came to see me ever so many times."

"No," said Guy. "I never for an instant suspected you, Mrs. Day."

"Why not?" asked Valentine in a disappointed tone. "Of course I know I'm not clever . . ."

"Oh, it wasn't that. It was simply because you had no earthly motive."

"Then why did you ask me so many questions?"

"Well, there was your husband . . ."

"But he hadn't any more motive."

"No, he hadn't," said Guy stoutly. "But well, he's an artistic type. . ."

"Oh, I say," said Adam.

"And we always suspect people with long hair." That reef avoided, Guy went quickly on. "I think the crucial point in my investigations was when I played darts with Smallbone and picked up a dud dart. I didn't think anything of it at the time, but, I suppose because I'm a trained jigsaw-ist, the fact—the shape of the piece—stuck at the back of my mind and floated to the surface when I discovered the crack in the matchboarding. That reduced my suspects to the people who had had the opportunity to remove the dart from the public bar. I got Conway to make a list of them, and Mrs. Scaife's name was there, but I'd never suspected her, and I didn't suspect her then—half-witted of me, but you must remember in my favor that, while all you people were glaringly on the scene of the crime, she wasn't, in addition to which she had supplied me with what sounded like a perfectly good alibi—an absolutely natural one and not too perfect. Then came her first and fatal mistake. At Crescy's party she got rattled. Crescy's book on toxicology was discovered by her husband; she learned that I knew about it, and Crescy's story about forgetting who had borrowed it didn't take her in at all. She decided that sooner or later, Cres—Mrs. Hardwick—would split on her, so she planned another poisoning. She staged it to look like suicide, hoping that the police, already suspicious of Mrs. Hardwick, would assume her guilty and the case would be closed. But, as I told you, I'd never been able to see Mrs. Hardwick as a poisoner, and now there was one little thing that made me quite sure. In Dixon Mann's book the page on nicotine poisoning was dog-eared and I knew that Crescy, an author and a lover of books, would never have marked a page in that way. There was another little piece fitted into my jigsaw."

Guy ceased speaking to take a drink. Adam said, "That was bright of you. Did it put you on to Janet? Now I come to think of it, she *was* the sort of person who would dog-ear a book. Didn't care a damn about books except as a source of information . . . mad on efficiency, and there's no more efficient marker than a dog-ear."

"No," said Guy. "That didn't occur to me. I went back from Little Bottom Cottage to The Dog and got out the list of the people who had had the opportunity to remove the dart from the public bar. One of them was right out of the case now—Mark Scaife—because he wasn't at Crescy's party, and all the oddments, like the brewers' vanman, were out, too. I should have said that, before I started on that list, a rather desperate snoop round had put me wise to the fact, which you all know from the trial, that the murderer had used the electric fan as a peep-hole—all along it had been obvious that he, or she, must have known exactly how Scaife was sitting—the sharp instrument had to be driven into the neck, otherwise it would have given up its lethal dose as it passed through the old man's clothing. The ironic thing is that if Scaife hadn't asked for the fan to have been turned off earlier in the evening, he might have been alive now."

"You don't think she would have tried again?" asked David.

"I'm sure she would. It was her custom to go into Melchester once a week to the pictures, and I think she would have tried again and again. For all we know, she may have tried before. A determined female. Well, as I sat here studying that list, her name leaped out at me. As far as I was concerned, Mark Scaife and Mrs. Hardwick were washed out; Mr. Day hadn't a motive, but here was someone I hadn't considered, and I set out to bust her alibi."

"You told me you were busting an alibi," said Peter, "but I jumped to the conclusion that it was Mark Scaife's."

"No. I was on the right track then. My enquiries confirmed that Mrs. Scaife had come back from Melchester on the bus, as she said, but there was no evidence that she went in. When I first thought of her, I'd remembered another little piece of jigsaw—Smallbone's bicycle had disappeared on the night of the crime. It was found propped up against a curb in Melchester. That fitted in."

"What I don't see," said Bridget, "is how she knew that she'd find a woman's bicycle ready to hand. It was by sheer chance that Smallbone was using his sister's."

"Mrs. Chandler rides a bike," Guy told her. "Janet was obviously counting on that, but it was in the car park, while Smallbone's had been left practically at the door. I daresay she thought it *was* Mrs. Chandler's—anyhow it didn't matter whose it was as long as it would take her into Melchester. Well . . . we're getting near the end . . . the next thing I did was to get a warrant to search the Hall. I found everything I wanted, a sponge that had been near spilt powdered pumice, nicotine in a shed. As you know from the trial the powdered pumice was one of our clues."

"That's what seems so odd," said Eve. "Why didn't she hide it?"

"Because of her husband. Put yourself in her place. At first, no doubt, she thought she had committed the perfect crime and there was no need to hide anything, but when we began to enquire about nicotine, supposing she'd hidden it and Edward had missed it—they were both keen gardeners and terribly tidy people—wouldn't he have wondered where it had gone?"

"Yes, of course."

"Then we sifted the household ashes—I took a chance that she'd burned the dart—and we found the ribbon-threader. I'd noticed, by the way, what a well-equipped workbasket Mrs. Scaife possessed. While the sifting was going on, I'd been upstairs and gone through her wardrobe. On the lining of the pocket in her green and brown jacket I found a brown stain which smelt of tobacco and I think I was justified in taking the risk that the analyst would declare it to be nicotine. Well, then I had to get a warrant for her arrest, and that was that, and I suppose the moral is that murder doesn't pay."

"One thing," said David. "Why didn't she take the dart away with her? Surely it was madness to leave it in the pub and run all sorts of risks collecting it again."

"Yes," Guy answered. "Leaving it in the pub was a great mistake. But what could she do? She wanted to leave it sticking in the wound for as long as possible in order to make sure that the blood would absorb the poison. She couldn't hang about in the lobby when she was supposed to be in Melchester. It would have been absolutely fatal if she'd been seen."

He threw back the rest of his ale and Peter refilled his tankard. Cresy said, "I wish I'd known her better. I wish I knew why she did it. Was it because Scaife was beastly to her and she hated him, or because she couldn't bear to see him mucking up the farm?"

"I think it was a bit of both," Guy answered. "She was mad about the land—crazy to possess the farm that her father-in-law was mismanaging. Then, in addition to frustrating every effort at improvement which she and Edward made, he kept her short of everything—even firewood, I believe, and I've no doubt he took every opportunity to insult and annoy her. With his death she would get a more comfortable life, her own way and the opportunity to run the place profitably—she was a conceited woman and perfectly certain that she could make a success of things. An unattractive character, but a strong one—all through the trial and afterwards, she was absolutely calm and self-contained. Like a rock. Strength incarnate. A steam roller, with no one in charge."

"I never liked her, did I, Adam," said Valentine. "She was grim."

"Not grim," said Cresy. "Drab. And, as Inspector Northeast said, completely self-contained. She mightn't have murdered Scaife if she had let off steam about the farm and things. Of course, I let off too much steam. My threats about wringing Scaife's neck . . . I expect they'd have hanged me if it hadn't been for you. You're a terribly wise youth, aren't you?" she said, her hand on Guy's arm.

"Not very wise," said Guy into his beer mug, "and a great deal older than you might suppose."

They gossiped for a while. Edward had gone to Canada; Mark had managed to enlist in the army; the Hall was for sale as a whole or in plots; Cresy had bought Little Bottom Cottage and people from London had bought Saunders' cottage for conversion and he had had to turn out of it after all. Presently Bridget and David went home. The Days followed them. Cresy said that she must go.

She and Guy had one for the road and then Guy said good-bye to Eve and Peter: Cresy, he said, should have police protection across the Green. They went out into the garden, which no longer smelt of chrysanthemums; it smelt of frost, a frightening smell, said Cresy, a smell of world's end. Under the dead moon and all the stars they walked across the thin snow-carpet on the Green. "I shall never forget this place," Guy said. "I shall never forget having tea and crumpets with you." Cresy didn't say, as he wildly hoped she'd say, come down one day and have tea and crumpets again. No, she decided; you go back to London, my lad, and find a nice girl. "We'll say good-bye here," she said firmly. "You don't want to come all the way down the lane," and she held out her hand and said, "I'm eternally grateful. I should have hated to be hanged." Guy held her thin, hard hand and said, "I didn't do anything. Do take care of yourself, won't you? and do send for me if you're ever in a show like this again. Or any sort of a mess. I'll come, wherever I am. You will, won't you?"

He pressed her hand and Cresy, stifling a scream of pain, said, "Yes, I will, but I'm going to live a quiet life and keep out of trouble from now on. It's too nerve-racking. Good-bye, my dear."

"Good-bye," said Guy. "It's made a difference, you know, knowing you. It's—well, it's made a difference knowing that a person like you exists. Rather unfortunate. It sets up a standard that no one else can reach."

Cresy said sharply, "That's nonsense. I may be clever, but I'm not nice, or kind." She got her hand away at last, said, "Good-bye and thank you. I'm going to run to get warm," and ran.

Detective-Inspector Northeast watched her till she disappeared from sight. Then he turned and walked back across the Green. A cold wind blew in his face; long since, the moon had died of cold; the stars were cold, and cold the frozen earth beneath his feet.

THE END

Other Rue Morgue vintage mysteries

Great Black Kanba
by Constance & Gwenyth Little

"If you love train mysteries as much as I do, hop on the Trans-Australia Railway in *Great Black Kanba*, a fast and funny 1944 novel by the talented team of Constance and Gwenyth Little. The back cover has a creative line: 'call it Cornell Woolrich on laughing gas.'"—Jon L. Breen, *Ellery Queen's Mystery Magazine*. "I have decided to add *Kanba* to my favorite mysteries of all time list!...a zany ride I'll definitely take again and again."—Diane Plumley in the Murder Ink newsletter.

A young American woman who's lost her memory comes to on baord an Australian train and discovers she could be a murderer in this 1944 novel by the queens of the wacky cozy. Not only does the young woman have a bump on her head and no memory, she also has no idea how she came to be on a train crossing the Nulabor Plain of Australia with a group of boisterous, argumentative Aussies who appear to be her relatives. Nor does she recall ever having met the young doctor who says he's her fiance. Which is a little awkward, since there's another man on the train who says she'd agreed to marry him, and a love letter in her pcoketbook from yet another beau.

She also discovers that she may be a cold-blooded killer. Even worse, she may have really bad taste in clothes, given the outfit she's wearing. When some of her fellow passengers are killed, an Australian cop thinks she would make a great suspect and the only reason she isn't arrested is that the train keeps passing into other jurisdictions. The pasengers also have to keep changing trains, since each Australian state uses a different railroad gauge.

And then there's the matter of the bakring lizard in her compartment. The lizard belongs to Uncle Joe, an amateur painter who awakes every morning to discover that someone has defaced his latest masterpiece. It all adds up to some delightful mischief—call it Cornell Woolrich on laughing ghas—which is what you would expect from the pens of the two Australian-born Little sisters.

0-915230-22-4 $14

The Black Honeymoon
by Constance & Gwenyth Little

Can you murder someone with feathers? If you don't believe that feathers can kill, then you probably haven't read one of the 21 mysteries by the two Little sisters, the reigning queens of the cozy screwball mystery from the 1930s to the 1950s. No, Uncle Richard wasn't tickled to death—though we can't make the same guarantee for readers—but the hyper-allergic rich man did manage to sneeze himself into the hereafter in his hospital room.

Suspicion falls on his nurse, young Miriel Mason, who recently married the dead man's nephew, Ian Ross, an army officer on furlough. Ian managed to sweep Miriel off her feet and to the altar—well, at least to city hall—before she had a chance to check his bank balance, which was nothing to boast about. In fact, Ian cheerfully explains that they'll have to honeymoon in the old family mansion and hope that his relations can leave the two lovebirds alone.

But when Miriel discovers that Ian's motive for marriage may have had nothing to do with her own charms, she decides to postpone at least one aspect of the honeymoon, installing herself and her groom in separate bedrooms. To clear herself of Richard's murder, Miriel summons private detective Kelly, an old crony of her father's, who gets himself hired as a servant in the house even though he can't cook, clean or serve. While Kelly snoops, the body count continues to mount at an alarming rate. Nor is Miriel's hapless father much help. Having squandered the family fortune, he now rents out rooms in his mansion and picks up a little extra cash doing Miriel's laundry.

Originally published in 1944, *The Black Honeymoon* is filled with tantalizing questions: Who is moaning in the attic. . .what is the terrible secret in the family Bible. . .why does Aunt Violet insist on staying in her room. . .will Kelly get fired for incompetence before he nabs the killer. . .will Miriel and Ian ever consummate their marriage? Combining the charm and laughs of a Frank Capra movie with the eccentric characters of a George S. Kaufmann play, *The Black Honeymoon* is a delight from start to finish.   **0-915230-21-6**   **$14**

The Black Gloves
by Constance & Gwenyth Little

"I'm relishing every madcap moment."—*Murder Most Cozy*

Welcome to the Vickers estate near East Orange, New Jersey, where the middle class is destroying the neighborhood, erecting their horrid little cottages, playing on the Vickers tennis court, and generally disrupting the comfortable life of Hammond Vickers no end.

It's bad enough that he had to shell out good money to get his daughter Lissa a divorce in Reno only to have her brute of an ex-husband show up on his doorstep. But why does there also have to be a corpse in the cellar? And lights going on and off in the attic?

Lissa, on the other hand, welcomes the newcomers into the neighborhood, having spotted a likely candidate for a summer beau among them. But when she hears coal being shoveled in the cellar and finds a blue dandelion near a corpse, what's a girl gonna do but turn detective, popping into people's cottages and dipping dandelions into their inkwells looking for a color match. And she'd better catch the killer fast, because Detective Sergeant Timothy Frobisher says that only a few nail files are standing between her and jail.

Originally published in 1939, *The Black Gloves* was one of 21 wacky mysteries written by the Little sisters and is a sparkling example of the light-hearted cozy mystery that flourished between the Depression and the Korean War. It won't take you long to understand why these long out-of-print titles have so many ardent fans.   **0-915230-20-8**   **$14**

The Rue Morgue Press intends to eventually publish all 21 of the Little mysteries.

Murder, Chop Chop
by James Norman

"The book has the butter-wouldn't-melt-in-his-mouth cool of Rick in *Casablanca*."
—*The Rocky Mountain News*. "Amuses the reader no end."—*Mystery News*. "This long out-of-print masterpiece is intricately plotted, full of eccentric characters and very humorous indeed. Highly recommended."—*Mysteries by Mail*

You'll find a cipher or two to crack, a train with a mind of its own, and Chiang Kai-shek's false teeth to cloud the waters in this 1942 classic tale of detection and adventure set during the Sino-Japanese war, with the sleuthing honors going to a gigantic Mexican guerrilla fighter named Gimiendo Quinto and a beautiful Eurasian known as Mountain of Virtue.

0-915230-16-X $13

Cook Up a Crime
by Charlotte Murray Russell

"Some wonderful old-time recipes...highly recommended."—*Mysteries by Mail*.

Meet Jane Amanda Edwards, a self-styled "full-fashioned" spinster who complains she hasn't looked at herself in a full-length mirror since Helen Hokinson started drawing for *The New Yorker*. But you can always count on Jane to look into other people's affairs, especially when there's a juicy murder case to investigate. In this 1951 title Jane goes looking for recipes (included between chapters) and finds a body instead. As usual, in one of the longest running jokes in detective fiction, her lily-of-the-field brother Arthur is found clutching the murder weapon. **0-915230-18-6**   **$13**

The Man from Tibet
by Clyde B. Clason

"The novels of American classicist Clason have been unavailable for years, a lapse happily remedied with the handsome trade paperback reprint of (Westborough's)best known case. Clason spun ornate puzzles in the manner of Carr and Queen and spread erudition as determinedly as Van Dine."—Jon L. Breen, *Ellery Queen's Mystery Magazine*. "A highly original and practical locked-room murder method."— Robert C.S. Adey.

The elderly historian, Prof. Theocritus Lucius Westborough, solves a cozy 1938 locked room mystery involving a Tibetan lama in Chicago in which the murder weapon may well be an eighth century manuscript. A fair-play puzzler for fans of John Dickson Carr. With an extensive bibliography, it is also one of the first popular novels to examine in depth forbidden Tibet and Tibetan Buddhism.   **0-915230-17-8**   **$14**

As part of its vintage mystery series, The Rue Morgue Press intends to publish more titles by many of the authors appearing in this catalog as well as books by Manning Coles (the four ghost books), Joanna Cannan, Glyn Carr and other important writers whose books have been unavailable for many years.

Murder is a Collector's Item
by Elizabeth Dean

"Completely enjoyable"—*New York Times*. "Fast and funny."—*The New Yorker.*
Murder is a Collector's Item froths over with the same effervescent humor as the
best Hepburn-Grant films. — Sujata Massey, Agatha award winning author of
The Salaryman's Wife and *Zen Attitude.*

Twenty-six-year-old Emma Marsh isn't much at spelling or geography and
perhaps she butchers the odd literary quotation or two, but she's a keen judge
of character and more than able to hold her own when it comes to selling
antiques or solving murders. When she stumbles upon the body of a rich collector on the floor of the Boston antiques shop where she works, suspicion quickly
falls upon her missing boss. Emma knows Jeff Graham is no murderer, but
veteran homicide cop Jerry Donovan doesn't share her conviction.

With a little help from Hank Fairbanks, her wealthy boyfriend and would-
be criminologist, Emma turns sleuth and cracks the case, but not before a host
of cops, reporters and customers drift through the shop on Charles Street,
trading insults and sipping scotch as they talk clues, prompting a *New York Times*
reviewer to remark that Emma "drinks far more than a nice girl should."

Emma does a lot of things that women didn't do in detective novels of the
1930s. In an age of menopausal spinsters, deadly sirens, admiring wives and air-
headed girlfriends, pretty, big-footed Emma Marsh stands out. She's a precur-
sor of the independent women sleuths that finally came into their own in the
last two decades of this century.

Originally published in 1939, *Murder is a Collector's Item* was the first of three
books featuring Emma. Smoothly written and sparkling with dry, sophisticated
humor, it combines an intriguing puzzle with an entertaining portrait of a self-
possessed young woman on her own in Boston toward the end of the Great
Depression. Author Dean, who worked in a Boston antiques shop, offers up an
insider's view of what that easily impressed *Times* reviewer called the "goofy"
world of antiques. Lovejoy, the rogue antiques dealer in Jonathan Gash's mysteries, would have loved Emma. **0-915230-19-4** **$14**

The Rue Morgue Press

Rue Morgue Presss books are published under the editorial direction of
Tom & End Schantz. For more information on the press and future titles, write
The Rue Morgue Press, P O Box 4119, Boulder, Colorado 80306